Charlie and the Chocolate Factory

The golden ticket
that started it all . . .

Charlie went on wolfing the candy. He couldn't stop. And in less than half a minute, the whole thing had disappeared down his throat. He was quite out of breath, but he felt marvelously, extraordinarily happy. He reached out a hand to take the change. Then he paused. His eyes were just above the level of the counter. They were staring at the little silver coins lying there. The coins were all dimes. There were nine of them altogether. Surely it wouldn't matter if he spent just one more. . . .

"I think," he said quietly, "I think . . . I'll have just one more of those candy bars. The same kind as before, please."

"Why not?" the fat shopkeeper said, reaching behind him again and taking another Whipple-Scrumptious Fudgemallow Delight from the shelf. He laid it on the counter.

Charlie picked it up and tore off the wrapper . . . and *suddenly* . . . from underneath the wrapper . . . there came a brilliant flash of gold.

Charlie's heart stood still.

Puffin Books by Roald Dahl

Roald Dahl

Charlie and the Chocolate Factory

AND

Charlie and the Great Glass Elevator

illustrated by Quentin Blake

PUFFIN BOOKS
An Imprint of Penguin Group (USA) Inc.

PUFFIN BOOKS
Published by the Penguin Group
Penguin Young Readers Group, 345 Hudson Street, New York, New York 10014, U.S.A.
Penguin Group (Canada), 90 Eglinton Avenue East, Suite 700,
Toronto, Ontario, Canada M4P 2Y3 (a division of Pearson Penguin Canada Inc.)
Penguin Books Ltd, 80 Strand, London WC2R 0RL, England
Penguin Ireland, 25 St Stephen's Green, Dublin 2, Ireland (a division of Penguin Books Ltd)
Penguin Group (Australia), 250 Camberwell Road, Camberwell, Victoria 3124, Australia
(a division of Pearson Australia Group Pty Ltd)
Penguin Books India Pvt Ltd, 11 Community Centre,
Panchsheel Park, New Delhi - 110 017, India
Penguin Group (NZ), 67 Apollo Drive, Rosedale, North Shore 0632, New Zealand
(a division of Pearson New Zealand Ltd)
Penguin Books (South Africa) (Pty) Ltd, 24 Sturdee Avenue,
Rosebank, Johannesburg 2196, South Africa

Registered Offices: Penguin Books Ltd, 80 Strand, London WC2R 0RL, England

Charlie and the Chocolate Factory was first published in the United States of America
by Alfred A. Knopf, Inc., 1964
Charlie and the Chocolate Factory was first published in Puffin Books
by arrangement with Alfred A. Knopf, Inc., 1988
Reissued in Puffin Books, 2007

Charlie and the Great Glass Elevator was first published in the United States of America
by Alfred A. Knopf, Inc., 1972
Charlie and the Great Glass Elevator was first published in Puffin Books
by arrangement with Alfred A. Knopf, Inc., 1988
Reissued in Puffin Books, 2007

This bind-up edition published by Puffin Books,
a division of Penguin Young Readers Group, 2010

3 5 7 9 10 8 6 4 2

THE LIBRARY OF CONGRESS HAS CATALOGED THE 1988 PUFFIN BOOKS EDITION OF
CHARLIE AND THE CHOCOLATE FACTORY UNDER CATALOG CARD NUMBER: 88-42886

THE LIBRARY OF CONGRESS HAS CATALOGED THE 1988 PUFFIN BOOKS EDITION OF
CHARLIE AND THE GREAT GLASS ELEVATOR UNDER CATALOG CARD NUMBER: 88-42881

Puffin Books ISBN 978-0-14-241740-9

Set in ITC Garamond Book
Printed in the United States of America

For Theo

CONTENTS

There are five children in this book:

AUGUSTUS GLOOP
A greedy boy

VERUCA SALT
A girl who is spoiled by her parents

VIOLET BEAUREGARDE
A girl who chews gum all day long

MIKE TEAVEE
A boy who does nothing but watch television

and

CHARLIE BUCKET
The hero

1
Here Comes Charlie

THESE TWO VERY OLD PEOPLE are the father and mother of Mr. Bucket. Their names are Grandpa Joe and Grandma Josephine.

And *these* two very old people are the father and
mother of Mrs. Bucket. Their names are Grandpa George
and Grandma Georgina.

This is Mr. Bucket.   This is Mrs. Bucket.
Mr. and Mrs. Bucket have a small boy whose name is
Charlie Bucket.

This is Charlie.

How d'you do? And how d'you do? And how d'you do again?

He is pleased to meet you.

The whole of this family—the six grownups (count them) and little Charlie Bucket—live together in a small wooden house on the edge of a great town.

The house wasn't nearly large enough for so many people, and life was extremely uncomfortable for them all. There were only two rooms in the place altogether, and there was only one bed. The bed was given to the four old grandparents because they were so old and tired. They were so tired, they never got out of it.

Grandpa Joe and Grandma Josephine on this side, Grandpa George and Grandma Georgina on this side.

Mr. and Mrs. Bucket and little Charlie Bucket slept in the other room, upon mattresses on the floor.

In the summertime, this wasn't too bad, but in the winter, freezing cold drafts blew across the floor all night long, and it was awful.

There wasn't any question of them being able to buy a better house—or even one more bed to sleep in. They were far too poor for that.

Mr. Bucket was the only person in the family with a job. He worked in a toothpaste factory, where he sat all day long at a bench and screwed the little caps onto the tops of the tubes of toothpaste after the tubes had been filled. But a toothpaste cap-screwer is never paid very much money, and poor Mr. Bucket, however hard he worked, and however fast he screwed on the caps, was never able to make enough to buy one-half of the things that so large a family needed. There wasn't even enough money to buy proper food for them all. The only meals they could afford were bread and margarine for breakfast, boiled potatoes and cabbage for lunch, and cabbage soup for supper. Sundays were a bit better. They all looked forward to Sundays because then, although they had exactly the same, everyone was allowed a second helping.

The Buckets, of course, didn't starve, but every one of them—the two old grandfathers, the two old grandmothers, Charlie's father, Charlie's mother, and especially little Charlie himself—went about from morning till night with a horrible empty feeling in their tummies.

Charlie felt it worst of all. And although his father and

mother often went without their own share of lunch or supper so that they could give it to him, it still wasn't nearly enough for a growing boy. He desperately wanted something more filling and satisfying than cabbage and cabbage soup. The one thing he longed for more than anything else was . . . CHOCOLATE.

Walking to school in the mornings, Charlie could see great slabs of chocolate piled up high in the shop windows, and he would stop and stare and press his nose against the glass, his mouth watering like mad. Many times a day, he would see other children taking creamy candy bars out of their pockets and munching them greedily, and *that*, of course, was *pure* torture.

Only once a year, on his birthday, did Charlie Bucket ever get to taste a bit of chocolate. The whole family saved up their money for that special occasion, and when the great day arrived, Charlie was always presented with one small chocolate bar to eat all by himself. And each time he received it, on those marvelous birthday mornings, he would place it carefully in a small wooden box that he owned, and treasure it as though it were a bar of solid gold; and for the next few days, he would allow himself only to look at it, but never to touch it. Then at last, when he could stand it no longer, he would peel back a *tiny* bit of the paper wrapping at one corner to expose a *tiny* bit of chocolate, and then he would take a *tiny* nibble—just enough to allow the lovely sweet taste to spread out slowly over his tongue. The next day, he would take another tiny nibble, and so on, and so on. And in this way, Charlie would make his ten-cent bar of birthday chocolate last him for more than a month.

But I haven't yet told you about the one awful thing that tortured little Charlie, the lover of chocolate, more than *anything* else. This thing, for him, was far, far worse than seeing slabs of chocolate in the shop windows or watching other children munching creamy candy bars right in front of him. It was the most terrible torturing thing you could imagine, and it was this:

In the town itself, actually within *sight* of the house in which Charlie lived, there was an ENORMOUS CHOCOLATE FACTORY!

Just imagine that!

And it wasn't simply an ordinary enormous chocolate factory, either. It was the largest and most famous in the whole world! It was WONKA'S FACTORY, owned by a man called Mr. Willy Wonka, the greatest inventor and maker of chocolates that there has ever been. And what a tremendous, marvelous place it was! It had huge iron gates leading in to it, and a high wall surrounding it, and smoke belching from its chimneys, and strange whizzing sounds coming from deep inside it. And outside the walls, for half a mile around in every direction, the air was scented with the heavy rich smell of melting chocolate!

Twice a day, on his way to and from school, little Charlie Bucket had to walk right past the gates of the factory. And every time he went by, he would begin to walk very, very slowly, and he would hold his nose high in the air and take long deep sniffs of the gorgeous chocolatey smell all around him.

Oh, how he loved that smell!

And oh, how he wished he could go inside the factory and see what it was like!

2

Mr. Willy Wonka's Factory

IN THE EVENINGS, after he had finished his supper of watery cabbage soup, Charlie always went into the room of his four grandparents to listen to their stories, and then afterwards to say good night.

Every one of these old people was over ninety. They were as shriveled as prunes, and as bony as skeletons, and throughout the day, until Charlie made his appearance, they lay huddled in their one bed, two at either end, with nightcaps on to keep their heads warm, dozing the time away with nothing to do. But as soon as they heard the door opening, and heard Charlie's voice saying, "Good evening, Grandpa Joe and Grandma Josephine, and Grandpa George and Grandma Georgina," then all four of them would suddenly sit up, and their old wrinkled faces would light up with smiles of pleasure—and the talking would begin. For they loved this little boy. He was the only bright thing in their lives, and his evening visits were something that they looked forward to all day long. Often, Charlie's mother and father would come in as well, and stand by the door, listening to the stories that the old people told; and thus, for perhaps half an hour every night, this room would become a happy place, and the whole family would forget that it was hungry and poor.

One evening, when Charlie went in to see his grandparents, he said to them, "Is it *really* true that Wonka's

Chocolate Factory is the biggest in the world?"

"True?" cried all four of them at once. "Of course it's true! Good heavens, didn't you know *that*? It's about *fifty* times as big as any other!"

"And is Mr. Willy Wonka *really* the cleverest chocolate maker in the world?"

"My *dear* boy," said Grandpa Joe, raising himself up a little higher on his pillow, "Mr. Willy Wonka is the most *amazing,* the most *fantastic,* the most *extraordinary* chocolate maker the world has ever seen! I thought *everybody* knew that!"

"I knew he was famous, Grandpa Joe, and I knew he was very clever. . . ."

"Clever!" cried the old man. "He's more than that! He's a *magician* with chocolate! He can make *anything*— anything he wants! Isn't that a fact, my dears?"

The other three old people nodded their heads slowly up and down, and said, *"Absolutely* true. *Just* as true as can be."

And Grandpa Joe said, "You mean to say I've never *told* you about Mr. Willy Wonka and his factory?"

"Never," answered little Charlie.

"Good heavens above! I don't know what's the matter with me!"

"Will you tell me now, Grandpa Joe, please?"

"I certainly will. Sit down beside me on the bed, my dear, and listen carefully."

Grandpa Joe was the oldest of the four grandparents. He was ninety-six and a half, and that is just about as old as anybody can be. Like all extremely old people, he was delicate and weak, and throughout the day he spoke very little. But in the evenings, when Charlie, his beloved grandson, was in the room, he seemed in some marvelous way to grow quite young again. All his tiredness fell away from him, and he became as eager and excited as a young boy.

"Oh, what a man he is, this Mr. Willy Wonka!" cried Grandpa Joe. "Did you know, for example, that he has himself invented more than two hundred new kinds of candy bars, each with a different center, each far sweeter and creamier and more delicious than anything the other chocolate factories can make!"

"Perfectly true!" cried Grandma Josephine. "And he sends them to *all* the four corners of the earth! Isn't that so, Grandpa Joe?"

"It is, my dear, it is. And to all the kings and presidents of the world as well. But it isn't only candy bars that he makes. Oh, dear me, no! He has some really *fantastic* inventions up his sleeve, Mr. Willy Wonka has! Did you know that he's invented a way of making chocolate ice cream so that it stays cold for hours and hours without being in the icebox?

You can even leave it lying in the sun all morning on a hot day and it won't go runny!"

"But that's *impossible*!" said little Charlie, staring at his grandfather.

"Of course it's impossible!" cried Grandpa Joe. "It's completely *absurd*! But Mr. Willy Wonka has done it!"

"Quite right!" the others agreed, nodding their heads. "Mr. Wonka has done it."

"And then again," Grandpa Joe went on, speaking very slowly now so that Charlie wouldn't miss a word, "Mr. Willy Wonka can make marshmallows that taste of violets, and rich caramels that change color every ten seconds as you suck them, and little feathery sweets that melt away deliciously the moment you put them between your lips. He can make chewing gum that never loses its taste, and candy balloons that you can blow up to enormous sizes before you pop them with a pin and gobble them up. And, by a most secret method, he can make lovely blue birds' eggs with black spots on them, and when you put one of these in your mouth, it gradually gets smaller

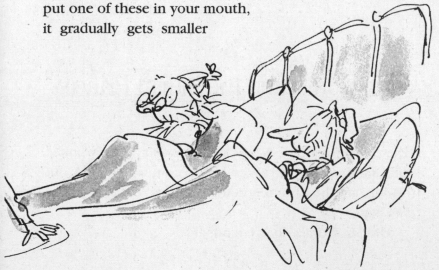

and smaller until suddenly there is nothing left except a tiny little pink sugary baby bird sitting on the tip of your tongue."

Grandpa Joe paused and ran the point of his tongue slowly over his lips. "It makes my mouth water just *thinking* about it," he said.

"Mine, too," said little Charlie. "But *please* go on."

While they were talking, Mr. and Mrs. Bucket, Charlie's mother and father, had come quietly into the room, and now both were standing just inside the door, listening.

"Tell Charlie about that crazy Indian prince," said Grandma Josephine. "He'd like to hear that."

"You mean Prince Pondicherry?" said Grandpa Joe, and he began chuckling with laughter.

"*Completely* dotty!" said Grandpa George.

"But *very* rich," said Grandma Georgina.

"What did he do?" asked Charlie eagerly.

"Listen," said Grandpa Joe, "and I'll tell you."

3

Mr. Wonka and the Indian Prince

"PRINCE PONDICHERRY wrote a letter to Mr. Willy Wonka," said Grandpa Joe, "and asked him to come all the way out to India and build him a colossal palace entirely out of chocolate."

"Did Mr. Wonka do it, Grandpa?"

"He did, indeed. And what a palace it was! It had one hundred rooms, and *everything* was made of either dark or light chocolate! The bricks were chocolate, and the cement holding them together was chocolate, and the windows were chocolate, and all the walls and ceilings were made of chocolate, so were the carpets and the pictures and the furniture and the beds; and when you turned on the taps in the bathroom, hot chocolate came pouring out.

"When it was all finished, Mr. Wonka said to Prince Pondicherry, 'I warn you, though, it won't last very long, so you'd better start eating it right away.'

"'Nonsense!' shouted the Prince. 'I'm not going to eat my palace! I'm not even going to nibble the staircase or lick the walls! I'm going to *live* in it!'

"But Mr. Wonka was right, of course, because soon after this, there came a very hot day with a boiling sun, and the whole palace began to melt, and then it sank slowly to the ground, and the crazy prince, who was dozing in the living room at the time, woke up to find himself swimming around in a huge brown sticky lake of chocolate."

Little Charlie sat very still on the edge of the bed, staring at his grandfather. Charlie's face was bright, and his eyes were stretched so wide you could see the whites all around. "Is all this *really* true?" he asked. "Or are you pulling my leg?"

"It's true!" cried all four of the old people at once. "Of course it's true! Ask anyone you like!"

"And I'll tell you something else that's true," said Grandpa Joe, and now he leaned closer to Charlie, and lowered his voice to a soft, secret whisper. *"Nobody . . . ever . . . comes . . . out!"*

"Out of where?" asked Charlie.

"And . . . nobody . . . ever . . . goes . . . in!"

"In *where*?" cried Charlie.

"Wonka's factory, of course!"

"Grandpa, what *do* you mean?"

"I mean *workers,* Charlie."

"Workers?"

"All factories," said Grandpa Joe, "have workers streaming in and out of the gates in the mornings and evenings—except Wonka's! Have *you* ever seen a single person going into that place—or coming out?"

Little Charlie looked slowly around at each of the four old faces, one after the other, and they all looked back at him. They were friendly smiling faces, but they were also quite serious. There was no sign of joking or leg-pulling on any of them.

"Well? Have *you*?" asked Grandpa Joe.

"I . . . I really don't know, Grandpa," Charlie stammered. "Whenever *I* walk past the factory, the gates seem to be closed."

"Exactly!" said Grandpa Joe.

"But there *must* be people working there. . . ."

"Not *people,* Charlie. Not *ordinary* people, anyway."

"Then who?" cried Charlie.

"Ah-ha. . . . That's it, you see. . . . That's another of Mr. Willy Wonka's clevernesses."

"Charlie, dear," Mrs. Bucket called out from where she was standing by the door, "it's time for bed. That's enough for tonight."

"But mother, I *must* hear. . . ."

"Tomorrow, my darling. . . ."

"That's right," said Grandpa Joe, "I'll tell you the rest of it tomorrow evening."

4

The Secret Workers

THE NEXT EVENING, Grandpa Joe went on with his story.

"You see, Charlie," he said, "not so very long ago there used to be thousands of people working in Mr. Willy Wonka's factory. Then one day, all of a sudden, Mr. Wonka had to ask *every single one of them* to leave, to go home, never to come back."

"But why?" asked Charlie.

"Because of spies."

"Spies?"

"Yes. All the other chocolate makers, you see, had begun to grow jealous of the wonderful candies that Mr. Wonka was making, and they started sending in spies to steal his secret recipes. The spies took jobs in the Wonka factory, pretending that they were ordinary workers, and while they were there, each one of them found out exactly how a certain special thing was made."

"And did they go back to their own factories and tell?" asked Charlie.

"They must have," answered Grandpa Joe, "because

soon after that, Fickelgruber's factory started making an ice cream that would never melt, even in the hottest sun. Then Mr. Prodnose's factory came out with a chewing gum that never lost its flavor however much you chewed it. And then Mr. Slugworth's factory began making candy balloons that you could blow up to huge sizes before you popped them with a pin and gobbled them up. And so on, and so on. And Mr. Willy Wonka tore his beard and shouted, 'This is terrible! I shall be ruined! There are spies everywhere! I shall have to close the factory!'"

"But he didn't do that!" Charlie said.

"Oh, yes he did. He told *all* the workers that he was sorry, but they would have to go home. Then, he shut the main gates and fastened them with a chain. And suddenly, Wonka's giant chocolate factory became silent and deserted. The chimneys stopped smoking, the machines stopped whirring, and from then on, not a single chocolate or candy was made. Not a soul went in or out, and even Mr. Willy Wonka himself disappeared completely.

"Months and months went by," Grandpa Joe went on, "but still the factory remained closed. And everybody said, 'Poor Mr. Wonka. He was so nice. And he made such marvelous things. But he's finished now. It's all over.'

"Then something astonishing happened. One day, early in the morning, thin columns of white smoke were seen to be coming out of the tops of the tall chimneys of the factory! People in the town stopped and stared. 'What's going on?' they cried. 'Someone's lit the furnaces! Mr. Wonka must be opening up again!' They ran to the gates, expecting to see them wide open and Mr. Wonka standing there to welcome his workers back.

"But no! The great iron gates were still locked and chained as securely as ever, and Mr. Wonka was nowhere to be seen.

"'But the factory *is* working!' the people shouted. 'Listen! You can hear the machines! They're all whirring again! And you can smell the smell of melting chocolate in the air!'"

Grandpa Joe leaned forward and laid a long bony finger on Charlie's knee, and he said softly, "But most mysterious of all, Charlie, were the shadows in the windows of the factory. The people standing on the street outside could see small dark shadows moving about behind the frosted glass windows."

"Shadows of whom?" said Charlie quickly.

"That's exactly what everybody else wanted to know.

"'The place is full of workers!' the people shouted. 'But nobody's gone in! The gates are locked! It's crazy! Nobody ever comes out, either!'

"But there was no question at all," said Grandpa Joe, "that the factory *was* running. And it's gone on running ever since, for these last ten years. What's more, the chocolates and candies it's been turning out have become more fantastic and delicious all the time. And of course *now,* when Mr. Wonka invents some new and wonderful candy, neither Mr. Fickelgruber nor Mr. Prodnose nor Mr. Slugworth nor anybody else is able to copy it. No spies can go into the factory to find out how it is made."

"But Grandpa, *who,*" cried Charlie, "*who* is Mr. Wonka using to do all the work in the factory?"

"Nobody knows, Charlie."

"But that's *absurd!* Hasn't someone asked Mr. Wonka?"

"Nobody sees him any more. He never comes out. The only things that come out of that place are chocolates and candies. They come out through a special trap door in the wall, all packed and addressed, and they are picked up every day by Post Office trucks."

"But Grandpa, what *sort* of people are they that work in there?"

"My dear boy," said Grandpa Joe, "that is one of the great mysteries of the chocolate-making world. We know only one thing about them. They are very small. The faint shadows that sometimes appear behind the windows, especially late at night when the lights are on, are those of *tiny* people, people no taller than my knee. . . ."

"There aren't any such people," Charlie said.

Just then, Mr. Bucket, Charlie's father, came into the room. He was home from the toothpaste factory, and he was waving an evening newspaper rather excitedly. "Have you heard the news?" he cried. He held up the paper so that they could see the huge headline. The headline said:

WONKA FACTORY TO BE OPENED AT LAST TO LUCKY FEW

5
The Golden Tickets

"YOU MEAN people are actually going to be allowed to go inside the factory?" cried Grandpa Joe. "Read us what it says—quickly!"

"All right," said Mr. Bucket, smoothing out the newspaper. "Listen."

𝕰𝖛𝖊𝖓𝖎𝖓𝖌 𝕭𝖚𝖑𝖑𝖊𝖙𝖎𝖓

Mr. Willy Wonka, the candy-making genius whom nobody has seen for the last ten years, sent out the following notice today:

I, Willy Wonka, have decided to allow five children —just *five,* mind you, and no more—to visit my factory this year. These lucky five will be shown around personally by me, and they will be allowed to see all the secrets and the magic of my factory. Then, at the end of the tour, as a special present, all of them will be given enough chocolates and candies to last them for the rest of their lives! So watch out for the Golden Tickets! Five Golden Tickets have been printed on golden paper, and these five Golden Tickets have been hidden underneath the ordinary wrapping paper of five ordinary candy bars. These five candy bars may be anywhere—in any shop in any street in any town in any country in the world—upon any counter where Wonka's candies are sold. And the five lucky finders of these five Golden Tickets are the *only* ones who will be allowed to visit my factory and see what it's like *now* inside! Good luck to you all, and happy hunting! (Signed Willy Wonka.)

"The man's dotty!" muttered Grandma Josephine.

"He's brilliant!" cried Grandpa Joe. "He's a magician! Just imagine what will happen now! The whole world will be searching for those Golden Tickets! Everyone will be buying Wonka's candy bars in the hope of finding one! He'll sell more than ever before! Oh, how exciting it would be to find one!"

"And all the chocolate and candies that you could eat for the rest of your life—*free!*" said Grandpa George. "Just imagine that!"

"They'd have to deliver them in a truck!" said Grandma Georgina.

"It makes me quite ill to think of it," said Grandma Josephine.

"Nonsense!" cried Grandpa Joe. "Wouldn't it be *something*, Charlie, to open a bar of candy and see a Golden Ticket glistening inside!"

"It certainly would, Grandpa. But there isn't a hope," Charlie said sadly. "I only get one bar a year."

"You never know, darling," said Grandma Georgina. "It's your birthday next week. You have as much chance as anybody else."

"I'm afraid that simply isn't true," said Grandpa George. "The kids who are going to find the Golden Tickets are the ones who can afford to buy candy bars every day. Our Charlie gets only one a year. There isn't a hope."

6
The First Two Finders

THE VERY NEXT DAY, the first Golden Ticket was found. The finder was a boy called Augustus Gloop, and Mr. Bucket's evening newspaper carried a large picture of him on the front page. The picture showed a nine-year-old boy who was so enormously fat he looked as though he had been blown up with a powerful pump. Great flabby folds of fat bulged out from every part of his body, and his face was like a monstrous ball of dough with two small greedy curranty eyes peering out upon the world. The town in which Augustus Gloop lived, the newspaper said, had gone wild with excitement over their hero. Flags were flying from all the windows, children had been given a holiday from school, and a parade was being organized in honor of the famous youth.

"I just *knew* Augustus would find a Golden Ticket," his mother had told the newspapermen. "He eats *so many* candy bars a day that it was almost *impossible* for him *not* to find one. Eating is his hobby, you know. That's *all* he's interested in. But still, that's better than being a *hooligan* and shooting off *zip guns* and things like that in his spare time, isn't it? And what I always say is, he wouldn't go on eating like he does unless he *needed* nourishment, would he? It's all *vitamins,* anyway. What a *thrill* it will be for him to visit Mr. Wonka's marvelous factory! We're just as *proud* as can be!"

"What a revolting woman," said Grandma Josephine.

"And what a repulsive boy," said Grandma Georgina.

"Only four Golden Tickets left," said Grandpa George. "I wonder who'll get *those.*"

And now the whole country, indeed, the whole world, seemed suddenly to be caught up in a mad candy-buying spree, everybody searching frantically for those precious remaining tickets. Fully grown women were seen going into sweetshops and buying ten Wonka candy bars at a time, then tearing off the wrappers on the spot and peering eagerly underneath for a glint of golden paper. Children were taking hammers and smashing their piggy banks and running out to the shops with handfuls of money. In one city, a famous gangster robbed a bank of five thousand dollars and spent the whole lot on candy bars that same afternoon. And when the police entered his house to arrest him, they found him sitting on the floor amidst mountains of candy, ripping off the wrappers with the blade of a long dagger. In far-off Russia, a woman called Charlotte Russe claimed to have found the second ticket, but it turned out to be a clever fake. In England, the famous scientist, Professor Foulbody, invented a machine which would tell you at once, without opening the wrapper of a candy bar, whether or not there was a Golden Ticket hidden underneath it. The machine had a mechanical arm that shot out with tremendous force and grabbed hold of anything that had the slightest bit of gold inside it, and for a moment, it looked like the answer to everything. But unfortunately, while the Professor was showing off the machine to the public at the candy counter of a large department store, the mechanical arm shot out and made a grab for the gold filling in the back tooth of a duchess who was standing nearby. There was an ugly scene, and the machine was smashed by the crowd.

Suddenly, on the day before Charlie Bucket's birthday, the newspapers announced that the second Golden Ticket had been found. The lucky person was a small girl called Veruca Salt who lived with her rich parents in a great city far away. Once again, Mr. Bucket's evening newspaper carried a big picture of the finder. She was sitting between her beaming father and mother in the living room of their house, waving the Golden Ticket above her head, and grinning from ear to ear.

Veruca's father, Mr. Salt, had eagerly explained to the newspapermen exactly how the ticket was found. "You see, fellers," he had said, "as soon as my little girl told me that she simply *had* to have one of those Golden Tickets, I went out into the town and started buying up all the Wonka candy bars I could lay my hands on. *Thousands* of them, I must have bought. *Hundreds* of thousands! Then I had them loaded onto trucks and sent directly to my *own* factory. I'm in the peanut business, you see, and I've got about a hundred women working for me over at my joint, shelling peanuts for roasting and salting. That's what they do all day long, those women, they sit there shelling peanuts. So I says to them, 'Okay, girls,' I says, 'from now on, you can stop shelling peanuts and start shelling the wrappers off these crazy candy bars instead!' And they did. I had every worker in the place yanking the paper off those bars of chocolate full speed ahead from morning till night.

"But three days went by, and we had no luck. Oh, it was terrible! My little Veruca got more and more upset each day, and every time I went home she would scream at me, *'Where's my Golden Ticket! I want my Golden Ticket!'* And she would lie for hours on the floor, kicking and yelling in the most disturbing way. Well, sir, I just hated to see my little girl feeling unhappy like that, so I vowed I would keep up the search until I'd got her what she wanted. Then suddenly . . . on the evening of the fourth day, one of my women workers yelled, 'I've got it! A Golden Ticket!' And I said, 'Give it to me, quick!' and she did, and I rushed it home and gave it to my darling Veruca, and now she's all smiles, and we have a happy home once again."

"That's even worse than the fat boy," said Grandma Josephine.

"She needs a real good spanking," said Grandma Georgina.

"I don't think the girl's father played it quite fair, Grandpa, do you?" Charlie murmured.

"He spoils her," Grandpa Joe said. "And no good can ever come from spoiling a child like that, Charlie, you mark my words."

"Come to bed, my darling," said Charlie's mother. "Tomorrow's your birthday, don't forget that, so I expect you'll be up early to open your present."

"A Wonka candy bar!" cried Charlie. "It is a Wonka candy bar, isn't it?"

"Yes, my love," his mother said. "Of course it is."

"Oh, wouldn't it be wonderful if I found the third Golden Ticket inside it?" Charlie said.

"Bring it in here when you get it," Grandpa Joe said. "Then we can all watch you taking off the wrapper."

7
Charlie's Birthday

"HAPPY BIRTHDAY!" cried the four old grandparents as Charlie came into their room early the next morning.

Charlie smiled nervously and sat down on the edge of the bed. He was holding his present, his only present, very carefully in his two hands. WONKA'S WHIPPLE-SCRUMPTIOUS FUDGEMALLOW DELIGHT, it said on the wrapper.

The four old people, two at either end of the bed,

propped themselves up on their pillows and stared with anxious eyes at the candy bar in Charlie's hands.

Mr. and Mrs. Bucket came in and stood at the foot of the bed, watching Charlie.

The room became silent. Everybody was waiting now for Charlie to start opening his present. Charlie looked down at the candy bar. He ran his fingers slowly back and forth along the length of it, stroking it lovingly, and the shiny paper wrapper made little sharp crackly noises in the quiet room.

Then Mrs. Bucket said gently, "You mustn't be too disappointed, my darling, if you don't find what you're looking for underneath that wrapper. You really can't expect to be as lucky as all that."

"She's quite right," Mr. Bucket said.

Charlie didn't say anything.

"After all," Grandma Josephine said, "in the whole wide world there are only three tickets left to be found."

"The thing to remember," Grandma Georgina said, "is that whatever happens, you'll still have the bar of candy."

"Wonka's Whipple-Scrumptious Fudgemallow Delight!" cried Grandpa George. "It's the best of them all! You'll just *love* it!"

"Yes," Charlie whispered. "I know."

"Just forget all about those Golden Tickets and enjoy the candy," Grandpa Joe said. "Why don't you do that?"

They all knew it was ridiculous to expect this one poor little candy bar to have a magic ticket inside it, and they were trying as gently and as kindly as they could to prepare Charlie for the disappointment. But there was one other thing that the grownups also knew, and it was this: that however *small* the chance might be of striking lucky, *the chance was there.*

The chance *had* to be there.

This particular candy bar had as much chance as any other of having a Golden Ticket.

And that was why all the grandparents and parents in the room were actually just as tense and excited as Charlie was, although they were pretending to be very calm.

"You'd better go ahead and open it up, or you'll be late for school," Grandpa Joe said.

"You might as well get it over with," Grandpa George said.

"Open it, my dear," Grandma Georgina said. "Please open it. You're making me jumpy."

Very slowly, Charlie's fingers began to tear open one small corner of the wrapping paper.

The old people in the bed all leaned forward, craning their scraggy necks.

Then suddenly, as though he couldn't bear the suspense any longer, Charlie tore the wrapper right down the middle . . . and on to his lap, there fell . . . a light-brown creamy-colored chocolate candy bar.

There was no sign of a Golden Ticket anywhere.

"Well—that's *that!*" said Grandpa Joe brightly. "It's just what we expected."

Charlie looked up. Four kind old faces were watching him intently from the bed. He smiled at them, a small sad smile, and then he shrugged his shoulders and picked up the candy bar and held it out to his mother, and said, "Here Mother, have a bit. We'll share it. I want everybody to taste it."

"Certainly not!" his mother said.

And the others all cried, "No, no! We wouldn't dream of it! It's *all* yours!"

"Please," begged Charlie, turning around and offering it to Grandpa Joe.

But neither he nor anyone else would take even a tiny bite.

"It's time to go to school, my darling," Mrs. Bucket said, putting an arm around Charlie's skinny shoulders. "Come on, or you'll be late."

8
Two More Golden Tickets Found

THAT EVENING, Mr. Bucket's newspaper announced the finding of not only the third Golden Ticket, but the fourth as well. TWO GOLDEN TICKETS FOUND TODAY, screamed the headlines. ONLY ONE MORE LEFT.

"All right," said Grandpa Joe, when the whole family was gathered in the old people's room after supper, "let's hear who found them."

"The third ticket," read Mr. Bucket, holding the newspaper up close to his face because his eyes were bad and he couldn't afford glasses, "the third Ticket was found by a Miss Violet Beauregarde. There was great excitement in the Beauregarde household when our reporter arrived to interview the lucky young lady—cameras were clicking and flashbulbs were flashing and people were pushing and jostling and trying to get a bit closer to the famous girl. And the famous girl was standing on a chair in the living-room waving the Golden Ticket madly at arm's length as though she were flagging a taxi. She was talking very fast and very loudly to everyone, but it was not easy to hear all that she said because she was chewing so ferociously upon a piece of gum at the same time.

"'I'm a gumchewer, normally,' she shouted, 'but when I heard about these ticket things of Mr. Wonka's, I laid off the gum and switched to candy bars in the hope of striking lucky. *Now,* of course, I'm right back on gum. I just *adore* gum. I can't do without it. I munch it all day long except for a few minutes at mealtimes when I take it out and stick it behind my ear for safekeeping. To tell you the honest truth, I simply wouldn't feel *comfortable* if I didn't have that little wedge of gum to chew on every moment of the day, I really wouldn't. My mother says it's not ladylike and it looks ugly to see a girl's jaws going up and down like mine do all the time, but I don't agree. And who's she to criticize, anyway, because if you ask me, I'd say that *her* jaws are going up and down almost as much as mine are just from *yelling* at me every minute of the day.'

"'Now, Violet,' Mrs. Beauregarde said from a far corner of the room where she was standing on the piano to avoid being trampled by the mob.

"'All right, Mother, keep your hair on!' Miss Beauregarde shouted. 'And now,' she went on, turning to the reporters again, 'it may interest you to know that this piece of gum I'm chewing right at this moment is one I've been working on for over *three months solid.* That's a record, that is. It's beaten the record held by my best friend, Miss Cornelia Prinzmetel. And was she mad! It's my most treasured possession now, this piece of gum is. At nights, I just stick it on the end of the bedpost, and it's as good as ever in the mornings—a bit hard at first, maybe, but it soon softens up again after I've given it a few good chews. Before I started chewing for the world record, I used to change my piece of gum once a day. I used to do it in our elevator on the way home from school. Why the elevator? Because I liked sticking the gooey piece that I'd just finished with onto one of the elevator buttons. Then the next person who came along and pressed the button got my old gum on the end of his or her finger. Ha-ha! And what a racket they kicked up, some of them. You get the best results with women who have expensive gloves on. Oh yes, I'm thrilled to be going to Mr. Wonka's factory. And I understand that afterwards he's going to give me enough gum to last me for the rest of my whole life. Whoopee! Hooray!"

"*Beastly* girl," said Grandma Josephine.

"Despicable!" said Grandma Georgina. "She'll come to a sticky end one day, chewing all that gum, you see if she doesn't."

"And who got the fourth Golden Ticket, Daddy?" Charlie asked.

"Now, let me see," said Mr. Bucket, peering at the newspaper again. "Ah yes, here we are. The fourth Golden Ticket," he read, "was found by a boy called Mike Teavee."

"Another bad lot, I'll be bound," muttered Grandma Josephine.

"Don't interrupt, Grandma," said Mrs. Bucket.

"The Teavee household," said Mr. Bucket, going on with his reading, "was crammed, like all the others, with excited visitors when our reporter arrived, but young Mike Teavee, the lucky winner, seemed extremely annoyed by the whole business. 'Can't you fools see I'm watching television?' he said angrily, 'I wish you wouldn't interrupt!'

"The nine-year-old boy was seated before an enormous television set, with his eyes glued to the screen, and he was watching a film in which one bunch of gangsters was shooting up another bunch of gangsters with machine guns. Mike Teavee himself had no less than eighteen toy pistols of various sizes hanging from belts around his body, and every now and again he would leap up into the air and fire off half a dozen rounds from one or another of these weapons.

"'Quiet!' he shouted, when someone tried to ask him a question. 'Didn't I *tell* you not to interrupt! This show's an absolute whiz-banger! It's terrific! I watch it every day. I watch all of them every day, even the crummy ones, where there's no shooting. I like the gangsters best.

They're terrific, those gangsters! Especially when they start pumping each other full of lead, or flashing the old stilettos, or giving each other the one-two-three with their knuckle-dusters! Oh boy, what wouldn't I give to be doing that myself! It's the *life*, I tell you! It's terrific!'"

"That's quite enough!" snapped Grandma Josephine. "I can't *bear* to listen to it!"

"Nor me," said Grandma Georgina. "Do *all* children behave like this nowadays—like these brats we've been hearing about?"

"Of course not," said Mr. Bucket, smiling at the old lady in the bed. "Some do, of course. In fact, quite a lot of them do. But not *all*."

"And now there's only *one ticket left!*" said Grandpa George.

"Quite so," sniffed Grandma Georgina. "And just as sure as I'll be having cabbage soup for supper tomorrow, that ticket'll go to some nasty little beast who doesn't deserve it!"

9

Grandpa Joe Takes a Gamble

THE NEXT DAY, when Charlie came home from school and went in to see his grandparents, he found that only Grandpa Joe was awake. The other three were all snoring loudly.

"Ssshh!" whispered Grandpa Joe, and he beckoned Charlie to come closer. Charlie tiptoed over and stood beside the bed. The old man gave Charlie a sly grin, and then he started rummaging under his pillow with one hand; and when the hand came out again, there was an ancient leather purse clutched in the fingers. Under cover of the bedclothes, the old man opened the purse and tipped it upside down. Out fell a single silver ten-cent piece. "It's my secret hoard," he whispered. "The others don't know I've got it. And now, you and I are going to have one more fling at finding that last ticket. How about it, eh? But you'll have to help me."

"Are you *sure* you want to spend your money on that, Grandpa?" Charlie whispered.

"Of course I'm sure!" spluttered the old man excitedly. "Don't stand there arguing! I'm just as crazy as you are to find that ticket! Here—take the money and run down the street to the nearest store and buy the first Wonka candy bar you see and bring it straight back to me, and we'll open it together."

Charlie took the little silver coin, and slipped quickly out of the room. In five minutes, he was back.

"Have you got it?" whispered Grandpa Joe, his eyes shining with excitement.

Charlie nodded and held out the bar of candy. WONKA'S NUTTY CRUNCH SURPRISE, it said on the wrapper.

"Good!" the old man whispered, sitting up in the bed and rubbing his hands. "Now—come over here and sit close to me and we'll open it together. Are you ready?"

"Yes," Charlie said. "I'm ready."

"All right. You tear off the first bit."

"No," Charlie said, "you paid for it. You do it all."

The old man's fingers were trembling most terribly as they fumbled with the candy bar. "We don't have a hope, really," he whispered, giggling a bit. "You do know we don't have a hope, don't you?"

"Yes," Charlie said. "I know that."

They looked at each other, and both started giggling nervously.

"Mind you," said Grandpa Joe, "there is just that *tiny* chance that it *might* be the one, don't you agree?"

"Yes," Charlie said. "Of course. Why don't you open it Grandpa?"

"All in good time, my boy, all in good time. Which end do you think I ought to open first?"

"That corner. The one furthest from you. Just tear off a *tiny* bit, but not quite enough for us to see anything."

"Like that?" said the old man.

"Yes. Now a little bit more."

"You finish it," said Grandpa Joe. "I'm too nervous."

"No, Grandpa. You must do it yourself."

"Very well, then. Here goes." He tore off the wrapper.

They both stared at what lay underneath.

It was a bar of candy—nothing more.

All at once, they both saw the funny side of the whole thing, and they burst into peals of laughter.

"What the heck's going on!" cried Grandma Josephine, waking up suddenly.

"Nothing," said Grandpa Joe. "You go on back to sleep."

10
The Family Begins to Starve

DURING THE NEXT TWO WEEKS, the weather turned very cold. First came the snow. It began very suddenly one morning just as Charlie Bucket was getting dressed for school. Standing by the window, he saw the huge flakes drifting slowly down out of an icy sky that was the color of steel.

By evening, it lay four feet deep around the tiny house, and Mr. Bucket had to dig a path from the front door to the road.

After the snow, there came a freezing gale that blew for days and days without stopping. And oh, how bitter cold it was! Everything that Charlie touched seemed to be made of ice, and each time he stepped outside the door, the wind was like a knife on his cheek.

Inside the house, little jets of freezing air came rushing in through the sides of the windows and under the doors, and there was no place to go to escape them. The four old ones lay silent and huddled in their bed, trying to keep the cold out of their bones. The excitement over the Golden Tickets had long since been forgotten. Nobody in the family gave a thought now to anything except the two vital problems of trying to keep warm and trying to get enough to eat.

There is something about very cold weather that gives one an enormous appetite. Most of us find ourselves beginning to crave rich steaming stews and hot apple pies and all kinds of delicious warming dishes; and because we are all a great deal luckier than we realize, we usually get what we want—or near enough. But Charlie Bucket never got what he wanted because the family couldn't afford it, and as the cold weather went on and on, he became ravenously and desperately hungry. Both bars of candy, the birthday one and the one Grandpa Joe had bought, had long since been nibbled away, and all he got now were those thin, cabbagy meals three times a day.

Then all at once, the meals became even thinner.

The reason for this was that the toothpaste factory, the place where Mr. Bucket worked, suddenly went bust and had to close down. Quickly, Mr. Bucket tried to get another job. But he had no luck. In the end, the only way in which he managed to earn a few pennies was by shoveling snow in the streets. But it wasn't enough to buy even a quarter of the food that seven people needed. The situation became desperate. Breakfast was a single slice of bread for each person now, and lunch was maybe half a boiled potato.

Slowly but surely, everybody in the house began to starve.

And every day, little Charlie Bucket, trudging through the snow on his way to school, would have to pass Mr. Willy Wonka's giant chocolate factory. And every day, as he came near to it, he would lift his small pointed nose high in the air and sniff the wonderful sweet smell of melting chocolate. Sometimes, he would stand motionless outside the gates for several minutes on end, taking deep swallowing breaths as though he were trying to *eat* the smell itself.

"That child," said Grandpa Joe, poking his head up from under the blanket one icy morning, "that child has

got to have more food. It doesn't matter about us. We're too old to bother with. But a *growing boy!* He can't go on like this! He's beginning to look like a skeleton!"

"What can one *do?*" murmured Grandma Josephine miserably. "He refuses to take any of ours. I hear his mother tried to slip her own piece of bread onto his plate at breakfast this morning, but he wouldn't touch it. He made her take it back."

"He's a fine little fellow," said Grandpa George. "He deserves better than this."

The cruel weather went on and on.

And every day, Charlie Bucket grew thinner and thinner. His face became frighteningly white and pinched. The skin was drawn so tightly over the cheeks that you could see the shapes of the bones underneath. It seemed doubtful whether he could go on much longer like this without becoming dangerously ill.

And now, very calmly, with that curious wisdom that seems to come so often to small children in times of hardship, he began to make little changes here and there in some of the things that he did, so as to save his strength. In the mornings, he left the house ten minutes earlier so that he could walk slowly to school, without ever having to run. He sat quietly in the classroom during recess, resting himself, while the others rushed outdoors and threw snowballs and wrestled in the snow. Everything he did now, he did slowly and carefully, to prevent exhaustion.

Then one afternoon, walking back home with the icy wind in his face (and incidentally feeling hungrier than he had ever felt before), his eye was caught suddenly by a piece of paper that was lying in the gutter, in the snow.

The paper was of a greenish color, and there was something vaguely familiar about it. Charlie stepped off the curb and bent down to examine it. Part of it was buried under the snow, but he saw at once what it was.

It was a dollar bill!

Quickly he looked around him.

Had somebody just dropped it?

No—that was impossible because of the way part of it was buried.

Several people went hurrying past him on the sidewalk, their chins sunk deep in the collars of their coats, their feet crunching in the snow. None of them was searching for any money; none of them was taking the slightest notice of the small boy crouching in the gutter.

Then was it *his,* this dollar?

Could he *have* it?

Carefully, Charlie pulled it out from under the snow. It was damp and dirty, but otherwise perfect.

A WHOLE dollar!

He held it tightly between his shivering fingers, gazing down at it. It meant one thing to him at that moment, only *one* thing. It meant FOOD.

Automatically, Charlie turned and began moving toward the nearest shop. It was only ten paces away . . . it was a newspaper and stationery store, the kind that sells almost everything, including candy and cigars . . . and what he would *do,* he whispered quickly to himself . . . he would buy one luscious bar of candy and eat it *all* up, every bit of it, right then and there . . . and the rest of the money he would take straight back home and give to his mother.

11
The Miracle

CHARLIE ENTERED THE STORE and laid the damp dollar bill on the counter.

"One Wonka's Whipple-Scrumptious Fudgemallow Delight," he said, remembering how much he had loved the one he had on his birthday.

The man behind the counter looked fat and well-fed. He had big lips and fat cheeks and a very fat neck. The fat around his neck bulged out all around the top of his collar like a rubber ring. He turned and reached behind him

for the candy bar, then he turned back again and handed it to Charlie. Charlie grabbed it and quickly tore off the wrapper and took an enormous bite. Then he took another . . . and another . . . and oh, the joy of being able to cram large pieces of something sweet and solid into one's mouth! The sheer blissful joy of being able to fill one's mouth with rich solid food!

"You look like you wanted that one, sonny," the shopkeeper said pleasantly.

Charlie nodded, his mouth bulging with chocolate

The shopkeeper put Charlie's change on the counter. "Take it easy," he said. "It'll give you a gut-ache if you swallow it like that without chewing."

Charlie went on wolfing the candy. He couldn't stop.

And in less than half a minute, the whole thing had disappeared down his throat. He was quite out of breath, but he felt marvelously, extraordinarily happy. He reached out a hand to take the change. Then he paused. His eyes were just above the level of the counter. They were staring at the little silver coins lying there. The coins were all dimes. There were nine of them altogether. Surely it wouldn't matter if he spent just one more. . . .

"I think," he said quietly, "I think . . . I'll have just one more of those candy bars. The same kind as before, please."

"Why not?" the fat shopkeeper said, reaching behind him again and taking another Whipple-Scrumptious Fudgemallow Delight from the shelf. He laid it on the counter.

Charlie picked it up and tore off the wrapper . . . and *suddenly* . . . from underneath the wrapper . . . there came a brilliant flash of gold.

Charlie's heart stood still.

"It's a Golden Ticket!" screamed the shopkeeper, leaping about a foot in the air. "You've got a Golden Ticket! You've found the last Golden Ticket! Hey, what do you know! Come and look at this, everybody! The kid's found Wonka's last Golden Ticket! There it is! It's right there in his hands!"

It seemed as though the shopkeeper might be going to have a fit. "In my shop, too!" he yelled. "He found it right here in my own little shop! Somebody call the newspapers quick and let them know! Watch out now, sonny! Don't tear it as you unwrap it! That thing's precious!"

In a few seconds, there was a crowd of about twenty people clustering around Charlie, and many more were pushing their way in from the street. Everybody wanted to get a look at the Golden Ticket and at the lucky finder.

"Where is it?" somebody shouted. "Hold it up so all of us can see it!"

"There it is, there!" someone else shouted. "He's holding it in his hands! See the gold shining!"

"How did *he* manage to find it, I'd like to know?" a large boy shouted angrily. "*Twenty* bars a day I've been buying for weeks and weeks!"

"Think of all the free stuff he'll be getting too!" another boy said enviously. "A lifetime supply!"

"He'll need it, the skinny little shrimp!" a girl said, laughing.

Charlie hadn't moved. He hadn't even unwrapped the Golden Ticket from around the candy bar. He was standing very still, holding it tightly with both hands while the crowd pushed and shouted all around him. He felt quite dizzy. There was a peculiar floating sensation coming over him, as though he were floating up in the air like a balloon. His feet didn't seem to be touching the ground at all. He could hear his heart thumping away loudly somewhere in his throat.

At that point, he became aware of a hand resting lightly on his shoulder, and when he looked up, he saw a tall man standing over him. "Listen," the man whispered. "I'll buy it from you. I'll give you fifty dollars. How about it, eh? And I'll give you a new bicycle as well. Okay?"

"Are you *crazy*?" shouted a woman who was standing equally close. "Why, I'd give him *five hundred* dollars for that ticket! You want to sell that ticket for five hundred dollars, young man?"

"That's *quite* enough of that!" the fat shopkeeper

shouted, pushing his way through the crowd and taking Charlie firmly by the arm. "Leave the kid alone, will you! Make way there! Let him out!" And to Charlie, as he led him to the door, he whispered, "Don't you let *anybody* have it! Take it straight home, quickly, before you lose it! Run all the way and don't stop till you get there, you understand?"

Charlie nodded.

"You know something," the fat shopkeeper said, pausing a moment and smiling at Charlie, "I have a feeling you needed a break like this. I'm awfully glad you got it. Good luck to you, sonny."

"Thank you," Charlie said, and off he went, running through the snow as fast as his legs would go. And as he flew past Mr. Willy Wonka's factory, he turned and waved at it and sang out, "I'll be seeing you! I'll be seeing you soon!" And five minutes later he arrived at his own home.

12

What It Said on the Golden Ticket

CHARLIE BURST THROUGH the front door, shouting, *"Mother! Mother! Mother!"*

Mrs. Bucket was in the old grandparents' room, serving them their evening soup.

"Mother!" yelled Charlie, rushing in on them like a hur-

ricane. "Look! I've got it! Look, Mother, look! The last Golden Ticket! It's mine! I found some money in the street and I bought two candy bars and the second one had the Golden Ticket and there were *crowds* of people all around me wanting to see it and the shopkeeper rescued me and I ran all the way home and here I am! *IT'S THE FIFTH GOLDEN TICKET, MOTHER, AND I'VE FOUND IT!*"

Mrs. Bucket simply stood and stared, while the four old grandparents, who were sitting up in bed balancing bowls of soup on their laps, all dropped their spoons with a clatter and froze against their pillows.

For about ten seconds there was absolute silence in the room. Nobody dared to speak or move. It was a magic moment.

Then, very softly, Grandpa Joe said, "You're pulling our legs, Charlie, aren't you? You're having a little joke?"

"I am *not*!" cried Charlie, rushing up to the bed and holding out the large and beautiful Golden Ticket for him to see.

Grandpa Joe leaned forward and took a close look, his nose almost touching the ticket. The others watched him, waiting for the verdict.

Then very slowly, with a slow and marvelous grin spreading all over his face, Grandpa Joe lifted his head and looked straight at Charlie. The color was rushing to his cheeks, and his eyes were wide open, shining with joy, and in the center of each eye, right in the very center, in the black pupil, a little spark of wild excitement was slowly dancing. Then the old man took a deep breath, and suddenly, with no warning whatsoever, an explosion seemed to take place inside him. He threw up his arms

and yelled *"Yippeeeeeeeeeeeeeeeeeeeeeeeeee!"* And at the same time, his long bony body rose up out of the bed and his bowl of soup went flying into the face of Grandma Josephine, and in one fantastic leap, this old fellow of ninety-six and a half, who hadn't been out of bed these last twenty years, jumped on to the floor and started doing a dance of victory in his pajamas.

"Yippeeeeeeeeee!" he shouted. "Three cheers for Charlie! Hip, hip, hooray!"

At this point, the door opened, and Mr. Bucket walked into the room. He was cold and tired, and he looked it. All day long, he had been shoveling snow in the streets.

"Cripes!" he cried. "What's going on in here?"

It didn't take them long to tell him what had happened.

"I don't believe it!" he said. "It's not possible."

"Show him the ticket, Charlie!" shouted Grandpa Joe, who was still dancing around the floor like a dervish in his striped pajamas. "Show your father the fifth and last Golden Ticket in the world!"

"Let me see it, Charlie," Mr. Bucket said, collapsing into a chair and holding out his hand. Charlie came forward with the precious document.

It was a very beautiful thing, this Golden Ticket, having been made, so it seemed, from a sheet of pure gold hammered out almost to the thinness of paper. On one side of it, printed by some clever method in jet-black letters, was the invitation itself—from Mr. Wonka.

"Read it aloud," said Grandpa Joe, climbing back into bed again at last. "Let's all hear exactly what it says."

Mr. Bucket held the lovely Golden Ticket up close

to his eyes. His hands were trembling slightly, and he seemed to be overcome by the whole business. He took several deep breaths. Then he cleared his throat, and said, "All right, I'll read it. Here we go:

'Greetings to you, the lucky finder of this golden ticket, from Mr. Willy Wonka! I shake you warmly by the hand! Tremendous things are in store for you! Many wonderful surprises await you! For now, I do invite you to come to my factory and be my guest for one whole day—you and all others who are lucky enough to find my Golden Tickets. I, Willy Wonka, will conduct you around the factory myself, showing you everything that there is to see, and afterwards, when it is time to leave, you will be escorted home by a procession of large trucks. These trucks, I can promise you, will be loaded with enough delicious eatables to last you and your entire household for many years. If, at any time thereafter, you should run out of supplies, you have only to come back to the factory and show this Golden Ticket, and I shall be happy to refill your cupboard with whatever you want. In this way, you will be able to keep yourself supplied with tasty morsels for the rest of your life. But this is by no means the most exciting thing that will happen on the day of your visit. I am preparing other surprises that are even more marvelous and more fantastic for you and for all my beloved Golden Ticket holders—mystic and marvelous surprises that will entrance, delight, intrigue, astonish, and perplex you beyond measure. In your wildest

dreams you could not imagine that such things could happen to you! Just wait and see! And now, here are your instructions: The day I have chosen for the visit is the first day in the month of February. On this day, and on no other, you must come to the factory gates at ten o'clock sharp in the morning. Don't be late! And you are allowed to bring with you either one or two members of your own family to look after you and to ensure that you don't get into mischief. One more thing—be certain to have this ticket with you, otherwise you will not be admitted.

(Signed) Willy Wonka.'"

"The first day of *February*!" cried Mrs. Bucket. "But that's *tomorrow*! Today is the last day of January, *I know it is!*"

"Cripes!" said Mr. Bucket. "I think you're right!"

"You're just in time!" shouted Grandpa Joe. "There's not a moment to lose. You must start making preparations at once! Wash your face, comb your hair, scrub your hands, brush your teeth, blow your nose, cut your nails, polish your shoes, iron your shirt, and for heaven's sake, get all that mud off your pants! You must get ready, my boy! You must get ready for the biggest day of your life!"

"Now don't overexcite yourself, Grandpa," Mrs. Bucket said. "And don't fluster poor Charlie. We must all try to keep very calm. Now the first thing to decide is this— who is going to go with Charlie to the factory?"

"*I* will!" shouted Grandpa Joe, leaping out of bed once again. "I'll take him! I'll look after him! You leave it to me!"

Mrs. Bucket smiled at the old man, then she turned to her husband and said, "How about you, dear? Don't you think *you* ought to go?"

"Well . . ." Mr. Bucket said, pausing to think about it, "no . . . I'm not so sure that I should."

"But you *must*."

"There's no *must* about it, my dear," Mr. Bucket said gently. "Mind you, I'd *love* to go. It'll be tremendously exciting. But on the other hand . . . I believe that the person who really *deserves* to go most of all is Grandpa Joe himself. He seems to know more about it than we do. Provided, of course, that he feels well enough. . . ."

"Yippeeeeee!" shouted Grandpa Joe, seizing Charlie by the hands and dancing round the room.

"He certainly *seems* well enough," Mrs. Bucket said, laughing. "Yes . . . perhaps you're right after all. Perhaps

Grandpa Joe should be the one to go with him. I certainly can't go myself and leave the other three old people all alone in bed for a whole day."

"Hallelujah!" yelled Grandpa Joe. "Praise the Lord!"

At that point, there came a loud knock on the front door. Mr. Bucket went to open it, and the next moment, swarms of newspapermen and photographers were pouring into the house. They had tracked down the finder of the fifth Golden Ticket, and now they all wanted to get the full story for the front pages of morning papers. For several hours, there was complete pandemonium in the little house, and it must have been nearly midnight before Mr. Bucket was able to get rid of them so that Charlie could go to bed.

13
The Big Day Arrives

THE SUN WAS SHINING BRIGHTLY on the morning of the big day, but the ground was still white with snow and the air was very cold.

Outside the gates of Wonka's factory, enormous crowds of people had gathered to watch the five lucky ticket holders going in. The excitement was tremendous. It was just before ten o'clock. The crowds were pushing and shouting, and policemen with arms linked were trying to hold them back from the gates.

Right beside the gates, in a small group that was carefully shielded from the crowds by the police, stood the five famous children, together with the grownups who had come with them.

The tall bony old figure of Grandpa Joe could be seen standing quietly among them, and beside him, holding tightly on to his hand, was little Charlie Bucket himself.

All the children, except Charlie, had both their mothers and fathers with them, and it was a good thing that they had, otherwise the whole party might have gotten out of hand. They were so eager to get going that their parents were having to hold them back by force to prevent them from climbing over the gates. "Be patient!" cried the fathers. "Be still! It's not *time* yet! It's not ten o'clock!"

Behind him, Charlie Bucket could hear the shouts of the people in the crowd as they pushed and fought to get a glimpse of the famous children.

"There's Violet Beauregarde!" he heard someone shouting. "That's her all right! I can remember her face from the newspapers!"

"And you know what?" somebody else shouted back. "She's still chewing that dreadful old piece of gum she's had for three months! You look at her jaws! They're still working on it!"

"Who's the big fat boy?"

"That's Augustus Gloop!"

"So it is!"

"Enormous, isn't he!"

"Fantastic!"

"Who's the kid with a picture of The Lone Ranger stenciled on his windbreaker?"

"That's Mike Teavee! He's the television fiend!"

"He must be crazy! Look at all those crazy pistols he's got hanging all over him!"

"The one *I* want to see is Veruca Salt!" shouted another voice in the crowd. "She's the girl whose father bought up half a million candy bars and then made the workers in his peanut factory unwrap every one of them until they found a Golden Ticket! He gives her anything she wants! Absolutely anything! She only has to start screaming for it and she gets it!"

"Dreadful, isn't it?"

"Shocking, I call it!"

"Which do you think is her?"

"That one! Over there on the left! The little girl in the silver mink coat!"

"Which one is Charlie Bucket?"

"Charlie Bucket? He must be that skinny little shrimp standing beside the old fellow who looks like a skeleton. Right close to us. Just there! See him?"

"Why hasn't he got a coat on in this cold weather?"

"Don't ask me. Maybe he can't afford to buy one."

"Jeepers! He must be freezing!"

Charlie, standing only a few paces away from the speaker, gave Grandpa Joe's hand a squeeze, and the old man looked down at Charlie and smiled.

Somewhere in the distance, a church clock began striking ten.

Very slowly, with a loud creaking of rusty hinges, the

great iron gates of the factory began to swing open.

The crowd became suddenly silent. The children stopped jumping about. All eyes were fixed upon the gates.

"There he is!" somebody shouted. *"That's him!"*

And so it was!

14

Mr. Willy Wonka

MR. WONKA WAS STANDING all alone just inside the open gates of the factory.

And what an extraordinary little man he was!

He had a black top hat on his head.

He wore a tail coat made of a beautiful plum-colored velvet.

His trousers were bottle green.

His gloves were pearly gray.

And in one hand he carried a fine gold-topped walking cane.

Covering his chin, there was a small neat pointed black beard—a goatee. And his eyes—his eyes were most marvelously bright. They seemed to be sparkling and twinkling at you all the time. The whole face, in fact, was alight with fun and laughter.

And oh, how clever he looked! How quick and sharp and full of life! He kept making quick jerky little movements with his head, cocking it this way and that, and taking everything in with those bright twinkling eyes. He was like a squirrel in the quickness of his movements, like a quick clever old squirrel from the park.

Suddenly, he did a funny little skipping dance in the snow, and he spread his arms wide, and he smiled at the five children who were clustered near the gates, and he called out, "Welcome, my little friends! Welcome to the factory!"

His voice was high and flutey. "Will you come forward one at a time, please," he called out, "and bring your parents. Then show me your Golden Ticket and give me your name. Who's first?"

The big fat boy stepped up. "I'm Augustus Gloop," he said.

"Augustus!" cried Mr. Wonka, seizing his hand and pumping it up and down with terrific force. "My *dear* boy, how *good* to see you! Delighted! Charmed! Overjoyed to have you with us! And *these* are your parents? How nice! Come in! Come in! That's right! Step through the gates!"

Mr. Wonka was clearly just as excited as everybody else.

"My name," said the next child to go forward, "is Veruca Salt."

"My *dear* Veruca! How *do* you do? What a pleasure this is! You *do* have an interesting name, don't you? I always thought that a veruca was a sort of wart that you got on the sole of your foot! But I must be wrong, mustn't I? How pretty you look in that lovely mink coat! I'm so glad you could come! Dear me, this is going to be *such* an exciting day! I *do* hope you enjoy it! I'm sure you *will*! I *know* you will! Your father? How *are* you, Mr. Salt? And Mrs. Salt? Overjoyed to see you! Yes, the ticket is *quite* in order! Please go in!"

The next two children, Violet Beauregarde and Mike Teavee, came forward to have their tickets examined and then to have their arms practically pumped off their shoulders by the energetic Mr. Wonka.

And last of all, a small nervous voice whispered, "Charlie Bucket."

"Charlie!" cried Mr. Wonka. "Well, well, well! So *there*

you are! You're the one who found your ticket only yesterday, aren't you? Yes, yes. I read *all* about it in this morning's papers! *Just* in time, my dear boy! I'm so glad! So happy for you! And this? Your grandfather? Delighted to meet you, sir! Overjoyed! Enraptured! Enchanted! All right! Excellent! Is everybody in now? Five children? Yes! Good! Now will you please follow me! Our tour is about to begin! But *do* keep together! *Please* don't wander off by yourselves! I shouldn't like to lose any of you at *this* stage of the proceedings! Oh, dear me, no!"

Charlie glanced back over his shoulder and saw the great iron entrance gates slowly closing behind him. The crowds on the outside were still pushing and shouting. Charlie took a last look at them. Then, as the gates closed with a clang, all sight of the outside world disappeared.

"Here we are!" cried Mr. Wonka, trotting along in front of the group. "Through this big red door, please! *That's* right! It's nice and warm inside! I have to keep it warm inside the factory because of the workers! My workers are used to an *extremely* hot climate! They can't stand the cold! They'd perish if they went outdoors in this weather! They'd freeze to death!"

"But who *are* these workers?" asked Augustus Gloop.

"All in good time, my dear boy!" said Mr. Wonka, smiling at Augustus. "Be patient! You shall see everything as we go along! Are all of you inside? Good! Would you mind closing the door? Thank you."

Charlie Bucket found himself standing in a long corridor that stretched away in front of him as far as he could see. The corridor was so wide that a car could easily have been driven along it. The walls were pale pink, the lighting was soft and pleasant.

"How lovely and warm!" whispered Charlie.

"I know. And what a marvelous smell!" answered Grandpa Joe, taking a long deep sniff. All the most wonderful smells in the world seemed to be mixed up in the air around them—the smell of roasting coffee and burnt sugar and melting chocolate and mint and violets and crushed hazelnuts and apple blossom and caramel and lemon peel. . . .

And far away in the distance, from the heart of the great factory, came a muffled roar of energy as though some monstrous gigantic machine were spinning its wheels at breakneck speed.

"Now *this,* my dear children," said Mr. Wonka, raising his voice above the noise, "this is the main corridor. Will you please hang your coats and hats on those pegs over there, and then follow me. *That's* the way! Good! Everyone ready! Come on, then! Here we go!" He trotted off rapidly down the corridor with the tails of his plum-colored velvet coat flapping behind him, and the visitors all hurried after him.

It was quite a large party of people, when you came to think of it. There were nine grownups and five children, fourteen in all. So you can imagine that there was a good deal of pushing and shoving as they hustled and bustled down the passage, trying to keep up with the swift little figure in front of them. "Come *on!*" cried Mr. Wonka. "Get a move on, please! We'll *never* get round today if you dawdle like this!"

Soon, he turned right off the main corridor into another slightly narrower passage.

Then he turned left.

Then left again.

Then right.

Then left.

Then right.

Then right.

Then left.

The place was like a gigantic rabbit warren, with passages leading this way and that in every direction.

"Don't you let go my hand, Charlie," whispered Grandpa Joe.

"Notice how all these passages are sloping downwards!" called Mr. Wonka. "We are now going underground! *All* the most important rooms in my factory are deep down below the surface!"

"Why is that?" somebody asked.

"There wouldn't be *nearly* enough space for them up on top!" answered Mr. Wonka. "These rooms we are going to see are *enormous*! They're larger than football fields! No building in the *world* would be big enough to house them! But down here, underneath the ground, I've got *all* the space I want. There's no limit—so long as I hollow it out."

Mr. Wonka turned right.

He turned left.

He turned right again.

The passages were sloping steeper and steeper downhill now.

Then suddenly, Mr. Wonka stopped. In front of him, there was a shiny metal door. The party crowded round. On the door, in large letters, it said:

THE CHOCOLATE ROOM

15

The Chocolate Room

"AN IMPORTANT ROOM, THIS!" cried Mr. Wonka, taking a bunch of keys from his pocket and slipping one into the keyhole of the door. "*This* is the nerve center of the whole factory, the heart of the whole business! And so *beautiful*! I *insist* upon my rooms being beautiful! I can't *abide* ugliness in factories! *In* we go, then! But *do* be careful, my dear children! Don't lose your heads! Don't get overexcited! Keep very calm!"

Mr. Wonka opened the door. Five children and nine grownups pushed their ways in—and *oh,* what an amazing sight it was that now met their eyes!

They were looking down upon a lovely valley. There were green meadows on either side of the valley, and along the bottom of it there flowed a great brown river.

What is more, there was a tremendous waterfall halfway along the river—a steep cliff over which the water curled and rolled in a solid sheet, and then went crashing down into a boiling churning whirlpool of froth and spray.

Below the waterfall (and this was the most astonishing sight of all), a whole mass of enormous glass pipes were dangling down into the river from somewhere high up in the ceiling! They really were *enormous,* those pipes. There must have been a dozen of them at least, and they were sucking up the brownish muddy water from the river and carrying it away to goodness knows where. And because they were made of glass, you could see the liquid flowing and bubbling along inside them, and above the noise of the waterfall, you could hear the never-ending suck-suck-sucking sound of the pipes as they did their work.

Graceful trees and bushes were growing along the riverbanks—weeping willows and alders and tall clumps of rhododendrons with their pink and red and mauve blossoms. In the meadows there were thousands of buttercups.

"There!" cried Mr. Wonka, dancing up and down and pointing his gold-topped cane at the great brown river. "It's *all* chocolate! Every drop of that river is hot melted chocolate of the finest quality. The *very* finest quality. There's enough chocolate in there to fill *every* bathtub in the *entire* country! *And* all the swimming pools as well! Isn't it *terrific*? And just look at my pipes! They suck up the chocolate and carry it away to all the other rooms in the factory where it is needed! Thousands of gallons an hour, my dear children! Thousands and thousands of gallons!"

The children and their parents were too flabbergasted to speak. They were staggered. They were dumfounded. They were bewildered and dazzled. They were com-

pletely bowled over by the hugeness of the whole thing. They simply stood and stared.

"The waterfall is *most* important!" Mr. Wonka went on. "It mixes the chocolate! It churns it up! It pounds it and beats it! It makes it light and frothy! No other factory in the world mixes its chocolate by waterfall! But it's the *only* way to do it properly! The *only* way! And do you like my trees?" he cried, pointing with his stick. "And my lovely bushes? Don't you think they look pretty? I told you I hated ugliness! And of course they are *all* eatable! All made of something different and delicious! And do you like my meadows? Do you like my grass and my buttercups? The grass you are standing on, my dear little ones, is made of a new kind of soft, minty sugar that I've just invented! I call it swudge! Try a blade! Please do! It's delectable!"

Automatically, everybody bent down and picked one blade of grass—everybody, that is, except Augustus Gloop, who took a big handful.

And Violet Beauregarde, before tasting her blade of grass, took the piece of world-record-breaking chewing gum out of her mouth and stuck it carefully behind her ear.

"Isn't it *wonderful*!" whispered Charlie. "Hasn't it got a wonderful taste, Grandpa?"

"I could eat the whole *field*!" said Grandpa Joe, grinning with delight. "I could go around on all fours like a cow and eat every blade of grass in the field!"

"Try a buttercup!" cried Mr. Wonka. "They're even *nicer*!"

Suddenly, the air was filled with screams of excitement. The screams came from Veruca Salt. She was pointing frantically to the other side of the river. "*Look*! Look over there!" she screamed. "What *is* it? He's moving! He's walking! It's a little *person*! It's a little *man*! Down there below the waterfall!"

Everybody stopped picking buttercups and stared across the river.

"*She's right, Grandpa!*" cried Charlie. "It *is* a little man! Can you *see* him?"

"I see him, Charlie!" said Grandpa Joe excitedly.

And now everybody started shouting at once.

"There's *two* of them!"

"My gosh, so there is!"

"There's more than two! There's one, two, three, four, five!"

"What are they *doing*?"

"Where do they *come* from?"

"Who *are* they?"

Children and parents alike rushed down to the edge of the river to get a closer look.

"Aren't they *fantastic*!"

"No higher than my knee!"

"Look at their funny long hair!"

The tiny men—they were no larger than medium-sized dolls—had stopped what they were doing, and now they were staring back across the river at the visitors. One of them pointed towards the children, and then he whispered something to the other four, and all five of them burst into peals of laughter.

"But they can't be *real* people," Charlie said.

"Of course they're real people," Mr. Wonka answered. "They're Oompa-Loompas."

16

The Oompa-Loompas

"Oompa-Loompas!" everyone said at once. *"Oompa-Loompas!"*

"Imported direct from Loompaland," said Mr. Wonka proudly.

"There's no such place," said Mrs. Salt.

"Excuse me, dear lady, but . . ."

"Mr. Wonka," cried Mrs. Salt. "I am a teacher of geography . . ."

"Then you'll know all about it," said Mr. Wonka. "And oh, what a terrible country it is! Nothing but thick jungles infested by the most dangerous beasts in the entire world—hornswogglers and snozzwangers and those terrible wicked whangdoodles. A whangdoodle would eat ten Oompa-Loompas for breakfast and come galloping back for a second helping. When I went out there, I found the little Oompa-Loompas living in tree-houses. They *had* to live in tree-houses to escape from the whangdoodles and the hornswogglers and the snozzwangers. And they were practically starving to death. They were living on green caterpillars, and the caterpillars tasted revolting, and the Oompa-Loompas spent every moment of their days climbing through the treetops looking for other things to mash up with the caterpillars to make them taste better—red beetles, for instance, and eucalyptus leaves, and the bark of the bong-bong tree, all of them beastly, but not quite so beastly as the caterpillars. Poor little Oompa-Loompas! The one food that they longed for more than any other was the cacao bean. But they couldn't get it. An Oompa-Loompa was lucky if he found three or four cacao beans a year. But oh, how they craved them. They used to dream about cacao beans all night and talk about them all day. You had only to *mention* the word 'cacao' to an Oompa-Loompa and he would start dribbling at the mouth. The cacao bean," Mr. Wonka continued, "which grows on the cacao tree, happens to be *the thing* from which all chocolate is made. You cannot make chocolate without the cacao bean. The cacao bean *is* chocolate. I myself use billions of cacao beans every week in this factory. And so, my dear children, as soon as

I discovered that the Oompa-Loompas were crazy for this particular food, I climbed up to their tree-house village and poked my head in through the door of the tree house belonging to the leader of the tribe. The poor little fellow, looking thin and starved, was sitting there trying to eat a bowl full of mashed-up green caterpillars without being sick. 'Look here,' I said (speaking not in English, of course, but in Oompa-Loompish), 'look here, if you and all your people will come back to my country and live in my factory, you can have *all* the cacao beans you want! I've got mountains of them in my storehouses! You can have cacao beans for every meal! You can gorge yourselves silly on them! I'll even pay your wages in cacao beans if you wish!'

"'You really mean it?' asked the Oompa-Loompa leader, leaping up from his chair.

"'Of course I mean it,' I said. 'And you can have choco-late as well. Chocolate tastes even better than cacao beans because it's got milk and sugar added.'

"The little man gave a great whoop of joy and threw his bowl of mashed caterpillars right out of the tree-house window. 'It's a deal!' he cried. 'Come on! Let's go!'

"So I shipped them all over here, every man, woman, and child in the Oompa-Loompa tribe. It was easy. I smug-gled them over in large packing cases with holes in them, and they all got here safely. They are wonderful workers. They all speak English now. They love dancing and music. They are always making up songs. I expect you will hear a good deal of singing today from time to time. I must warn you, though, that they are rather mischievous. They like jokes. They still wear the same kind of clothes they wore in the jungle. They insist upon that. The men, as you can see for yourselves across the river, wear only deer-skins. The women wear leaves, and the children wear nothing at all. The women use fresh leaves every day. . . ."

"Daddy!" shouted Veruca Salt (the girl who got every-thing she wanted). "*Daddy!* I want an Oompa-Loompa! I want you to get me an Oompa-Loompa! I want an Oompa-Loompa right away! I want to take it home with me! Go on, Daddy! Get me an Oompa-Loompa!"

"Now, now, my pet!" her father said to her, "we mustn't interrupt Mr. Wonka."

"But I want an Oompa-Loompa!" screamed Veruca.

"All *right*, Veruca, all *right*. But I can't get it for you this second. Please be patient. I'll see you have one before the day is out."

"Augustus!" shouted Mrs. Gloop. "Augustus, sweetheart,

I don't think you had better do *that*." Augustus Gloop, as you might have guessed, had quietly sneaked down to the edge of the river, and he was now kneeling on the river-bank, scooping hot melted chocolate into his mouth as fast as he could.

17
Augustus Gloop Goes up the Pipe

WHEN MR. WONKA turned round and saw what Augustus Gloop was doing, he cried out, "Oh, no! *Please*, Augustus, *please*! I beg of you not to do that. My chocolate must be untouched by human hands!"

"Augustus!" called out Mrs. Gloop. "Didn't you hear what the man said? Come away from that river at once!"

"This stuff is *tee*-riffic!" said Augustus, taking not the slightest notice of his mother or Mr. Wonka. "Oh boy, I need a bucket to drink it properly!"

"Augustus," cried Mr. Wonka, hopping up and down and waggling his stick in the air, "you *must* come away. You are dirtying my chocolate!"

"Augustus!" cried Mrs. Gloop.

"Augustus!" cried Mr. Gloop.

But Augustus was deaf to everything except the call of his enormous stomach. He was now lying full length on the ground with his head far out over the river, lapping up the chocolate like a dog.

"Augustus!" shouted Mrs. Gloop. "You'll be giving that nasty cold of yours to about a million people all over the country!"

"Be careful, Augustus!" shouted Mr. Gloop. "You're leaning too far out!"

Mr. Gloop was absolutely right. For suddenly there was a shriek, and then a splash, and into the river went Augustus Gloop, and in one second he had disappeared under the brown surface.

"Save him!" screamed Mrs. Gloop, going white in the face, and waving her umbrella about. "He'll drown! He can't swim a yard! Save him! Save him!"

"Good heavens, woman," said Mr. Gloop, "I'm not diving in there! I've got my best suit on!"

Augustus Gloop's face came up again to the surface, painted brown with chocolate. "Help! Help! Help!" he yelled. "Fish me out!"

"Don't just *stand* there!" Mrs. Gloop screamed at Mr. Gloop. "*Do* something!"

"I *am* doing something!" said Mr. Gloop, who was now taking off his jacket and getting ready to dive into the chocolate. But while he was doing this, the wretched boy was being sucked closer and closer toward the mouth of one of the great pipes that was dangling down into the river. Then all at once, the powerful suction took hold of him completely, and he was pulled under the surface and then into the mouth of the pipe.

The crowd on the riverbank waited breathlessly to see where he would come out.

"There he goes!" somebody shouted, pointing upwards.

And sure enough, because the pipe was made of glass, Augustus Gloop could be clearly seen shooting up inside it, head first, like a torpedo.

"Help! Murder! Police!" screamed Mrs. Gloop. "Augustus, come back at once! Where are you going?"

"It's a wonder to me," said Mr. Gloop, "how that pipe is big enough for him to go through it."

"It *isn't* big enough!" said Charlie Bucket. "Oh dear, look! He's slowing down!"

"So he is!" said Grandpa Joe.

"He's going to stick!" said Charlie.

"I think he is!" said Grandpa Joe.

"By golly, he *has* stuck!" said Charlie.

"It's his stomach that's done it!" said Mr. Gloop.

"He's blocked the whole pipe!" said Grandpa Joe.

"Smash the pipe!" yelled Mrs. Gloop, still waving her umbrella. "Augustus, come out of there at once!"

The watchers below could see the chocolate swishing around the boy in the pipe, and they could see it building up behind him in a solid mass, pushing against the blockage. The pressure was terrific. Something had to give. Something did give, and that something was Augustus. WHOOF! Up he shot again like a bullet in the barrel of a gun.

"He's disappeared!" yelled Mrs. Gloop. "Where does that pipe go to? Quick! Call the fire brigade!"

"Keep calm!" cried Mr. Wonka. "Keep calm, my dear lady, keep calm. There is no danger! No danger whatsoever! Augustus has gone on a little journey, that's all. A most interesting little journey. But he'll come out of it just fine, you wait and see."

"How can he possibly come out just fine!" snapped Mrs. Gloop. "He'll be made into marshmallows in five seconds!"

"Impossible!" cried Mr. Wonka. "Unthinkable! Inconceivable! Absurd! He could never be made into marshmallows!"

"And why not, may I ask?" shouted Mrs. Gloop.

"Because that pipe doesn't *go* to the Marshmallow Room!" Mr. Wonka answered. "It doesn't go anywhere near it! That pipe—the one Augustus went up—happens to lead directly to the room where I make a most delicious kind of strawberry-flavored chocolate-coated fudge. . . ."

"Then he'll be made into strawberry-flavored chocolate-coated fudge!" screamed Mrs. Gloop. "My poor Augustus! They'll be selling him by the pound all over the country tomorrow morning!"

"Quite right," said Mr. Gloop.

"I *know* I'm right," said Mrs. Gloop.

"It's beyond a joke," said Mr. Gloop.

"Mr. Wonka doesn't seem to think so!" cried Mrs. Gloop. "Just look at him! He's laughing his head off! How *dare* you laugh like that when my boy's just gone up the pipe! You monster!" she shrieked, pointing her umbrella at Mr. Wonka as though she were going to run him through. "You think it's a joke, do you? You think that sucking my boy up into your Fudge Room like that is just one great big colossal joke?"

"He'll be perfectly safe," said Mr. Wonka, giggling slightly.

"He'll be chocolate fudge!" shrieked Mrs. Gloop.

"Never!" cried Mr. Wonka.

"Of course he will!" shrieked Mrs. Gloop.

"I wouldn't allow it!" cried Mr. Wonka.

"And why not?" shrieked Mrs. Gloop.

"Because the taste would be terrible," said Mr. Wonka. "Just imagine it! Augustus-flavored chocolate-coated Gloop! No one would buy it."

"They most certainly would!" cried Mr. Gloop indignantly.

"I don't want to think about it!" shrieked Mrs. Gloop.

"Nor do I," said Mr. Wonka. "And I do promise you, madam, that your darling boy is perfectly safe."

"If he's perfectly safe, then where is he?" snapped Mrs. Gloop. "Lead me to him this instant!"

Mr. Wonka turned around and clicked his fingers sharply, *click, click, click,* three times. Immediately, an Oompa-Loompa appeared, as if from nowhere, and stood beside him.

The Oompa-Loompa bowed and smiled, showing beautiful white teeth. His skin was rosy-white, his long hair was golden-brown, and the top of his head came just above the height of Mr. Wonka's knee. He wore the usual deerskin slung over his shoulder.

"Now listen to me!" said Mr. Wonka, looking down at the tiny man, "I want you to take Mr. and Mrs. Gloop up to the Fudge Room and help them to find their son, Augustus. He's just gone up the pipe."

The Oompa-Loompa took one look at Mrs. Gloop and exploded into peals of laughter.

"Oh, do be quiet!" said Mr. Wonka. "Control yourself! Pull yourself together! Mrs. Gloop doesn't think it's at all funny!"

"You can say that again!" said Mrs. Gloop.

"Go straight to the Fudge Room," Mr. Wonka said to the Oompa-Loompa, "and when you get there, take a long stick and start poking around inside the big chocolate-mixing barrel. I'm almost certain you'll find him in there.

But you'd better look sharp! You'll have to hurry! If you leave him in the chocolate-mixing barrel too long, he's liable to get poured out into the fudge boiler, and that really *would* be a disaster, wouldn't it? My fudge would become *quite* uneatable!"

Mrs. Gloop let out a shriek of fury.

"I'm joking," said Mr. Wonka, giggling madly behind his beard. "I didn't mean it. Forgive me. I'm so sorry. Good-by, Mrs. Gloop! And Mr. Gloop! Good-by! Good-by! I'll see you later. . . ."

As Mr. and Mrs. Gloop and their tiny escort hurried away, the five Oompa-Loompas on the far side of the river suddenly began hopping and dancing about and beating wildly upon a number of very small drums. "Augustus Gloop!" they chanted. "Augustus Gloop! Augustus Gloop! Augustus Gloop!"

"Grandpa!" cried Charlie. "Listen to them, Grandpa! What *are* they doing?"

"Ssshh!" whispered Grandpa Joe. "I think they're going to sing us a song!"

"Augustus Gloop!" chanted the Oompa-Loompas.
"Augustus Gloop! Augustus Gloop!
The great big greedy nincompoop!
How long could we allow this beast
To gorge and guzzle, feed and feast
On everything he wanted to?
Great Scott! It simply wouldn't do!
However long this pig might live,
We're positive he'd never give
Even the smallest bit of fun

Or happiness to anyone.
So what we do in cases such
As this, we use the gentle touch,
And carefully we take the brat
And turn him into something that
Will give great pleasure to us all—
A doll, for instance, or a ball,
Or marbles or a rocking horse.
But this revolting boy, of course,
Was so unutterably vile,
So greedy, foul, and infantile,
He left a most disgusting taste
Inside our mouths, and so in haste
We chose a thing that, come what may,
Would take the nasty taste away.
'Come on!' we cried, 'The time is ripe
To send him shooting up the pipe!
He has to go! It has to be!'
And very soon, he's going to see
Inside the room to which he's gone
Some funny things are going on.
But don't, dear children, be alarmed;
Augustus Gloop will not be harmed,
Although, of course, we must admit
He will be altered *quite a bit.*
He'll be quite *changed from what he's been,*
When he goes through the fudge machine:
Slowly, the wheels go round and round,
The cogs begin to grind and pound;
A hundred knives to slice, slice, slice;
We add some sugar, cream, and spice;

We boil him for a minute more,
Until we're absolutely sure
That all the greed and all the gall
Is boiled away for once and all.
Then out he comes! And now! By grace!
A miracle has taken place!
This boy, who only just before
Was loathed by men from shore to shore,
This greedy brute, this louse's ear,
Is loved by people everywhere!
For who could hate or bear a grudge
Against a luscious bit of fudge?"

"I *told* you they loved singing!" cried Mr. Wonka. "Aren't they delightful? Aren't they charming? But you mustn't believe a word they said. It's all nonsense, every bit of it!"

"Are the Oompa-Loompas really joking, Grandpa?" asked Charlie.

"Of course they're joking," answered Grandpa Joe. "They *must* be joking. At least, I hope they're joking. Don't you?"

18

Down the Chocolate River

"OFF WE GO!" cried Mr. Wonka. "Hurry up, everybody! Follow me to the next room! And please don't worry about

Augustus Gloop. He's bound to come out in the wash. They always do. We shall have to make the next part of the journey by boat! Here she comes! Look!"

A steamy mist was rising up now from the great warm chocolate river, and out of the mist there appeared suddenly a most fantastic pink boat. It was a large open rowboat with a tall front and a tall back (like a Viking boat of old), and it was of such a shining sparkling glistening pink color that the whole thing looked as though it were made of bright, pink glass. There were many oars on either side of it, and as the boat came closer, the watchers on the riverbank could see that the oars were being pulled by masses of Oompa-Loompas—at least ten of them to each oar.

"This is my private yacht!" cried Mr. Wonka, beaming with pleasure. "I made her by hollowing out an enormous boiled sweet! Isn't she beautiful! See how she comes cutting through the river!"

The gleaming pink boiled-sweet boat glided up to the riverbank. One hundred Oompa-Loompas rested on their oars and stared up at the visitors. Then suddenly, for some reason best known to themselves, they all burst into shrieks of laughter.

"What's so funny?" asked Violet Beauregarde.

"Oh, don't worry about *them*!" cried Mr. Wonka. "They're always laughing! They think everything's a colossal joke! Jump into the boat, all of you! Come on! Hurry up!"

As soon as everyone was safely in, the Oompa-Loompas pushed the boat away from the bank and began to row swiftly down river.

"Hey, there! Mike Teavee!" shouted Mr. Wonka. "Please

do not lick the boat with your tongue! It'll only make it sticky!"

"Daddy," said Veruca Salt, "I want a boat like this! I want you to buy me a big pink boiled-sweet boat exactly like Mr. Wonka's! And I want lots of Oompa-Loompas to row me about, and I want a chocolate river and I want . . . I want . . ."

"She wants a good kick in the pants," whispered Grandpa Joe to Charlie. The old man was sitting in the back of the boat and little Charlie Bucket was right beside him. Charlie was holding tightly onto his grandfather's bony old hand. He was in a whirl of excitement. Everything that he had seen so far—the great chocolate river, the waterfall, the huge sucking pipes, the candy meadows, the Oompa-Loompas, the beautiful pink boat, and most of all, Mr. Willy Wonka himself—had been so astonishing that he began to wonder whether there could possibly be any more astonishments left. Where were they going now? What were they going to see? And what in the world was going to happen in the next room?

"Isn't is marvelous?" said Grandpa Joe, grinning at Charlie.

Charlie nodded and smiled up at the old man.

Suddenly, Mr. Wonka, who was sitting on Charlie's other side, reached down into the bottom of the boat, picked up a large mug, dipped it into the river, filled it with chocolate, and handed it to Charlie. "Drink this," he said. "It'll do you good! You looked starved to death!"

Then Mr. Wonka filled a second mug and gave it to Grandpa Joe. "You, too," he said. "You look like a skeleton! What's the matter? Hasn't there been anything to eat in your house lately?"

"Not much," said Grandpa Joe.

Charlie put the mug to his lips, and as the rich warm creamy chocolate ran down his throat into his empty tummy, his whole body from head to toe began to tingle with pleasure, and a feeling of intense happiness spread over him.

"You like it?" asked Mr. Wonka.

"Oh, it's wonderful!" Charlie said.

"The creamiest loveliest chocolate I've ever tasted!" said Grandpa Joe, smacking his lips.

"That's because it's been mixed by waterfall," Mr. Wonka told him.

The boat sped on down the river. The river was getting narrower. There was some kind of a dark tunnel ahead—a great round tunnel that looked like an enormous pipe—and the river was running right into the tunnel. And so was the boat! "Row on!" shouted Mr. Wonka, jumping up and waving his stick in the air. "Full speed ahead!" And with the Oompa-Loompas rowing faster than ever, the boat shot into the pitch-dark tunnel, and all the passengers screamed with excitement.

"How can they see where they're going?" shrieked Violet Beauregarde in the darkness.

"There's no knowing where they're going!" cried Mr. Wonka, hooting with laughter.

> "There's no earthly way of knowing
> Which direction they are going!
> There's no knowing where they're rowing,
> Or which way the river's flowing!
> Not a speck of light is showing,

So the danger must be growing,
For the rowers keep on rowing,
And they're certainly not showing
Any signs that they are slowing...."

"He's gone off his rocker!" shouted one of the fathers, aghast, and the other parents joined in the chorus of frightened shouting. "He's crazy!" they shouted.

"He's balmy!"

"He's nutty!"

"He's screwy!"

"He's batty!"

"He's dippy!"

"He's dotty!"

"He's daffy!"

"He's goofy!"

"He's beany!"

"He's buggy!"

"He's wacky!"

"He's loony!"

"No, he is *not*!" said Grandpa Joe.

"Switch on the lights!" shouted Mr. Wonka. And suddenly, on came the lights and the whole tunnel was brilliantly lit up, and Charlie could see that they were indeed inside a gigantic pipe, and the great upward-curving walls of the pipe were pure white and spotlessly clean. The river of chocolate was flowing very fast inside the pipe, and the Oompa-Loompas were all rowing like crazy, and the boat was rocketing along at a furious pace. Mr. Wonka was jumping up and down in the back of the boat and calling to the rowers to row faster and faster still. He seemed to love the sensation of whizzing through a white tunnel in a pink boat on a chocolate river, and he clapped his hands and laughed and kept glancing at his passengers to see if they were enjoying it as much as he.

"Look, Grandpa!" cried Charlie. "There's a door in the wall!" It was a green door and it was set into the wall of the tunnel just above the level of the river. As they flashed past it there was just enough time to read the writing on the door: STOREROOM NUMBER 54, it said. ALL THE CREAMS—DAIRY CREAM, WHIPPED CREAM, VIOLET CREAM, COFFEE CREAM, PINEAPPLE CREAM, VANILLA CREAM, AND HAIR CREAM.

"Hair cream?" cried Mike Teavee. "You don't use *hair cream*?"

"Row on!" shouted Mr. Wonka. "There's no time to answer silly questions!"

They streaked past a black door. STOREROOM NUMBER 71, it said on it. WHIPS—ALL SHAPES AND SIZES.

"*Whips!*" cried Veruca Salt. "What on earth do you use whips for?"

"For whipping cream, of course," said Mr. Wonka. "How can you whip cream without whips? Whipped cream isn't whipped cream at all unless it's been whipped with whips. Just as a poached egg isn't a poached egg unless it's been stolen from the woods in the dead of night! Row on, please!"

They passed a yellow door on which it said: STOREROOM NUMBER 77—ALL THE BEANS, CACAO BEANS, COFFEE BEANS, JELLY BEANS, AND HAS BEANS.

"*Has beans?*" cried Violet Beauregarde.

"You're one yourself!" said Mr. Wonka. "There's no time

for arguing! Press on, press on!" But five seconds later, when a bright red door came into sight ahead, he suddenly waved his gold-topped cane in the air and shouted, "Stop the boat!"

19

The Inventing Room—Everlasting Gobstoppers and Hair Toffee

WHEN MR. WONKA SHOUTED "Stop the boat!", the Oompa-Loompas jammed their oars into the river and backed water furiously. The boat stopped.

The Oompa-Loompas guided the boat alongside the red door. On the door it said, INVENTING ROOM—PRIVATE—KEEP OUT. Mr. Wonka took a key from his pocket, leaned over the side of the boat, and put the key in the keyhole.

"*This* is the most important room in the entire factory!" he said. "All my most secret new inventions are cooking and simmering in here! Old Fickelgruber would give his front teeth to be allowed inside just for three minutes! So would Prodnose and Slugworth and all the other rotten chocolate makers! But now, listen to me! I want no messing about when you go in! No touching, no meddling, and no tasting! Is that agreed?"

"Yes, yes!" the children cried. "We won't touch a thing!"

"Up to now," Mr. Wonka said, "nobody else, not even an

Oompa-Loompa, has ever been allowed in here!" He opened the door and stepped out of the boat into the room. The four children and their parents all scrambled after him.

"Don't touch!" shouted Mr. Wonka. "And don't knock anything over!"

Charlie Bucket stared around the gigantic room in which he now found himself. The place was like a witch's kitchen! All about him black metal pots were boiling and bubbling on huge stoves, and kettles were hissing and pans were sizzling, and strange iron machines were clanking and spluttering, and there were pipes running all over the ceiling and walls, and the whole place was filled with smoke and steam and delicious rich smells.

Mr. Wonka himself had suddenly become even more excited than usual, and anyone could see that this was the room he loved best of all. He was hopping about among the saucepans and the machines like a child among his Christmas presents, not knowing which thing to look at first. He lifted the lid from a huge pot and took a sniff; then he rushed over and dipped a finger into a barrel of sticky yellow stuff and had a taste; then he skipped across to one of the machines and turned half a dozen knobs this way and that; then he peered anxiously through the glass door of a gigantic oven, rubbing his hands and cackling with delight at what he saw inside. Then he ran over to another machine, a small shiny affair that kept going *phut-phut-phut-phut-phut,* and every time it went *phut,* a large green marble dropped out of it into a basket on the floor. At least it looked like a marble.

"Everlasting Gobstoppers!" cried Mr. Wonka proudly.

"They're completely new! I am inventing them for children who are given very little pocket money. You can put an Everlasting Gobstopper in your mouth and you can suck it and suck it and suck it and suck it and suck it and it will *never* get any smaller!"

"It's like gum!" cried Violet Beauregarde.

"It is *not* like gum," Mr. Wonka said. "Gum is for chewing, and if you tried chewing one of these Gobstoppers here you'd break your teeth off. But they taste terrific! And they change color once a week! And they *never* get any smaller! They *never* disappear! *NEVER!* At least I don't think they do. There's one of them being tested this very moment in the Testing Room next door. An Oompa-Loompa is sucking it. He's been sucking it for very nearly a year now without stopping, and it's still just as good as ever!

"Now, over here," Mr. Wonka went on, skipping excitedly across the room to the opposite wall, "over here I am inventing a completely new line in toffees!" He stopped beside a large saucepan. The saucepan was full of thick gooey purplish treacle, boiling and bubbling. By standing on his toes, little Charlie could just see inside it.

"That's Hair Toffee!" cried Mr. Wonka. "You eat just one tiny bit of that, and in exactly half an hour a brand-new luscious thick silky beautiful crop of hair will start growing out all over the top of your head! And a moustache! And a beard!"

"A beard!" cried Veruca Salt. "Who wants a beard, for heaven's sake?"

"It would suit you very well," said Mr. Wonka, "but unfortunately the mixture is not quite right yet. I've got it too strong. It works too well. I tried it on an Oompa-

Loompa yesterday in the Testing Room and immediately a huge beard started shooting out of his chin, and the beard grew so fast that soon it was trailing all over the floor in a thick hairy carpet. It was growing faster than we could cut it! In the end we had to use a lawn mower to keep it in check! But I'll get the mixture right soon! And when I do, then there'll be no excuse any more for little boys and girls going about with bald heads!"

"But Mr. Wonka," said Mike Teavee, "little boys and girls never *do* go about with . . ."

"Don't argue, my dear child, *please* don't argue!" cried Mr. Wonka. "It's such a waste of precious time! Now, over *here*, if you will all step this way, I will show you something that I am terrifically proud of. Oh, do be careful! Don't knock anything over! Stand back!"

20

The Great Gum Machine

MR. WONKA LED THE PARTY over to a gigantic machine that stood in the very center of the Inventing Room. It was a mountain of gleaming metal that towered high above the children and their parents. Out of the very top of it there sprouted hundreds and hundreds of thin glass tubes, and the glass tubes all curled downwards and came together in a bunch and hung suspended over an enormous round tub as big as a bath.

"Here we go!" cried Mr. Wonka, and he pressed three different buttons on the side of the machine. A second later, a mighty rumbling sound came from inside it, and the whole machine began to shake most frighteningly, and steam began hissing out of it all over, and then suddenly the watchers noticed that runny stuff was pouring down the insides of all the hundreds of little glass tubes and squirting out into the great tub below. And in every single tube the runny stuff was of a different color, so that all the colors of the rainbow (and many others as well) came sloshing and splashing into the tub. It was a lovely sight. And when the tub was nearly full, Mr. Wonka pressed another button, and immediately the runny stuff stopped running out of the tubes, the rumbling sound disappeared, and a whizzing whirring noise took its place; and then a giant whizzer started whizzing round inside the enormous tub, mixing up all the different colored liquids like an ice-cream soda. Gradually, the mixture began to froth. It became frothier and frothier, and it turned from blue to white to green to brown to yellow, then back to blue again.

"Watch!" said Mr. Wonka.

Click went the machine, and the whizzer stopped whizzing. And now there came a sort of sucking noise, and very quickly all the blue frothy mixture in the huge basin was sucked back into the stomach of the machine. There was a moment of silence. Then a few queer rumblings were heard. Then silence again. Then suddenly, the machine let out a monstrous mighty groan, and at the same moment a tiny drawer (no bigger than the drawer in a slot machine) popped out of the side of the machine, and in the drawer there lay something so small and thin and grey that everyone thought it must be a mistake. The think looked like a little strip of grey cardboard.

The children and their parents stared at the little grey strip lying in the drawer.

"You mean that's *all*?" said Mike Teavee, disgusted.

"That's all," answered Mr. Wonka, gazing proudly at the result. "Don't you know what it is?"

There was a pause. Then suddenly, Violet Beauregarde,

the goofy gum-chewing girl, let out a yell of excitement. "By gum, it's *gum*!" she shrieked. "It's a stick of chewing gum!"

"Right you are!" cried Mr. Wonka, slapping Violet hard on the back. "It's a stick of gum! It's a stick of the most *amazing* and *fabulous* and *sensational* gum in the world!"

21
Good-by Violet

"THIS GUM," Mr. Wonka went on, "is my latest, my greatest, my most fascinating invention! It's a chewing-gum meal! It's . . . it's . . . it's . . . that tiny little strip of gum lying there is a whole three-course dinner all by itself!"

"What sort of nonsense is this?" said one of the fathers.

"My dear sir!" cried Mr. Wonka. "When I start selling this gum in the shops it will change *everything*! It will be the end of all kitchens and all cooking! There will be no more marketing to do! No more buying of meat and groceries! There'll be no knives and forks at mealtimes! No plates! No washing up! No garbage! No mess! Just a little strip of Wonka's magic chewing gum—and that's all you'll ever need at breakfast, lunch, and supper! This piece of gum I've just made happens to be tomato soup, roast beef, and blueberry pie, but you can have almost anything you want!"

"What *do* you mean, it's tomato soup, roast beef, and blueberry pie?" said Violet Beauregarde.

"If you were to start chewing it," said Mr. Wonka, "then that is exactly what you would get on the menu. It's absolutely amazing! You can actually *feel* the food going down your throat and into your tummy! And you can taste it perfectly! And it fills you up! It satisfies you! It's terrific!"

"It's utterly impossible," said Veruca Salt.

"Just so long as it's gum," shouted Violet Beauregarde, "just so long as it's a piece of gum and I can chew it, then *that's* for me!" And quickly she took her own world-record piece of chewing gum out of her mouth and stuck it behind her left ear. "Come on, Mr. Wonka," she said, "hand over this magic gum of yours and we'll see if the thing works."

"Now, Violet," said Mrs. Beauregarde, her mother, "don't let's do anything silly, Violet."

"I want the gum!" Violet said obstinately. "What's so silly?"

"I would rather you didn't take it," Mr. Wonka told her gently. "You see, I haven't got it *quite right* yet. There are still one or two things. . . ."

"Oh, to heck with that!" said Violet, and suddenly, before Mr. Wonka could stop her, she shot out a fat hand and grabbed the stick of gum out of the little drawer and popped it into her mouth. At once, her huge well-trained jaws started chewing away on it like a pair of tongs.

"Don't!" said Mr. Wonka.

"Fabulous!" shouted Violet. "It's tomato soup! It's hot and creamy and delicious! I can feel it running down my throat!"

"Stop!" said Mr. Wonka. "The gum isn't ready yet! It's not right!"

"Of course it's right!" said Violet. "It's working beautifully! Oh my, what lovely soup this is!"

"Spit it out!" said Mr. Wonka.

"It's changing!" shouted Violet, chewing and grinning both at the same time. "The second course is coming up! It's roast beef! It's tender and juicy! Oh boy, what a flavor! The baked potato is marvelous, too! It's got a crispy skin and it's all filled with butter inside!"

"But how *in*-teresting, Violet," said Mrs. Beauregarde. "You *are* a clever girl."

"Keep chewing, kiddo!" said Mr. Beauregarde. "Keep right on chewing, baby! This is a great day for the Beauregardes! Our little girl is the first person in the world to have a chewing-gum meal!"

Everybody was watching Violet Beauregarde as she stood there chewing this extraordinary gum. Little Charlie Bucket was staring at her absolutely spellbound, watching her huge rubbery lips as they pressed and unpressed with the chewing, and Grandpa Joe stood beside him, gaping at the girl. Mr. Wonka was wringing his hands and saying, "No, no, no, no, no! It isn't ready for eating! It isn't right! You mustn't do it!"

"Blueberry pie and cream!" shouted Violet. "Here it comes! Oh my, it's perfect! It's beautiful! It's . . . it's exactly as though I'm swallowing it! It's as though I'm chewing and swallowing great big spoonfuls of the most marvelous blueberry pie in the world!"

"Good heavens, girl!" shrieked Mrs. Beauregarde suddenly, staring at Violet, "what's happening to your nose!"

"Oh, be quiet, mother, and let me finish!" said Violet.

"It's turning blue!" screamed Mrs. Beauregarde. "Your nose is turning blue as a blueberry!"

"Your mother is right!" shouted Mr. Beauregarde. "Your whole nose has gone purple!"

"What *do* you mean?" said Violet, still chewing away.

"Your cheeks!" screamed Mrs. Beauregarde. "They're turning blue as well! So is your chin! Your whole face is turning blue!"

"Spit that gum out at once!" ordered Mr. Beauregarde.

"Mercy! Save us!" yelled Mrs. Beauregarde. "The girl's going blue and purple all over! Even her hair is changing color! Violet, you're turning violet, Violet! What *is* happening to you!"

"I *told* you I hadn't got it quite right," sighed Mr. Wonka, shaking his head sadly.

"I'll say you haven't!" cried Mrs. Beauregarde. "Just look at the girl now!"

Everybody was staring at Violet. And what a terrible peculiar sight she was! Her face and hands and legs and neck, in fact the skin all over her body, as well as her great big mop of curly hair, had turned a brilliant, purplish-blue, the color of blueberry juice!

"It *always* goes wrong when we come to the dessert," sighed Mr. Wonka. "It's the blueberry pie that does it. But I'll get it right one day, you wait and see."

"Violet," screamed Mrs. Beauregarde, "you're swelling up!"

"I feel sick," Violet said.

"You're swelling up!" screamed Mrs. Beauregarde again.

"I feel most peculiar!" gasped Violet.

"I'm not surprised!" said Mr. Beauregarde.

"Great heavens, girl!" screeched Mrs. Beauregarde. "You're blowing up like a balloon!"

"Like a blueberry," said Mr. Wonka.

"Call a doctor!" shouted Mr. Beauregarde.

"Prick her with a pin!" said one of the other fathers.

"Save her!" cried Mrs. Beauregarde, wringing her hands.

But there was no saving her now. Her body was swelling up and changing shape at such a rate that within a minute it had turned into nothing less than an enormous round blue ball—a gigantic blueberry, in fact—and all that remained of Violet Beauregarde herself was a tiny pair of legs and a tiny pair of arms sticking out of the great round fruit and a little head on top.

"It *always* happens like that," sighed Mr. Wonka. "I've tried it twenty times in the Testing Room on twenty Oompa-Loompas, and every one of them finished up as a blueberry. It's most annoying. I just can't understand it."

"But I don't want a blueberry for a daughter!" yelled Mrs. Beauregarde. "Put her back to what she was this instant!"

Mr. Wonka clicked his fingers, and ten Oompa-Loompas appeared immediately at his side.

"Roll Miss Beauregarde into the boat," he said to them, "and take her along to the Juicing Room at once."

"The *Juicing Room*?" cried Mrs. Beauregarde. "What are they going to do to her there?"

"Squeeze her," said Mr. Wonka. "We've got to squeeze the juice out of her immediately. After that, we'll just have to see how she comes out. But don't worry, my dear Mrs. Beauregarde. We'll get her repaired if it's the last thing we do. I *am* sorry about it all, I really am. . . ."

Already the ten Oompa-Loompas were rolling the enormous blueberry across the floor of the Inventing Room toward the door that led to the chocolate river where the boat was waiting. Mr. and Mrs. Beauregarde hurried after them. The rest of the party, including little Charlie Bucket and Grandpa Joe, stood absolutely still and watched them go.

"Listen!" whispered Charlie. "Listen, Grandpa! The Oompa-Loompas in the boat outside are starting to sing!"

The voices, one hundred of them singing together, came loud and clear into the room:

> *"Dear friends, we surely all agree*
> *There's almost nothing worse to see*
> *Than some repulsive little bum*
> *Who's always chewing chewing gum.*
> *(It's very near as bad as those*

Who sit around and pick the nose).
So please believe us when we say
That chewing gum will never pay;
This sticky habit's bound to send
The chewer to a sticky end.
Did any of you ever know
A person called Miss Bigelow?
This dreadful woman saw no wrong
In chewing, chewing all day long.
She chewed while bathing in the tub,
She chewed while dancing at her club,
She chewed in church and on the bus;
It really was quite ludicrous!
And when she couldn't find her gum,
She'd chew up the linoleum,
Or anything that happened near—
A pair of boots, the postman's ear,
Or other people's underclothes,
And once she chewed her boy friend's nose.
She went on chewing till, at last,
Her chewing muscles grew so vast
That from her face her giant chin
Stuck out just like a violin.
For years and years she chewed away,
Consuming fifty packs a day,
Until one summer's eve, alas,
A horrid business came to pass.
Miss Bigelow went late to bed,
For half an hour she lay and read,
Chewing and chewing all the while
Like some great clockwork crocodile.

At last, she put her gum away
Upon a special little tray,
And settled back and went to sleep—
(She managed this by counting sheep).
But now, how strange! Although she slept,
Those massive jaws of hers still kept
On chewing, chewing through the night,
Even with nothing there to bite.
They were, you see, in such a groove
They positively had *to move.*
And very grim it was to hear
In pitch darkness, loud and clear,
This sleeping woman's great big trap
Opening and shutting, snap-snap-snap!
Faster and faster, chop-chop-chop,
The noise went on, it wouldn't stop.
Until at last her jaws decide

To pause and open extra wide,
And with the most tremendous *chew*
They bit the lady's tongue in two.
Thereafter, just from chewing gum,
Miss Bigelow was always dumb,
And spent her life shut up in some
Disgusting sanatorium.
And that *is why we'll try so hard*
To save Miss Violet Beauregarde
From suffering an equal fate.
She's still quite young. It's not too late,
Provided she survives the cure.
We hope she does. We can't be sure."

22

Along the Corridor

"WELL, WELL, WELL," sighed Mr. Willy Wonka, "two naughty little children gone. Three good little children left. I think we'd better get out of this room quickly before we lose anyone else!"

"But Mr. Wonka," said Charlie Bucket anxiously, "will Violet Beauregarde *ever* be all right again or will she always be a blueberry?"

"They'll de-juice her in no time flat!" declared Mr. Wonka. "They'll roll her into the de-juicing machine, and she'll come out just as thin as a whistle!"

"But will she still be blue all over?" asked Charlie.

"She'll be *purple*!" cried Mr. Wonka. "A fine rich purple from head to toe! But there you are! That's what comes from chewing disgusting gum all day long!"

"If you think gum is so disgusting," said Mike Teavee, "then why do you make it in your factory?"

"I do wish you wouldn't mumble," said Mr. Wonka. "I can't hear a word you're saying. Come on! Off we go! Hurry up! Follow me! We're going into the corridors again!" And so saying, Mr. Wonka scuttled across to the far end of the Inventing Room and went out through a small secret door hidden behind a lot of pipes and stoves. The three remaining children—Veruca Salt, Mike Teavee, and Charlie Bucket—together with the five remaining grown-ups, followed after him.

Charlie Bucket saw that they were now back in one of

those long pink corridors with many other pink corridors leading out of it. Mr. Wonka was rushing along in front, turning left and right and right and left, and Grandpa Joe was saying, "Keep a good hold of my hand, Charlie. It would be terrible to get lost in here."

Mr. Wonka was saying, "No time for any more messing about! We'll never get *anywhere* at the rate we've been going!" And on he rushed, down the endless pink corridors, with his black top hat perched on the top of his head and his plum-colored velvet coattails flying out behind him like a flag in the wind.

They passed another door, then another and another. There were doors every twenty paces or so along the corridor now, and they all had something written on them, and strange clanking noises were coming from behind several of them, and delicious smells came wafting through the keyholes, and sometimes little jets of colored steam shot out from the cracks underneath.

Grandpa Joe and Charlie were half running and half walking to keep up with Mr. Wonka, but they were able to read what it said on quite a few of the doors as they hurried by. EATABLE MARSHMALLOW PILLOWS, it said on one.

"Marshmallow pillows are terrific!" shouted Mr. Wonka as he dashed by. "They'll be all the rage when I get them into the shops! No time to go in, though! No time to go in!"

LICKABLE WALLPAPER FOR NURSERIES, it said on the next door.

"Lovely stuff, lickable wallpaper!" cried Mr. Wonka, rushing past. "It has pictures of fruits on it—bananas, apples, oranges, grapes, pineapples, strawberries, and snozzberries. . . ."

"*Snozzberries*?" said Mike Teavee.

"Don't interrupt!" said Mr. Wonka. "The wallpaper has pictures of all these fruits printed on it, and when you lick the picture of a banana, it tastes of banana. When you lick a strawberry, it tastes of strawberry. And when you lick a snozzberry, it tastes just exactly like a snozzberry. . . ."

"But what *does* a snozzberry taste like?"

"You're mumbling again," said Mr. Wonka. "Speak louder next time. On we go! Hurry up!"

HOT ICE CREAMS FOR COLD DAYS, it said on the next door.

"*Extremely* useful in the winter," said Mr. Wonka, rushing on. "Hot ice cream warms you up no end in freezing weather. I also make hot ice cubes for putting in hot drinks. Hot ice cubes make hot drinks hotter."

COWS THAT GIVE CHOCOLATE MILK, it said on the next door.

"Ah, my pretty little cows!" cried Mr. Wonka. "How I love those cows!"

"But why can't we *see* them?" asked Veruca Salt. "Why do we have to go rushing on past all these lovely rooms?"

"We shall stop in time!" called out Mr. Wonka. "Don't be so madly impatient!"

FIZZY LIFTING DRINKS, it said on the next door.

"Oh, those are fabulous!" cried Mr. Wonka. "They fill you with bubbles, and the bubbles are full of a special kind of gas, and this gas is so terrifically *lifting* that it lifts you right off the ground just like a balloon, and up you go until your head hits the ceiling—and there you stay."

"But how do you come down again?" asked little Charlie.

"You do a burp, of course," said Mr. Wonka. "You do a great big long rude burp, and *up* comes the gas and *down*

comes you! But don't drink it outdoors! There's no knowing how high up you'll be carried if you do that. I gave
some to an old Oompa-Loompa once out in the back yard
and he went up and up and up and disappeared out of
sight! It was very sad. I never saw him again."

"He should have burped," Charlie said.

"Of course he should have burped," said Mr. Wonka. "I
stood there shouting, 'Burp, you silly ass, burp, or you'll
never come down again! But he didn't or couldn't or
wouldn't, I don't know which. Maybe he was too polite.
He must be on the moon by now."

On the next door, it said, SQUARE CANDIES THAT LOOK
ROUND.

"Wait!" cried Mr. Wonka, skidding suddenly to a halt. "I
am very proud of my square candies that look round.
Let's take a peek."

23
Square Candies That Look Round

EVERYBODY STOPPED and crowded to the door. The top half
of the door was made of glass. Grandpa Joe lifted Charlie
up so that he could get a better view, and looking in, Charlie saw a long table, and on the table there were rows and
rows of small white square-shaped candies. The candies
looked very much like square sugar lumps—except that

each of them had a funny little pink face painted on one side. At the end of the table, a number of Oompa-Loompas were busily painting more faces on more candies.

"There you are!" cried Mr. Wonka. "Square candies that look round!"

"They don't look round to me," said Mike Teavee.

"They look square," said Veruca Salt. "They look completely square."

"But they *are* square," said Mr. Wonka. "I never said they weren't."

"You said they were *round*!" said Veruca Salt.

"I never said anything of the sort," said Mr. Wonka. "I said they *looked* round."

"But they *don't* look round!" said Veruca Salt. "They look square!"

"They look round," insisted Mr. Wonka.

"They most certainly do not look round!" cried Veruca Salt.

"Veruca, darling," said Mrs. Salt, "pay no attention to Mr. Wonka! He's lying to you!"

"My dear old fish," said Mr. Wonka, "go and boil your head!"

"How dare you speak to me like that!" shouted Mrs. Salt.

"Oh, do shut up," said Mr. Wonka. "Now watch this!" He took a key from his pocket, and unlocked the door, and flung it open . . . and suddenly . . . at the sound of the door opening, all the rows and rows of little square candies looked quickly round to see who was coming in. The tiny faces actually turned toward the door and stared at Mr. Wonka.

"There you are!" he cried triumphantly. "They're looking round! There's no argument about it! They are square candies that look round!"

"By golly, he's right!" said Grandpa Joe.

"Come on!" said Mr. Wonka, starting off down the corridor again. "On we go! We mustn't dawdle!"

BUTTERSCOTCH AND BUTTERGIN, it said on the next door they passed.

"Now *that* sounds a bit more interesting," said Mr. Salt, Veruca's father.

"Glorious stuff!" said Mr. Wonka. "The Oompa-Loompas all adore it. It makes them tiddly. Listen! You can hear them in there now, whooping it up."

Shrieks of laughter and snatches of singing could be heard coming through the closed door.

"They're drunk as lords," said Mr. Wonka. "They're drinking butterscotch and soda. They like that best of all.

Buttergin and tonic is also very popular. Follow me, please! We really mustn't keep stopping like this." He turned left. He turned right. They came to a long flight of stairs. Mr. Wonka slid down the bannisters. The three children did the same. Mrs. Salt and Mrs. Teavee, the only women now left in the party, were getting very out of breath. Mrs. Salt was a great fat creature with short legs, and she was blowing like a rhinoceros. "This way!" cried Mr. Wonka, turning left at the bottom of the stairs.

"Go *slower*!" panted Mrs. Salt.

"Impossible," said Mr. Wonka. "We should never get there in time if I did."

"Get where?" asked Veruca Salt.

"Never you mind," said Mr. Wonka. "You just wait and see."

24
Veruca in the Nut Room

MR. WONKA RUSHED ON down the corridor. THE NUT ROOM, it said on the next door they came to.

"All right," said Mr. Wonka, "stop here for a moment and catch your breath, and take a peek through the glass panel of this door. But don't go in! Whatever you do, don't go into THE NUT ROOM! If you go in, you'll disturb the squirrels!"

Everyone crowded around the door.

"Oh look, Grandpa, look!" cried Charlie.

"Squirrels!" shouted Veruca Salt.

"Jeepers!" said Mike Teavee.

It was an amazing sight. One hundred squirrels were seated upon high stools around a large table. On the table, there were mounds and mounds of walnuts, and the squirrels were all working away like mad, shelling the walnuts at a tremendous speed.

"These squirrels are specially trained for getting the nuts out of walnuts," Mr. Wonka explained.

"Why use squirrels?" Mike Teavee asked. "Why not use Oompa-Loompas?"

"Because," said Mr. Wonka, "Oompa-Loompas can't get walnuts out of walnut shells in one piece. They always break them in two. Nobody except squirrels can get walnuts *whole* out of walnut shells every time. It is extremely difficult. But in my factory, I insist upon using only whole walnuts. Therefore I have to have squirrels to do the job. Aren't they wonderful, the way they get those nuts out! And see how they first tap each walnut with their knuckles to be sure it's not a bad one! If it's bad, it makes a hollow sound, and they don't bother to open it. They just throw it down the garbage chute. There! Look! Watch that squirrel nearest to us! I think he's got a bad one now!"

They watched the little squirrel as he tapped the walnut shell with his knuckles. He cocked his head to one side, listening intently, then suddenly he threw the nut over his shoulder into a large hole in the floor.

"Hey, Mummy!" shouted Veruca Salt suddenly, "I've decided I want a squirrel! Get me one of those squirrels!"

"Don't be silly, sweetheart," said Mrs. Salt. "These all belong to Mr. Wonka."

"I don't care about that!" shouted Veruca. "I want one. All I've *got* at home is two dogs and four cats and six bunny rabbits and two parakeets and three canaries and a green parrot and a turtle and a bowl of goldfish and a cage of white mice and a silly old hamster! I want a *squirrel*!"

"All right, my pet," Mrs. Salt said soothingly. "Mummy'll get you a squirrel just as soon as she possibly can."

"But I don't want *any* old squirrel!" Veruca shouted. "I want a *trained* squirrel!"

At this point, Mr. Salt, Veruca's father, stepped forward. "Very well, Wonka," he said importantly, taking out a wallet full of money, "how much d'you want for one of these crazy squirrels? Name your price."

"They're not for sale," Mr. Wonka answered. "She can't have one."

"Who says I can't!" shouted Veruca. "I'm going in to grab me a squirrel this very minute!"

"Don't!" said Mr. Wonka quickly, but he was too late. The girl had already thrown open the door and rushed in.

The moment she entered the room, one hundred squirrels stopped what they were doing and turned their heads and stared at her with small black beady eyes.

Veruca Salt stopped also, and stared back at them.

Then her gaze fell upon a pretty little squirrel sitting nearest to her at the end of the table. The squirrel was holding a walnut in its paws.

"All right," Veruca said, "I'll have *you*!"

She reached out her hands to grab the squirrel . . . but as she did so . . . in that first split second when her hands started to go forward, there was a sudden flash of movement in the room, like a flash of brown lightning, and every single squirrel around the table took a flying leap towards her and landed on her body.

Twenty-five of them caught hold of her right arm, and pinned it down.

Twenty-five more caught hold of her left arm, and pinned that down.

Twenty-five caught hold of her right leg and anchored it to the ground.

Twenty-*four* caught hold of her left leg.

And the one remaining squirrel (obviously the leader of them all) climbed up on to her shoulder and started tap-tap-tapping the wretched girl's head with its knuckles.

"Save her!" screamed Mrs. Salt. "Veruca! Come back! What are they *doing* to her?"

"They're testing her to see if she's a bad nut," said Mr. Wonka. "You watch."

Veruca struggled furiously, but the squirrels held her tight and she couldn't move. The squirrel on her shoulder went tap-tap-tapping the side of her head with his knuckles.

Then all at once, the squirrels pulled Veruca to the ground and started carrying her across the floor.

"My goodness, she *is* a bad nut after all," said Mr. Wonka. "Her head must have sounded quite hollow."

Veruca kicked and screamed, but it was no use. The tiny strong paws held her tightly and she couldn't escape.

"Where are they taking her?" shrieked Mrs. Salt.

"She's going where all the other bad nuts go," said Mr. Willy Wonka. "Down the garbage chute."

"By golly, she *is* going down the chute!" said Mr. Salt, staring through the glass door at his daughter.

"Then save her!" cried Mrs. Salt.

"Too late," said Mr. Wonka. "She's gone!"

And indeed she had.

"But where?" shrieked Mrs. Salt, flapping her arms. "What happens to the bad nuts? Where does the chute go to?"

"That *particular* chute," Mr. Wonka told her, "runs directly into the great big main garbage pipe which carries away all the rubbish from every part of the factory— all the floor sweepings and potato peelings and rotten cabbages and fish heads and stuff like that."

"Who eats fish and cabbage and potatoes in *this* factory, I'd like to know?" said Mike Teavee.

"I do, of course," answered Mr. Wonka. "You don't think *I* live on cacao beans, do you?"

"But . . . but . . . but . . ." shrieked Mrs. Salt, "where does the great big pipe go to in the end?"

"Why, to the furnace, of course," Mr. Wonka said calmly. "To the incinerator."

Mrs. Salt opened her huge red mouth and started to scream.

"Don't worry," said Mr. Wonka, "there's always a chance that they've decided not to light it today."

"A *chance*!" yelled Mrs. Salt. "My darling Veruca! She'll . . . she'll . . . she'll be sizzled like a sausage!"

"Quite right, my dear," said Mr. Salt. "Now see here, Wonka," he added, "I think you've gone *just* a shade too far this time, I do indeed. My daughter may be a bit of a frump—I don't mind admitting it—but that doesn't mean you can roast her to a crisp. I'll have you know I'm extremely cross about this, I really am."

"Oh, don't be cross, my dear sir!" said Mr. Wonka. "I expect she'll turn up again sooner or later. She may not even have gone down at all. She may be stuck in the chute just below the entrance hole, and if *that's* the case, all you'll have to do is go in and pull her up again."

Hearing this, both Mr. and Mrs. Salt dashed into the Nut Room and ran over to the hole in the floor and peered in.

"Veruca!" shouted Mrs. Salt. "Are you down there!"

There was no answer.

Mrs. Salt bent further forward to get a closer look. She was now kneeling right on the edge of the hole with her head down and her enormous behind sticking up in the air like a giant mushroom. It was a dangerous position to be in. She needed only one tiny little push . . . one gentle nudge in the right place . . . and *that* is exactly what the squirrels gave her!

Over she toppled, into the hole head first, screeching like a parrot.

"Good gracious me!" said Mr. Salt as he watched his fat wife go tumbling down the hole, "*what* a lot of garbage there's going to be today!" He saw her disappearing into the darkness. "What's it like down there, Angina?" he called out. He leaned further forward.

The squirrels rushed up behind him. . . .

"Help!" he shouted.

But he was already toppling forward, and down the chute he went, just as his wife had done before him—and his daughter.

"Oh *dear*!" cried Charlie, who was watching with the others through the door, "what on earth's going to happen to them now?"

"I expect someone will catch them at the bottom of the chute," said Mr. Wonka.

"But what about the great fiery incinerator?" asked Charlie.

"They only light it every other day," said Mr. Wonka. "Perhaps this is one of the days when they let it go out. You never know . . . they might be lucky. . . ."

"Ssshh!" said Grandpa Joe. "Listen! Here comes another song!"

From far away down the corridor came the beating of drums. Then the singing began.

> *"Veruca Salt!"* sang the Oompa-Loompas.
> *"Veruca Salt, the little brute,*
>   *Has just gone down the garbage chute,*
>   *(And as we very rightly thought*
>   *That in a case like this we ought*
>   *To see the thing completely through,*
>   *We've polished off her parents, too.)*
>   *Down goes Veruca! Down the drain!*
>   *And here, perhaps, we should explain*
>   *That she will meet, as she descends,*
>   *A rather different set of friends*

To those that she has left behind—
These *won't be nearly so refined.*
A fish head, for example, cut
This morning from a halibut.
'Hello! Good morning! How d'you do?
How nice to meet you! How are you?'
And then a little further down
A mass of others gather round:
A bacon rind, some rancid lard,
A loaf of bread gone stale and hard,
A steak that nobody could chew,
An oyster from an oyster stew,
Some liverwurst so old and gray
One smelled it from a mile away,
A rotten nut, a reeky pear,
A thing the cat left on the stair,
And lots of other things as well,
Each with a rather horrid smell.
These *are Veruca's new found friends*
That she will meet as she descends,
And this *is the price she has to pay*
For going so very far astray.
But now, my dears, we think you might
Be wondering—is it really right
That every single bit of blame
And all the scolding and the shame
Should fall upon Veruca Salt?
Is *she* the only one at fault?
For though she's spoiled, and dreadfully so,
A girl can't spoil herself, you know.
Who *spoiled her, then? Ah, who indeed?*

Who pandered to her every need?
Who turned her into such a brat?
Who are the culprits? Who did that?
Alas! You needn't look so far
To find out who these sinners are.
They are (and this is very sad)
Her loving parents, MUM and DAD.
And that is why we're glad they fell
Into the garbage chute as well.

25

The Great Glass Elevator

"I'VE NEVER SEEN anything like it!" cried Mr. Wonka. "The children are disappearing like rabbits! But you mustn't worry about it! They'll *all* come out in the wash!"

Mr. Wonka looked at the little group that stood beside him in the corridor. There were only two children left now—Mike Teavee and Charlie Bucket. And there were three grownups, Mr. and Mrs. Teavee and Grandpa Joe. "Shall we move on?" Mr. Wonka asked.

"Oh, yes!" cried Charlie and Grandpa Joe, both together.

"My feet are getting tired," said Mike Teavee. "I want to watch television."

"If you're tired then we'd better take the elevator," said Mr. Wonka. "It's over here. Come on! In we go!" He skipped across the passage to a pair of double doors. The doors slid open. The two children and the grownups went in.

"Now then," cried Mr. Wonka, "which button shall we press first? Take your pick!"

Charlie Bucket stared around him in astonishment. This was the craziest elevator he had ever seen. There were buttons everywhere! The walls, and even the *ceiling,* were covered all over with rows and rows and rows of small, black push buttons! There must have been a thousand of them on each wall, and another thousand on the ceiling! And now Charlie noticed that every single button had a tiny printed label beside it telling you which room you would be taken to if you pressed it.

"This isn't just an ordinary up-and-down elevator!" announced Mr. Wonka proudly. "This elevator can go sideways and longways and slantways and any other way you can think of! It can visit any single room in the whole factory, no matter where it is! You simply press the button . . . and *zing*! . . . you're off!"

"*Fantastic*!" murmured Grandpa Joe. His eyes were shining with excitement as he stared at the rows and rows of buttons.

"The whole elevator is made of thick, clear glass!" Mr. Wonka declared. "Walls, doors, ceiling, floor, everything is made of glass so that you can see out!"

"But there's nothing to see," said Mike Teavee.

"Choose a button!" said Mr. Wonka. "The two children may press one button each. So take your pick! Hurry up! In every room, something delicious and wonderful is being made."

Quickly, Charlie started reading some of the labels alongside the buttons.

THE ROCK-CANDY MINE—10,000 FEET DEEP, it said on one.

COKERNUT-ICE SKATING RINKS, it said on another.

Then . . . STRAWBERRY-JUICE WATER PISTOLS.

TOFFEE-APPLE TREES FOR PLANTING OUT IN YOUR GARDEN—ALL SIZES.

EXPLODING CANDY FOR YOUR ENEMIES.

LUMINOUS LOLLIES FOR EATING IN BED AT NIGHT.

MINT JUJUBES FOR THE BOY NEXT DOOR—THEY'LL GIVE HIM GREEN TEETH FOR A MONTH.

CAVITY-FILLING CARAMELS—NO MORE DENTISTS.

STICKJAW FOR TALKATIVE PARENTS.

WRIGGLE-SWEETS THAT WRIGGLE DELIGHTFULLY IN YOUR TUMMY AFTER SWALLOWING.

INVISIBLE CHOCOLATE BARS FOR EATING IN CLASS.

CANDY-COATED PENCILS FOR SUCKING.

FIZZY LEMONADE SWIMMING POOLS.

MAGIC HAND-FUDGE—WHEN YOU HOLD IT IN YOUR HAND, YOU TASTE IT IN YOUR MOUTH.

RAINBOW DROPS—SUCK THEM AND YOU CAN SPIT IN SIX DIFFERENT COLORS.

"Come on, come on!" cried Mr. Wonka. "We can't wait all day!"

"Isn't there a *Television Room* in all this lot?" asked Mike Teavee.

"Certainly there's a television room," Mr. Wonka said. "That button over there." He pointed with his finger. Everybody looked. TELEVISION CHOCOLATE, it said on the tiny label beside the button.

"*Whoopee!*" shouted Mike Teavee. "That's for me!" He stuck out his thumb and pressed the button. Instantly, there was a tremendous whizzing noise. The doors clanged shut and the elevator leaped away as though it had been stung by a wasp. But it leapt *sideways*! And all the passengers (except Mr. Wonka, who was holding onto a strap from the ceiling) were flung off their feet onto the floor.

"Get up, get up!" cried Mr. Wonka, roaring with laughter. But just as they were staggering to their feet, the elevator changed directions and swerved violently round a corner. And over they went once more.

"Help!" shouted Mrs. Teavee.

"Take my hand, madam," said Mr. Wonka gallantly.

"There you are! Now grab this strap! Everybody grab a strap. The journey's not over yet!"

Old Grandpa Joe staggered to his feet and caught hold of a strap. Little Charlie, who couldn't possibly reach as high as that, put his arms around Grandpa Joe's legs and hung on tight.

The elevator rushed on at the speed of a rocket. Now it was beginning to climb. It was shooting up and up and up on a steep slanty course as if it were climbing a very steep hill. Then suddenly, as though it had come to the top of the hill and gone over a precipice, it dropped like a stone and Charlie felt his tummy coming right up into his throat, and Grandpa Joe shouted, "Yippee! Here we go!" And Mrs. Teavee cried out, "The rope has broken! We're going to crash!" And Mr. Wonka said, "Calm yourself, my dear lady," and patted her comfortingly on the arm. And then Grandpa Joe looked down at Charlie who was clinging to his legs, and he said, "Are you all right, Charlie?" Charlie shouted, "I love it! It's like being on a roller coaster!" And through the glass walls of the elevator, as it rushed along, they caught sudden glimpses of strange and wonderful things going on in some of the other rooms:

An enormous spout with brown sticky stuff oozing out of it onto the floor. . . .

A great, craggy mountain made entirely of fudge, with Oompa-Loompas (all roped together for safety) hacking huge hunks of fudge out of its sides. . . .

A machine with white powder spraying out of it like a snowstorm. . . .

A lake of hot caramel with steam coming off it. . . .

A village of Oompa-Loompas, with tiny houses and streets and hundreds of Oompa-Loompa children no more than four inches high playing in the streets. . . .

And now the elevator began flattening out again, but it seemed to be going faster than ever, and Charlie could hear the scream of the wind outside as it hurtled forward . . . and it twisted . . . and it turned . . . and it went up . . . and it went down . . . and . . .

"I'm going to be sick!" yelled Mrs. Teavee, turning green in the face.

"Please don't be sick," said Mr. Wonka.

"Try and stop me!" said Mrs. Teavee.

"Then you'd better take this," said Mr. Wonka, and he swept his magnificent black top hat of his head, and held it out, upside down, in front of Mrs. Teavee's mouth.

"Make this awful thing stop!" ordered Mr. Teavee.

"Can't do that," said Mr. Wonka. "It won't stop till we get there. I only hope no one's using the *other* elevator at this moment."

"What other elevator?" screamed Mrs. Teavee.

"The one that goes the opposite way on the same track as this one," said Mr. Wonka.

"Holy mackerel!" cried Mr. Teavee. "You mean we might have a collision?"

"I've always been lucky so far," said Mr. Wonka.

"Now I *am* going to be sick!" yelled Mrs. Teavee.

"No, no!" said Mr. Wonka. "Not now! We're nearly there! Don't spoil my hat!"

The next moment, there was a screaming of brakes, and the elevator began to slow down. Then it stopped altogether.

"Some ride!" said Mr. Teavee, wiping his great sweaty face with a handkerchief.

"Never again!" gasped Mrs. Teavee. And then the doors of the elevator slid open and Mr. Wonka said, "Just a minute now! Listen to me! I want everybody to be very careful in this room. There is dangerous stuff around in here and you *must not* tamper with it."

26
The Television-Chocolate Room

THE TEAVEE FAMILY, together with Charlie and Grandpa Joe, stepped out of the elevator into a room so dazzlingly bright and dazzlingly white that they screwed up their eyes in pain and stopped walking. Mr. Wonka handed each of them a pair of dark glasses and said, "Put these on quick! And don't take them off in here whatever you do! This light could blind you!"

As soon as Charlie had his dark glasses on, he was able to look around him in comfort. He saw a long narrow room. The room was painted white all over. Even the floor was white, and there wasn't a speck of dust anywhere. From the ceiling, huge lamps hung down and bathed the room in a brilliant blue-white light. The room was completely bare except at the far ends. At one of these ends there was an enormous camera on wheels, and a whole army of Oompa-Loompas was clustering around it, oiling its joints and adjusting its knobs and polishing its great glass lens. The Oompa-Loompas were all dressed in the most extraordinary way. They were wearing bright-red space suits, complete with helmets and goggles—at least they looked like space suits—and they were working in complete silence. Watching them, Charlie experienced a queer sense of danger. There was something dangerous about this whole business, and the Oompa-Loompas knew it. There was no chattering or singing among them here, and they moved about over the huge black camera slowly and carefully in their scarlet space suits.

At the other end of the room, about fifty paces away from the camera, a single Oompa-Loompa (also wearing a space suit) was sitting at a black table gazing at the screen of a very large television set.

"Here we go!" cried Mr. Wonka, hopping up and down with excitement. "This is the Testing Room for my very latest and greatest invention—Television Chocolate!"

"But what *is* Television Chocolate?" asked Mike Teavee.

"Good heavens, child, stop interrupting me!" said Mr. Wonka. "It works by television. I don't like television myself. I suppose it's all right in small doses, but children never seem to be able to take it in small doses. They want to sit there all day long staring and staring at the screen. . . ."

"That's me!" said Mike Teavee.

"Shut up!" said Mr. Teavee.

"Thank you," said Mr. Wonka. "I shall now tell you how this amazing television set of mine works. But first of all, do you know how ordinary television works? It is very simple. At one end, where the picture is being taken, you

have a large movie camera and you start photographing
something. The photographs are then split up into millions of tiny little pieces which are so small that you
can't see them, and these little pieces are shot out into
the sky by electricity. In the sky, they go whizzing around
all over the place until suddenly they hit the antenna on
the roof of somebody's house. They then go flashing
down the wire that leads right into the back of the television set, and in there they get jiggled and joggled
around until at last every single one of those millions of
tiny pieces is fitted back into its right place (just like a jig-
saw puzzle), and presto!—the photograph appears on
the screen. . . ."

"That isn't *exactly* how it works," Mike Teavee said.

"I am a little deaf in my left ear," Mr. Wonka said. "You must forgive me if I don't hear everything you say."

"I said, that isn't *exactly* how it works!" shouted Mike Teavee.

"You're a nice boy," Mr. Wonka said, "but you talk too much. Now then! The very first time I saw ordinary television working, I was struck by a tremendous idea. 'Look here!' I shouted, 'if these people can break up a *photograph* into millions of pieces and send the pieces whizzing through the air and then put them together again at the other end, why can't *I* do the same thing with a bar of chocolate? Why can't *I* send a real bar of chocolate whizzing through the air in tiny pieces and then put the pieces together at the other end, all ready to be eaten?"

"Impossible!" said Mike Teavee.

"You think so?" cried Mr. Wonka. "Well, watch this! I shall now send a bar of my very best chocolate from one end of this room to the other—by television! Get ready, there! Bring in the chocolate!"

Immediately, six Oompa-Loompas marched forward carrying on their shoulders the most enormous bar of chocolate Charlie had ever seen. It was about the size of the mattress he slept on at home.

"It has to be big," Mr. Wonka explained, "because whenever you send something by television, it always comes out much smaller than it was when it went in. Even with *ordinary* television, when you photograph a big man, he never comes out on your screen any taller than a pencil, does he? Here we go, then! Get ready! *No, no! Stop! Hold everything!* You there! Mike Teavee! Stand back! You're too close to the camera! There are dangerous rays coming out of that thing! They could break you up into million tiny pieces in one second! That's why the Oompa-Loompas are wearing space suits! The suits protect them! All right! That's better! Now, then! *Switch on!*"

One of the Oompa-Loompas caught hold of a large switch and pulled it down.

There was a blinding flash.

"The chocolate's gone!" shouted Grandpa Joe, waving his arms.

He was quite right! The whole enormous bar of chocolate had disappeared completely into thin air!

"It's on its way!" cried Mr. Wonka. "It is now rushing through the air above our heads in a million tiny pieces. Quick! Come over here!" He dashed over to the other end of the room where the large television set was standing, and the others followed him. "Watch the screen!" he cried. "Here it comes! Look!"

The screen flickered and lit up. Then suddenly, a small bar of chocolate appeared in the middle of the screen.

"Take it!" shouted Mr. Wonka, growing more and more excited.

"How can you take it?" asked Mike Teavee, laughing.

"It's just a picture on a television screen!"

"Charlie Bucket!" cried Mr. Wonka. "*You* take it! Reach out and grab it!"

Charlie put out his hand and touched the screen, and suddenly, miraculously, the bar of chocolate came away in his fingers. He was so surprised he nearly dropped it.

"Eat it!" shouted Mr. Wonka. "Go on and eat it! It'll be delicious! It's the same bar! It's gotten smaller on the journey, that's all!"

"It's absolutely fantastic!" gasped Grandpa Joe. "It's . . . it's . . . it's a miracle!"

"Just imagine," cried Mr. Wonka, "when I start using this across the country . . . you'll be sitting at home watching television and suddenly a commercial will flash onto the screen and a voice will say, 'EAT WONKA'S CHOCOLATES! THEY'RE THE BEST IN THE WORLD! IF YOU DON'T BELIEVE US, TRY ONE FOR YOURSELF—*NOW*!' And you simply reach out and take one! How about that, eh?"

"Terrific!" cried Grandpa Joe. "It will change the world!"

27
Mike Teavee Is Sent by Television

MIKE TEAVEE was even more excited than Grandpa Joe at seeing a bar of chocolate being sent by television.

"But Mr. Wonka," he shouted, "can you send *other things* through the air in the same way? Breakfast cereal, for instance?"

"Oh, my sainted aunt!" cried Mr. Wonka. "Don't mention that disgusting stuff in front of me! Do you *know* what breakfast cereal is made of? It's made of all those little curly wooden shavings you find in pencil sharpeners!"

"But could you send it by television if you wanted to, as you do chocolate?" asked Mike Teavee.

"Of course I could!"

"And what about people?" asked Mike Teavee. "Could you send a real live person from one place to another in the same way?"

"A *person*!" cried Mr. Wonka. "Are you off your rocker?"

"But *could* it be done?"

"Good heavens, child, I really don't know . . . I suppose it *could* . . . yes, I'm pretty sure it could . . . of course it could . . . I wouldn't like to risk it, though . . . it might have some very nasty results. . . ."

But Mike Teavee was already off and running. The moment he heard Mr. Wonka saying, "I'm pretty sure it could . . . of course it could," he turned away and started running as fast as he could towards the other end of the room where the great camera was standing. "Look at me!" he shouted as he ran. "I'm going to be the first person in the world to be sent by television!"

"No, no, no, no!" cried Mr. Wonka.

"Mike!" screamed Mrs. Teavee. "Stop! Come back! You'll be turned into a million tiny pieces!"

But there was no stopping Mike Teavee now. The crazy

boy rushed on, and when he reached the enormous camera, he jumped straight for the switch, scattering Oompa-Loompas right and left as he went.

"See you later, alligator!" he shouted, and he pulled down the switch, and as he did so, he leaped out into the full glare of the mighty lens.

There was a blinding flash.

Then there was silence.

Then Mrs. Teavee ran forward . . . but she stopped dead in the middle of the room . . . and she stood there . . . she stood staring at the place where her son had been . . . and her great red mouth opened wide and she screamed, "He's gone! He's gone!"

"Great heavens, he *has* gone!" shouted Mr. Teavee.

Mr. Wonka hurried forward and placed a hand gently on Mrs. Teavee's shoulder. "We shall have to hope for the best," he said. "We must pray that your little boy will come out unharmed at the other end."

"Mike!" screamed Mrs. Teavee, clasping her head in her hands. "Where are you?"

"I'll tell you where he is," said Mr. Teavee, "he's whizzing around above our heads in a million tiny pieces!"

"Don't talk about it!" wailed Mrs. Teavee.

"We must watch the television set," said Mr. Wonka. "He may come through any moment."

Mr. and Mrs. Teavee and Grandpa Joe and little Charlie and Mr. Wonka all gathered round the television and stared tensely at the screen. The screen was quite blank.

"He's taking a heck of a long time to come across," said Mr. Teavee, wiping his brow.

"Oh dear, oh dear," said Mr. Wonka, "I do hope that no part of him gets left behind."

"What on earth do you mean?" asked Mr. Teavee sharply.

"I don't wish to alarm you," said Mr. Wonka, "but it does sometimes happen that only about half the little pieces find their way into the television set. It happened last week. I don't know why, but the result was that only half a bar of chocolate came through."

Mrs. Teavee let out a scream of horror. "You mean only a half of Mike is coming back to us?" she cried.

"Let's hope it's the top half," said Mr. Teavee.

"Hold everything!" said Mr. Wonka. "Watch the screen! Something's happening!"

The screen had suddenly begun to flicker.

Then some wavy lines appeared.

Mr. Wonka adjusted one of the knobs and the wavy lines went away.

And now, very slowly, the screen began to get brighter and brighter.

"Here he comes!" yelled Mr. Wonka. "Yes, that's him all right!"

"Is he all in one piece?" cried Mrs. Teavee.

"I'm not sure," said Mr. Wonka. "It's too early to tell."

Faintly at first, but becoming clearer and clearer every second, the picture of Mike Teavee appeared on the screen. He was standing up and waving at the audience and grinning from ear to ear.

"But he's a midget!" shouted Mr. Teavee.

"Mike," cried Mrs. Teavee, "are you all right? Are there any bits of you missing?"

"Isn't he going to get any bigger?" shouted Mr. Teavee.

"Talk to me, Mike!" cried Mrs. Teavee. "Say something! Tell me you're all right!"

A tiny little voice, no louder than the squeaking of a mouse, came out of the television set. "Hi, Mum!" it said. "Hi, Pop! Look at *me*! I'm the first person ever to be sent by television!"

"Grab him!" ordered Mr. Wonka. "Quick!"

Mrs. Teavee shot out a hand and picked the tiny figure of Mike Teavee out of the screen.

"Hooray!" cried Mr. Wonka. "He's all in one piece! He's completely unharmed!"

"You call *that* unharmed?" snapped Mrs. Teavee, peering at the little speck of a boy who was now running to and fro across the palm of her hand, waving his pistols in the air.

He was certainly not more than an inch tall.

"He's *shrunk*!" said Mr. Teavee.

"Of course he's shrunk," said Mr. Wonka. "What did you expect?"

"This is terrible!" wailed Mrs. Teavee. "What *are* we going to do?"

And Mr. Teavee said, "We can't send him back to school like this! He'll get trod upon! He'll get squashed!"

"He won't be able to do *anything*!" cried Mrs. Teavee.

"Oh, yes I will!" squeaked the tiny voice of Mike Teavee. "I'll still be able to watch television!"

"Never again!" shouted Mr. Teavee. "I'm throwing the television set right out the window the moment we get home. I've had enough of television!"

When he heard this, Mike Teavee flew into a terrible tantrum. He started jumping up and down on the palm of his mother's hand, screaming and yelling and trying to bite her fingers. "I want to watch television!" he squeaked. "I want to watch television! I want to watch television! I want to watch television!"

"Here! Give him to me!" said Mr. Teavee, and he took the tiny boy and shoved him into the breast pocket of his jacket and stuffed a handkerchief on top. Squeals and yells came from inside the pocket, and the pocket shook as the furious little prisoner fought to get out.

"Oh, Mr. Wonka," wailed Mrs. Teavee, "how can we make him grow?"

"Well," said Mr. Wonka, stroking his beard and gazing thoughtfully at the ceiling, "I must say that's a wee bit tricky. But small boys are extremely springy and elastic. They stretch like mad. So what we'll do, we'll put him in a special machine I have for testing the stretchiness of chewing gum! Maybe that will bring him back to what he was."

"Oh, thank you!" said Mrs. Teavee.

"Don't mention it, dear lady."

"How far d'you think he'll stretch?" asked Mr. Teavee.

"Maybe miles," said Mr. Wonka. "Who knows? But he's

going to be awfully thin. Everything gets thinner when you stretch it."

"You mean like chewing gum?" asked Mr. Teavee.

"Exactly."

"How thin will he be?" asked Mrs. Teavee anxiously.

"I haven't the foggiest idea," said Mr. Wonka. "And it doesn't really matter, anyway, because we'll soon fatten him up again. All we'll have to do is give him a triple over-dose of my wonderful Supervitamin Candy. Supervitamin Candy contains huge amounts of vitamin A and vitamin B. It also contains vitamin C, vitamin D, vitamin E, vitamin F, vitamin G, vitamin I, vitamin J, vitamin K, vitamin L, vita-min M, vitamin N, vitamin O, vitamin P, vitamin Q, vitamin R, vitamin T, vitamin U, vitamin V, vitamin W, vitamin X, vit-amin Y, *and*, believe it or not, vitamin Z! The only two vit-amins it doesn't have in it are vitamin S, because it makes you sick, and vitamin H, because it makes you grow horns out of the top of your head, like a bull. But it *does* have in it a very small amount of the rarest and most magical vit-amin of them all—vitamin Wonka."

"And what will *that* do to him?" asked Mr. Teavee anx-iously.

"It'll make his toes grow out until they're as long as his fingers. . . ."

"Oh, no!" cried Mrs. Teavee.

"Don't be silly," said Mr. Wonka. "It's most useful. He'll be able to play the piano with his feet."

"But Mr. Wonka. . . ."

"No arguments, *please*!" said Mr. Wonka. He turned away and clicked his fingers three times in the air. An

Oompa-Loompa appeared immediately and stood beside him. "Follow these orders," said Mr. Wonka, handing the Oompa-Loompa a piece of paper on which he had written full instructions. "And you'll find the boy in his father's pocket. Off you go! Good-by, Mr. Teavee! Good-by, Mrs. Teavee! And please don't look so worried! They all come out in the wash, you know; every one of them. . . ."

At the end of the room, the Oompa-Loompas around the giant camera were already beating their tiny drums and beginning to jog up and down to the rhythm.

"There they go again!" said Mr. Wonka. "I'm afraid you can't stop them singing."

Little Charlie caught Grandpa Joe's hand, and the two of them stood beside Mr. Wonka in the middle of the long bright room, listening to the Oompa-Loompas. And this is what they sang:

> "The most important thing we've learned,
> So far as children are concerned,
> Is never, NEVER, NEVER let
> Them near your television set—
> Or better still, just don't install
> The idiotic thing at all.
> In almost every house we've been,
> We've watched them gaping at the screen.
> They loll and slop and lounge about,
> And stare until their eyes pop out.
> (Last week in someone's place we saw
> A dozen eyeballs on the floor.)

They sit and stare and stare and sit
Until they're hypnotised by it,
Until they're absolutely drunk
With all that shocking ghastly junk.
Oh yes, we know it keeps them still,
They don't climb out the window sill,
They never fight or kick or punch,
They leave you free to cook the lunch
And wash the dishes in the sink—
But did you ever stop to think,
To wonder just exactly what
This does to your beloved tot?
IT ROTS THE SENSES IN THE HEAD!
IT KILLS IMAGINATION DEAD!
IT CLOGS AND CLUTTERS UP THE MIND!
IT MAKES A CHILD SO DULL AND BLIND
HE CAN NO LONGER UNDERSTAND
A FANTASY, A FAIRYLAND!
HIS BRAIN BECOMES AS SOFT AS CHEESE!
HIS POWERS OF THINKING RUST AND FREEZE!
HE CANNOT THINK—HE ONLY SEES!
'All right!' you'll cry. 'All right!' you'll say,
'But if we take the set away,
What shall we do to entertain
Our darling children? Please explain!'
We'll answer this by asking you,
'What used the darling ones to do?
'How used they keep themselves contented
Before this monster was invented?'
Have you forgotten? Don't you know?

We'll say it very loud and slow:
THEY ... USED ... TO ... READ! They'd READ and
READ,
AND READ and READ, and then proceed
To READ some more. Great Scott! Gadzooks!
One half their lives was reading books!
The nursery shelves held books galore!
Books cluttered up the nursery floor!
And in the bedroom, by the bed,
More books were waiting to be read!
Such wondrous, fine, fantastic tales
Of dragons, gypsies, queens, and whales
And treasure isles, and distant shores
Where smugglers rowed with muffled oars,
And pirates wearing purple pants,
And sailing ships and elephants,
And cannibals crouching 'round the pot,
Stirring away at something hot.
(It smells so good, what can it be!
Good gracious, it's Penelope.)
The younger ones had Beatrix Potter
With Mr. Tod, the dirty rotter,
And Squirrel Nutkin, Pigling Bland,
And Mrs. Tiggy-Winkle and—
Just How The Camel Got His Hump,
And How The Monkey Lost His Rump,
And Mr. Toad, and bless my soul,
There's Mr. Rat and Mr. Mole—
Oh, books, what books they used to know,
Those children living long ago!

So please, oh please, *we beg, we pray,*
Go throw your TV set away,
And in its place you can install
A lovely bookshelf on the wall.
Then fill the shelves with lots of books,
Ignoring all the dirty looks,
The screams and yells, the bites and kicks,
And children hitting you with sticks—
Fear not, because we promise you
That, in about a week or two
Of having nothing else to do,
They'll now begin to feel the need
Of having something good to read.
And once they start—oh boy, oh boy!
You *watch the slowly growing joy*
That fills their hearts. They'll grow so keen
They'll wonder what they'd ever seen
In that ridiculous machine,
That nauseating, foul, unclean,
Repulsive television screen!
And later, each and every kid
Will love you more for what you did.
P.S. Regarding Mike Teavee,
We very much regret that we
Shall simply have to wait and see
If we can get him back his height.
But if we can't—it serves him right.

28
Only Charlie Left

"WHICH ROOM SHALL IT BE NEXT?" said Mr. Wonka as he turned away and darted into the elevator. "Come on! Hurry up! We *must* get going! And how many children are there left now?"

Little Charlie looked at Grandpa Joe, and Grandpa Joe looked back at little Charlie.

"But Mr. Wonka," Grandpa Joe called after him, "there's . . . there's only Charlie left now."

Mr. Wonka swung round and stared at Charlie.

There was a silence. Charlie stood there holding tightly onto Grandpa Joe's hand.

"You mean you're the *only* one left?" Mr. Wonka said, pretending to be surprised.

"Why yes," whispered Charlie. "Yes."

Mr. Wonka suddenly exploded with excitement. "But my *dear boy,*" he cried out, "*that means you've won*!" He rushed out of the elevator and started shaking Charlie's hand so furiously it nearly came off. "Oh, I do congratulate you!" he cried. "I really do! I'm absolutely delighted! It couldn't be better! How wonderful this is! I had a hunch, you know, right from the beginning, that it was going to be you! Well *done,* Charlie, well *done*! This is terrific! Now the fun is really going to start! But we mustn't dilly! We mustn't dally! There's even less time to lose now than there was before! We have an *enormous* number of

things to do before the day is out! Just think of the
arrangements that have to be made! And the people we
have to fetch! But luckily for us, we have the great glass
elevator to speed things up! Jump in, my dear Charlie,
jump in! You too, Grandpa Joe, sir! No, no, *after* you!
That's the way! Now then! This time *I* shall choose the
button we are going to press!" Mr. Wonka's bright twinkling blue eyes rested for a moment on Charlie's face.

Something crazy is going to happen now, Charlie thought. But he wasn't frightened. He wasn't even nervous. He was just terrifically excited. And so was Grandpa Joe. The old man's face was shining with excitement as he watched every move that Mr. Wonka made. Mr. Wonka was reaching for a button high up on the glass ceiling of the elevator. Charlie and Grandpa Joe both craned their necks to read what it said on the little label beside the button.

It said . . . UP AND OUT.

Up and *out*, thought Charlie. *What sort of a room is that?*

Mr. Wonka pressed the button.

The glass doors closed.

"Hold on!" cried Mr. Wonka.

Then *WHAM*! The elevator shot straight up like a rocket! "Yippee!" shouted Grandpa Joe. Charlie was clinging to Grandpa Joe's legs and Mr. Wonka was holding onto a strap from the ceiling, and up they went, up, up, up, straight up this time, with no twistings or turnings, and Charlie could hear the whistling of the air outside as the elevator went faster and faster. "Yippee!" shouted Grandpa Joe again. "Yippee! Here we go!"

"Faster!" cried Mr. Wonka, banging the wall of the elevator with his hand. "Faster! Faster! If we don't go any faster than this, we shall never get through!"

"Through what?" shouted Grandpa Joe. "What have we got to get through?"

"Aha!" cried Mr. Wonka. "You wait and see! I've been *longing* to press this button for years! But I've never done it until now! I was tempted many times! Oh yes, I was tempted! But I couldn't bear the thought of making a great big hole in the roof of the factory! Here we go, boys! Up and out!"

"But you don't mean . . ." shouted Grandpa Joe, ". . . you don't *really* mean that this elevator. . . ."

"Oh yes, I do!" answered Mr. Wonka. "You wait and see! Up and out!"

"But . . . but . . . but . . . it's made of glass!" shouted Grandpa Joe. "It'll break into a million pieces!"

"I suppose it might," said Mr. Wonka, cheerful as ever, "but it's pretty thick glass, all the same."

The elevator rushed on, going up and up and up, faster and faster and faster. . . .

The suddenly, CRASH!—and the most tremendous noise of splintering wood and broken tiles came from directly above their heads, and Grandpa Joe shouted, "Help! It's the end! We're done for!" and Mr. Wonka said, "No, we're not! We're through! We're out!" Sure enough, the elevator had shot right up through the roof of the factory and was now rising into the sky like a rocket, and the sunshine was pouring in through the glass roof. In five seconds they were a thousand feet up in the sky.

"The elevator's gone mad!" shouted Grandpa Joe.

"Have no fear, my dear sir," said Mr. Wonka calmly, and he pressed another button. The elevator stopped. It stopped and hung in mid-air, hovering like a helicopter, hovering over the factory and over the very town itself which lay spread out below them like a picture postcard! Looking down through the glass floor on which he was standing, Charlie could see the small far-away houses and the streets and the snow that lay thickly over everything.

It was an eerie and frightening feeling to be standing on clear glass high up in the sky. It made you feel that you weren't standing on anything at all.

"Are we all right?" cried Grandpa Joe. "How does this thing stay up?"

"Candy power!" said Mr. Wonka. "One million candy power! Oh, look," he cried, pointing down, "there go the other children! They're returning home!"

29

The Other Children Go Home

"WE *MUST* GO DOWN and take a look at our little friends before we do anything else," said Mr. Wonka. He pressed a different button, and the elevator dropped lower, and soon it was hovering just above the entrance gates to the factory.

Looking down now, Charlie could see the children and their parents standing in a little group just inside the gates. "I can only see three," he said. "Who's missing?"

"I expect it's Mike Teavee," Mr. Wonka said. "But he'll be coming along soon. Do you see the trucks?" Mr. Wonka pointed to a line of gigantic covered vans parked in a line nearby.

"Yes," Charlie said. "What are *they* for?"

"Don't you remember what it said on the Golden Tickets? Every child goes home with a lifetime's supply of candy. There's one truckload for each of them, loaded to the brim. Ah-ha," Mr. Wonka went on, "there goes our friend Augustus Gloop! D'you see him? He's getting into the first truck with his mother and father!"

"You mean he's *really* all right?" asked Charlie, astonished. "Even after going up that awful pipe?"

"He's very much all right," said Mr. Wonka.

"He's changed!" said Grandpa Joe, peering down through the glass wall of the elevator. "He used to be fat! Now he's thin as a straw!"

"Of course he's changed," said Mr. Wonka, laughing. "He got squeezed in the pipe. Don't you remember? And look! There goes Miss Violet Beauregarde, the great gum-chewer! It seems as though they managed to de-juice her after all. I'm so glad. And how healthy she looks! Much better than before!"

"But she's purple in the face!" cried Grandpa Joe.

"So she is," said Mr. Wonka. "Ah, well, there's nothing we can do about that."

"Good gracious!" cried Charlie. "Look at poor Veruca Salt and Mr. Salt and Mrs. Salt! They're simply *covered* with garbage!"

"And here comes Mike Teavee!" said Grandpa Joe. "Good heavens! What *have* they done to him? He's about ten feet tall and thin as a wire!"

"They've overstretched him on the gum-stretching machine," said Mr. Wonka. "How very careless."

"But how dreadful for him!" cried Charlie.

"Nonsense," said Mr. Wonka, "he's very lucky. Every basketball team in the country will be trying to get him. But now," he added, "it is time we left these four silly children. I have something very important to talk to you about, my dear Charlie." Mr. Wonka pressed another button, and the elevator swung upwards into the sky.

30

Charlie's Chocolate Factory

THE GREAT GLASS ELEVATOR was now hovering high over the town. Inside the elevator stood Mr. Wonka, Grandpa Joe, and little Charlie.

"How I love my chocolate factory," said Mr. Wonka, gazing down. Then he paused, and he turned around and looked at Charlie with a most serious expression on his face. "Do *you* love it, too, Charlie?" he asked.

"Oh, yes," cried Charlie, "I think it's the most wonderful place in the whole world!"

"I am very pleased to hear you say that," said Mr. Wonka, looking more serious than ever. He went on staring at Charlie. "Yes," he said, "I am very pleased indeed to hear you say that. And now I shall tell you why." Mr. Wonka cocked his head to one side and all at once the tiny twinkling wrinkles of a smile appeared around the corners of his eyes, and he said, "You see, my dear boy, I have decided to make you a present of the whole place.

As soon as you are old enough to run it, the entire factory will become yours."

Charlie stared at Mr. Wonka. Grandpa Joe opened his mouth to speak, but no words came out.

"It's quite true," Mr. Wonka said, smiling broadly now. "I really am giving it to you. That's all right, isn't it?"

"*Giving* it to him?" gasped Grandpa Joe. "You must be joking."

"I'm not joking, sir. I'm deadly serious."

"But . . . but . . . why should you want to give your factory to little Charlie?"

"Listen," Mr. Wonka said, "I'm an old man. I'm much older than you think. I can't go on forever. I've got no children of my own, no family at all. So who is going to run the factory when I get too old to do it myself? *Someone's* got to keep it going—if only for the sake of the Oompa-Loompas. Mind you, there are thousands of clever men who would give anything for the chance to come in and take over from me, but I don't *want* that sort of person. I don't want a grown-up person at all. A grownup won't listen to me; he won't learn. He will try to do things his own way and not mine. So I have to have a child. I want a good sensible loving child, one to whom I can tell all my most precious candy-making secrets—while I am still alive."

"So *that* is why you sent out the Golden Tickets!" cried Charlie.

"Exactly!" said Mr. Wonka. "I decided to invite five children to the factory, and the one I liked best at the end of the day would be the winner!"

"But Mr. Wonka," stammered Grandpa Joe, "do you

really and truly mean that you are giving the whole of this enormous factory to little Charlie? After all. . . ."

"There's no time for arguments!" cried Mr. Wonka. "We must go at once and fetch the rest of the family—Charlie's father and his mother and anyone else that's around! They can all live in the factory from now on! They can all help to run it until Charlie is old enough to do it by himself! Where do you live, Charlie?"

Charlie peered down through the glass elevator at the snow-covered houses that lay below. "It's over there," he said, pointing. "It's that little cottage right on the edge of the town, the tiny little one. . . ."

"I see it!" cried Mr. Wonka, and he pressed some more buttons and the elevator shot down toward Charlie's house.

"I'm afraid my mother won't come with us," Charlie said sadly.

"Why ever not?"

"Because she won't leave Grandma Josephine and Grandma Georgina and Grandpa George."

"But they must come too."

"They can't," Charlie said. "They're very old and they haven't been out of bed for twenty years."

"Then we'll take the bed along as well, with them in it," said Mr. Wonka. "There's plenty of room in this elevator for a bed."

"You couldn't get the bed out of the house," said Grandpa Joe. "It won't go through the door."

"You mustn't despair!" cried Mr. Wonka. "Nothing is impossible! You watch!"

The elevator was now hovering over the roof of the Bucket's little house.

"What are you going to do?" cried Charlie.

"I'm going right on in to fetch them," said Mr. Wonka.

"How?" asked Grandpa Joe.

"Through the roof," said Mr. Wonka, pressing another button.

"No!" shouted Charlie.

"Stop!" shouted Grandpa Joe.

CRASH went the elevator, right down through the roof of the house into the old people's bedroom. Showers of dust and broken tiles and bits of wood and cockroaches and spiders and bricks and cement went raining down on the three old ones who were lying in bed, and each of them thought that the end of the world was come. Grandma Georgina fainted, Grandma Josephine dropped her false teeth, Grandpa George put his head under the blanket, and Mr. and Mrs. Bucket came rushing in from the next room.

"Save us!" cried Grandma Josephine.

"Calm yourself, my darling wife," said Grandpa Joe, stepping out of the elevator. "It's only us."

"Mother!" cried Charlie, rushing into Mrs. Bucket's arms. "Mother! Mother! Listen to what's happened! We're all going back to live in Mr. Wonka's factory and we're going to help him to run it and he's given it *all* to me and . . . and . . . and . . . and. . . ."

"What *are* you talking about?" said Mrs. Bucket.

"Just look at our house!" cried poor Mr. Bucket. "It's in ruins!"

"My dear sir," said Mr. Wonka, jumping forward and shaking Mr. Bucket warmly by the hand, "I'm so very glad to meet you. You mustn't worry about your house. From now on, you're never going to need it again, anyway."

"Who *is* this crazy man?" screamed Grandma Josephine. "He could have killed us all."

"This," said Grandpa Joe, "is Mr. Willy Wonka himself."

It took quite a time for Grandpa Joe and Charlie to

explain to everyone exactly what had been happening to them all day. And even then they all refused to ride back to the factory in the elevator.

"I'd rather die in my bed!" shouted Grandma Josephine.

"So would I!" cried Grandma Georgina.

"I refuse to go!" announced Grandpa George.

So Mr. Wonka and Grandpa Joe and Charlie, taking no notice of their screams, simply pushed the bed into the elevator. They pushed Mr. and Mrs. Bucket in after it. Then they got in themselves. Mr. Wonka pressed a button. The doors closed. Grandma Georgina screamed. And the elevator rose up off the floor and shot through the hole in the roof, out into the open sky.

Charlie climbed onto the bed and tried to calm the three old people who were still petrified with fear. "Please don't be frightened," he said. "It's quite safe. And we're going to the most wonderful place in the world!"

"Charlie's right," said Grandpa Joe.

"Will there be anything to eat when we get there?" asked Grandma Josephine. "I'm starving! The whole family is starving!"

"Anything to *eat*?" cried Charlie, laughing. "Oh, you just wait and see!"

Charlie and the Great Glass Elevator

For my daughters

Tessa   Ophelia   Lucy

and for my godson

Edmund Pollinger

CONTENTS

1
Mr. Wonka Goes Too Far

THE LAST TIME WE SAW CHARLIE, he was riding high above his home town in the Great Glass Elevator. Only a short while before, Mr. Wonka had told him that the whole gigantic fabulous Chocolate Factory was his, and now our small friend was returning in triumph with his entire family to take over. The passengers in the Elevator (just to remind you) were:

> *Charlie Bucket,*
> *   our hero.*
> *Mr. Willy Wonka,*
> *   chocolate-maker extraordinary.*
> *Mr. and Mrs. Bucket,*
> *   Charlie's father and mother.*
> *Grandpa Joe and Grandma Josephine,*
> *   Mr. Bucket's father and mother.*
> *Grandpa George and Grandma Georgina,*
> *   Mrs. Bucket's father and mother.*

Grandma Josephine, Grandma Georgina and Grandpa George were still in bed, the bed having been pushed on board just before take off. Grandpa Joe, as you remember, had gotten out of bed to go around the Chocolate Factory with Charlie.

The Great Glass Elevator was a thousand feet up and cruising nicely. The sky was a brilliant blue. Everybody on board was wildly excited at the thought of going to live in the famous Chocolate Factory. Grandpa Joe was singing. Charlie was jumping up and down. Mr. and Mrs. Bucket were smiling for the first time in years, and the three old ones in the bed were grinning at one another with pink toothless gums.

"What in the world keeps this thing up in the air?" croaked Grandma Josephine.

"Skyhooks," said Mr. Wonka.

"You amaze me," said Grandma Josephine.

"Dear lady," said Mr. Wonka, "you are new to the scene. When you have been with us a little longer, nothing will amaze you."

"These skyhooks," said Grandma Josephine. "I assume

one end is hooked onto this contraption we're riding in. Right?"

"Right," said Mr. Wonka.

"What's the other end hooked onto?" said Grandma Josephine.

"Every day," said Mr. Wonka, "I get deafer and deafer. Remind me, please, to call up my ear doctor the moment we get back."

"Charlie," said Grandma Josephine. "I don't think I trust this gentleman very much."

"Nor do I," said Grandma Georgina. "He footles around."

Charlie leaned over the bed and whispered to the two old women. "Please," he said, "don't spoil everything. Mr. Wonka is a fantastic man. He's my friend. I love him."

"Charlie's right," whispered Grandpa Joe, joining the group. "Now you be quiet, Josie, and don't make trouble."

"We must hurry!" said Mr. Wonka. "We have so much time and so little to do! No! Wait! Strike that! Reverse it! Thank you! Now back to the factory!" he cried, clapping his hands once and springing two feet in the air with two feet. "Back we fly to the factory! But we must go *up* before we can come down! We must go *higher and higher*!"

"What did I tell you!" said Grandma Josephine. "The man's cracked!"

"Be quiet, Josie," said Grandpa Joe. "Mr. Wonka knows exactly what he's doing."

"He's cracked as a crab!" said Grandma Georgina.

"We must go higher!" said Mr. Wonka. "We must go tremendously high! Hold onto your stomachs!" He pressed a brown button. The Elevator shuddered, and then with a fearful whooshing noise it shot vertically upward like a rocket. Everybody clutched hold of everybody else and as the great machine gathered speed, the rushing whooshing sound of the wind outside grew louder and louder and shriller and shriller until it became a piercing shriek and you had to yell to make yourself heard.

"Stop!" yelled Grandma Josephine. "Joe, you make him stop! I want to get off!"

"Save us!" yelled Grandma Georgina.

"Go down!" yelled Grandpa George.

"No, no!" Mr. Wonka yelled back. "We've got to go up!"

"But why?" they all shouted at once. "Why up and not down?"

"Because the higher we are when we start coming down, the faster we'll be going when we hit," said Mr. Wonka. "We've got to be going at an absolutely sizzling speed when we hit!"

"When we hit *what?*" they cried.

"The factory, of course," answered Mr. Wonka.

"You must be whackers!" said Grandma Josephine. "We'll all be pulpified!"

"We'll be scrambled like eggs!" said Grandma Georgina.

"That," said Mr. Wonka, "is a chance we shall have to take."

"You're joking," said Grandma Josephine. "Tell us you're joking."

"Madam," said Mr. Wonka, "I never joke."

"Oh, my dears!" cried Grandma Georgina. "We'll be *lixivated*, every one of us!"

"More than likely," said Mr. Wonka.

Grandma Josephine screamed and disappeared under the bedclothes. Grandma Georgina clutched Grandpa George so tight he changed shape. Mr. and Mrs. Bucket stood hugging each other, speechless with fright. Only Charlie and Grandpa Joe kept moderately cool. They had traveled a long way with Mr. Wonka and had grown accustomed to surprises. But as the Great Elevator continued to streak upward, farther and farther away from the earth, even Charlie began to feel a trifle nervous. "Mr. Wonka!" he yelled above the noise. "What I don't understand is *why* we've got to come down at such a terrific speed."

"My dear boy," Mr. Wonka answered, "if we don't come down at a terrific speed, we'll never burst our way back in through the roof of the factory. It's not easy to punch a hole in a roof as strong as that."

"But there's a hole in it already," said Charlie. "We made it when we came out."

"Then we shall make another," said Mr. Wonka. "Two holes are better than one. Any mouse will tell you that."

Higher and higher rushed the Great Glass Elevator until soon they could see the countries and oceans of the earth spread out below them like a map. It was all very beautiful, but when you are standing on a glass floor looking down, it gives you a nasty feeling. Even Charlie was beginning to feel frightened now. He hung on tightly to Grandpa Joe's hand and looked up anxiously into the old man's face. "I'm scared, Grandpa," he said.

Grandpa Joe put an arm around Charlie's shoulders

and held him close. "So am I, Charlie," he said.

"Mr. Wonka!" Charlie shouted. "Don't you think this is about high enough?"

"Very nearly," Mr. Wonka answered. "But not quite. Don't talk to me now, please. Don't disturb me. I must watch things very carefully at this stage. Split-second timing, my boy, that's what it's got to be. You see this green button. I must press it at exactly the right instant. If I'm just half a second late, then we'll go *too high!*"

"What happens if we go too high?" asked Grandpa Joe.

"Do please stop talking and let me concentrate!" Mr. Wonka said.

At that precise moment, Grandma Josephine poked her head out from under the sheets and peered over the edge of the bed. Through the glass floor she saw the entire continent of North America nearly two hundred miles below and looking no bigger than a piece of candy. "*Someone's* got to stop this maniac," she screeched, and she shot out a wrinkled old hand and grabbed Mr. Wonka by the coattails and yanked him backward onto the bed.

"No, no," cried Mr. Wonka, struggling to free himself. "Let me go! I have things to see to! Don't disturb the pilot!"

"You madman," shrieked Grandma Josephine, shaking Mr. Wonka so fast that his head became a blur. "You get us back home this instant!"

"Let me go!" cried Mr. Wonka. "I've got to press that button or we'll go too high! Let me go! Let me go!" But Grandma Josephine hung on. "Charlie!" shouted Mr. Wonka. "Press the button! The green one! Quick, quick, quick!"

Charlie leaped across the Elevator and banged his

thumb down on the green button. But as he did so, the Elevator gave a mighty groan and rolled over onto its side, and the rushing whooshing noise stopped altogether and an eerie silence took its place.

"Too late!" cried Mr. Wonka. "Oh, my goodness me, we're cooked!" As he spoke, the bed with the three old ones in it and Mr. Wonka on top lifted gently off the floor and hung suspended in mid-air. Charlie and Grandpa Joe and Mr. and Mrs. Bucket also floated upward so that in a twink the entire company, as well as the bed, were floating around like balloons inside the Great Glass Elevator.

"*Now* look what you've done!" said Mr. Wonka, floating about.

"What happened?" Grandma Josephine called out. She

had floated clear of the bed and was hovering near the ceiling in her nightshirt.

"Did we go too far?" Charlie asked.

"Too *far?*" cried Mr. Wonka. "I'll say we went too far! You know where we've gone, my friends? We've gone into orbit!"

They gaped, they gasped, they stared. They were too flabbergasted to speak.

"We are now rushing around the earth at seventeen thousand miles an hour," Mr. Wonka said. "How does that grab you?"

"I'm choking!" gasped Grandma Georgina. "I can't breathe!"

"Of course you can't," said Mr. Wonka. "There's no air up here." He sort of swam across under the ceiling to a button marked OXYGEN. He pressed it. "You'll be all right now," he said. "Breathe away."

"This is the queerest feeling," Charlie said, swimming about. "I feel like a bubble."

"It's great," said Grandpa Joe. "It feels as though I don't weigh anything at all."

"You don't," said Mr. Wonka. "None of us weighs anything—not even one ounce."

"What piffle!" said Grandma Georgina. "I weigh eighty-seven pounds exactly."

"Not now you don't," said Mr. Wonka. "You are completely weightless."

The three old ones, Grandpa George, Grandma Georgina and Grandma Josephine were trying frantically to get back into the bed, but without success. The bed was floating about in mid-air. They, of course, were also floating, and every time they got above the bed and tried to lie down, they simply floated up out of it. Charlie and Grandpa Joe were hooting with laughter. "What's so funny?" said Grandma Josephine.

"We've got you out of bed at last," said Grandpa Joe.

"Shut up and help us back!" snapped Grandma Josephine.

"Forget it," said Mr. Wonka. "You'll never stay down. Just keep floating around and be happy."

"The man's a madman!" cried Grandma Georgina. "Watch out, I say, or he'll lixivate the lot of us!"

2

Space Hotel "U.S.A."

MR. WONKA'S GREAT GLASS ELEVATOR was not the only thing orbiting the earth at that particular time. Two days earlier, the United States of America had successfully launched its first Space Hotel, a gigantic sausage-shaped capsule no less than one thousand feet long. It was called Space Hotel "U.S.A." and it was the marvel of the space age. It had inside it a tennis court, a swimming pool, a gymnasium, a children's playroom and five hundred luxury bedrooms, each with a private bath. It was fully air-conditioned. It was also equipped with a gravity-making machine so that you didn't float about inside it. You could walk normally.

This extraordinary object was now speeding round

and round the earth at a height of two hundred and forty miles. Guests were to be taken up and down by a taxi service of commuter capsules blasting off from Cape Kennedy every hour on the hour, Monday through Friday. But as yet there was nobody on board at all, not even an astronaut. The reason for this was that no one had really believed such an enormous thing would ever get off the ground without blowing up.

But the launching had been a great success and now that the Space Hotel was safely in orbit, there was a tremendous hustle and bustle to send up the first guests. It was rumored that the President of the United States himself was going to be among the first to stay in the hotel, and of course there was a mad rush by all sorts of other people across the world to book rooms. Several kings and queens had cabled the White House in Washington for reservations, and a Texas millionaire called Orson Cart, who was about to marry a Hollywood starlet called Helen Highwater, was offering one hundred thousand dollars a day for the honeymoon suite.

But you cannot send guests to a hotel unless there are lots of people there to look after them, and that explains why there was yet another interesting object orbiting the earth at that moment. This was the large Commuter Capsule containing the entire staff for Space Hotel "U.S.A." There were managers, assistant managers, desk clerks, waitresses, bellhops, chambermaids, pastry chefs and hall porters. The capsule they were traveling in was manned by the three famous astronauts, Shuckworth, Shanks and Showler, all of them handsome, clever and brave.

"In exactly one hour," said Shuckworth, speaking to the

passengers over the loudspeaker, "we shall link up with Space Hotel 'U.S.A.,' your happy home for the next ten years. And any moment now, if you look straight ahead, you should catch your first glimpse of this magnificent spaceship. Ah-ha! I see something there! That must be it, folks! There's definitely something up there ahead of us!"

Shuckworth, Shanks and Showler, as well as the managers, assistant managers, desk clerks, waitresses, bellhops, chambermaids, pastry chefs, hall porters, all stared excitedly through the windows. Shuckworth fired a couple of small rockets to make the capsule go faster, and they began to catch up very quickly.

"Hey," yelled Showler. "That isn't our Space Hotel."

"Holy rats!" cried Shanks. "What in the name of Nebuchadnezzar is it?"

"Quick! Give me the telescope!" yelled Shuckworth. With one hand, he focused the telescope and with the other he flipped the switch connecting him to Ground Control.

"Hello, Houston!" he cried into the mike. "There's something crazy going on up here. There's a thing orbiting ahead of us and it's not like any spaceship I've ever seen, that's for sure!"

"Describe it at once," ordered Ground Control in Houston.

"It's . . . it's all made of glass and it's kind of square and it's got lots of people inside it! They're all floating about like fish in a tank!"

"How many astronauts on board?"

"None," said Shuckworth. "They can't possibly be astronauts."

"What makes you say that?"

"Because at least three of them are in nightshirts!"

"Don't be a fool, Shuckworth!" snapped Ground Control. "Pull yourself together, man! This is serious!"

"I swear it!" cried poor Shuckworth. "There's three of them in nightshirts! Two old women and one old man! I can see them clearly! I can even see their faces! Jeepers, they're older than Moses! They're about ninety years old!"

"You've gone mad, Shuckworth," shouted Ground Control. "You're fired. Give me Shanks!"

"Shanks speaking," said Shanks. "Now listen here, Houston. There's these three old birds in nightshirts floating around in this crazy glass box and there's a funny little guy with a pointed beard wearing a black top hat and a plum-colored velvet tailcoat and bottle-green trousers . . ."

"Stop!" screamed Ground Control.

"Hold the phone!" said Shanks. "There's also a little boy about ten years old."

"That's no boy, you idiot!" shouted Ground Control. "That's an astronaut in disguise! It's a midget astronaut dressed up as a little boy! Those old people are astronauts too! They're all in disguise!"

"But who *are* they?" cried Shanks.

"How the heck would I know?" said Ground Control. "Are they heading for our Space Hotel?"

"That's exactly where they are heading," cried Shanks. "I can see the Space Hotel now about a mile ahead."

"They're going to blow it up!" yelled Ground Control. "This is desperate! This is . . ." Suddenly his voice was cut off and Shanks heard another quite different voice in his earphones. It was deep and rasping.

"I'll take charge of this," said the deep rasping voice. "Are you there, Shanks?"

"Of course I'm here," said Shanks. "But how dare you butt in! Keep your big nose out of this! Who are you anyway?"

"This is the President of the United States," said the voice.

"And this is the Wizard of Oz," said Shanks. "Who are you kidding?"

"Cut the piffle, Shanks!" snapped the President. "This is a national emergency!"

"Good grief!" said Shanks, turning to Shuckworth and Showler. "It really *is* the President. It's President Gilligrass himself! Well, *hello there*, Mr. President, sir. How are *you* today?"

"How many people are there in that glass capsule?" rasped the President.

"Eight," said Shanks. "All floating."

"Floating?!"

14 ❧

"We're outside the pull of gravity up here, Mr. President. Everything floats. We'd be floating ourselves if we weren't strapped down. Didn't you know that?"

"Of course I knew it," said the President. "What else can you tell me about that glass capsule?"

"There's a bed in it," said Shanks. "A big double bed, and that's floating too."

"A bed?" barked the President. "Whoever heard of a bed in a spacecraft!"

"I swear it's a bed!" said Shanks.

"You must be loopy, Shanks!" declared the President. "You're dotty as a doughnut! Let me talk to Showler!"

"Showler here, Mr. President," said Showler, taking the mike from Shanks. "It is a great honor to talk to you, Mr. President, sir."

"Oh, shut up!" said the President. "Just tell me what you see."

"It's a bed all right, Mr. President. I can see it through my telescope. It's got sheets and blankets and a mattress . . ."

"That's not a bed, you driveling thickwit!" yelled the President. "Can't you understand it's a trick! It's a bomb! It's a bomb disguised as a bed! They're going to blow up our magnificent Space Hotel!"

"Who's *they*, Mr. President, sir?" said Showler.

"Don't talk so much and let me think!" said the President. There were a few moments of silence. Showler waited tensely. So did Shanks and Shuckworth. So did the managers and assistant managers and desk clerks and waitresses and bellhops and chambermaids and pastry chefs and hall porters. And down in the huge Control Room at Houston, one hundred controllers sat motionless in front of their dials and monitors, waiting to see what orders the President would give next to the astronauts.

"I've just thought of something," said the President. "Don't you have a television camera up there on the front of your spacecraft, Showler?"

"Sure do, Mr. President."

"Then switch it on, you nit, and let all of us down here get a look at this object!"

"I never thought of that," said Showler. "No *wonder* you're the President. Here goes!" He reached out and switched on the T.V. camera in the nose of the spacecraft, and at that moment, five hundred million people all over the world who had been listening in on their radios, rushed to their television sets.

On their screens they saw exactly what Shuckworth and Shanks and Showler were seeing—a weird glass box in splendid orbit around the earth, and inside the box, seen not too clearly but seen nonetheless, were seven grown-ups and one small boy and a big double bed, all floating. Three of the grown-ups were barelegged and wearing nightshirts. And far off in the distance, beyond the glass box, the T.V. watchers could see the enormous, glistening, silvery shape of Space Hotel "U.S.A."

But it was the sinister glass box itself that everyone was staring at, and the cargo of sinister creatures inside it—eight astronauts so tough and strong they didn't even bother to wear spacesuits. Who were these people and where did they come from? And what in heaven's name was that big evil-looking thing disguised as a double bed? The President had said it was a bomb and he was probably right. But what were they going to do with it? All across America and Canada and Russia and Japan and India and China and Africa and England and France and Germany and everywhere else in the world a kind of panic began to take hold of the television watchers.

"Keep well clear of them, Showler!" ordered the President over the radio link.

"Sure will, Mr. President!" Showler answered. "I *sure will*!"

3

The Link-Up

INSIDE THE GREAT GLASS ELEVATOR there was also a good deal of excitement. Charlie and Mr. Wonka and all the others could see clearly the huge silvery shape of Space Hotel "U.S.A." about a mile ahead of them. And behind them was the smaller (but still pretty enormous) Commuter Capsule. The Great Glass Elevator (not looking at all great now beside these two monsters) was in the middle. And of course everybody, even Grandma Josephine, knew very well what was going on. They even knew that the three astronauts in charge of the Commuter Capsule were called Shuckworth, Shanks and Showler. The whole world knew about these things. Newspapers and television had been shouting about almost nothing else for the past six months. Operation Space Hotel was the event of the century.

"What a load of luck!" cried Mr. Wonka. "We've landed

ourselves slap in the middle of the biggest space operation of all time!"

"We've landed ourselves in the middle of a nasty mess!" said Grandma Josephine. "Turn back at once!"

"*No,* Grandma," said Charlie. "We've *got* to watch it now! We *must* see the Commuter Capsule linking up with the Space Hotel!"

Mr. Wonka floated right up close to Charlie. "Let's beat them to it, Charlie," he whispered. "Let's get there first and go aboard the Space Hotel ourselves!"

Charlie gaped. Then he gulped. Then he said softly, "It's impossible. You've got to have all sorts of special gadgets to link up with another spacecraft, Mr. Wonka."

"My Elevator could link up with a crocodile if it had to," said Mr. Wonka. "Just leave it to me, my boy!"

"Grandpa Joe!" cried Charlie. "Did you hear that? We're going to link up with the Space Hotel and go on board!"

"Yippeeeeee!" shouted Grandpa Joe. "What a brilliant thought, sir! What a staggering idea!" He grabbed Mr. Wonka's hand and started shaking it like a thermometer.

"Be quiet, you balmy old bat!" said Grandma Josephine. "We're in a hot enough stew already! I want to go home!"

"Me, too!" said Grandma Georgina.

"What if they come after us?" said Mr. Bucket, speaking for the first time.

"What if they capture us?" said Mrs. Bucket.

"What if they shoot us?" said Grandma Georgina.

"What if my beard were made of green spinach?" cried Mr. Wonka. "Bunkum and tummyrot! You'll never get anywhere if you go about what-iffing like that. Would Columbus have discovered America if he'd said 'What if I sink on the way over? What if I meet pirates? What if I never come back?' He wouldn't even have started! We want no what-iffers around here, right Charlie? Off we go, then! But wait . . . this is a very tricky maneuver and I'm going to need help. We have to press lots of buttons, all in different parts of the Elevator. I shall take those two over there, the white and the black." Mr. Wonka made a funny blowing noise with his mouth and glided effortlessly, like a huge bird, across the Elevator to the white and black buttons, and there he hovered. "Grandpa Joe, sir, kindly station yourself beside that silver button there . . . yes, that's the one. And you, Charlie, go up and stay floating beside that little golden button near the ceiling. I must tell you that each of these buttons fires booster rockets from different places outside the Elevator. That's how we change direction. Grandpa Joe's rockets turn us to starboard, to the right. Charlie's turn us to port, to the left. Mine make us go higher or lower or faster or slower. All ready?"

"No! Wait!" cried Charlie, who was floating exactly

midway between the floor and the ceiling. "How do I get up? I can't get up to the ceiling!" He was thrashing his arms and legs violently, like a drowning swimmer, but getting nowhere.

"My dear boy," said Mr. Wonka. "You can't *swim* in this stuff. It isn't water you know. It's air and very thin air at that. There's nothing to push against. So you have to use jet propulsion. Watch me. First, you take a deep breath, then you make a small round hole with your mouth and you blow as hard as you can. If you blow downward, you jet propel yourself up. If you blow left, you shoot off to the right, and so on. You maneuver yourself like a spacecraft, but using your mouth as a booster rocket."

Suddenly everyone began practicing this business of flying about, and the whole Elevator was filled with the blowings and snortings of the passengers. Grandma Georgina, in her red flannel nightgown with two skinny bare legs sticking out of the bottom was trumpeting and spitting like a rhinoceros and flying from one side of the Elevator to the other, shouting, "Out of my way! Out of my way!" and crashing into poor Mr. and Mrs. Bucket with terrible speed. Grandpa George and Grandma Josephine were doing the same. And well may you wonder what the millions of people down on earth were thinking as they watched these crazy happenings on their television screens. You must realize they couldn't see things very clearly. The Great Glass Elevator was only about the size of a grapefruit on their screens, and the people inside, slightly blurred through the glass, were no bigger than the pits of the grapefruit. Even so, the watchers below could see them buzzing about wildly like insects in a glass box.

"What in the world are they doing?" shouted the President of the United States, staring at the screen.

"Looks like some kind of a war dance, Mr. President," answered astronaut Showler over the radio.

"You mean they're Indians!" said the President.

"I didn't say that, sir."

"Oh, yes you did, Showler."

"Oh, no I didn't, Mr. President."

"Silence!" said the President. "You're muddling me up."

Back in the Elevator, Mr. Wonka was saying, "*Please! Please!* Do stop flying about! Keep still everybody, so we can get on with the docking!"

"You miserable old mackerel!" said Grandma Georgina, sailing past him. "Just when we start having a bit of fun, you want to stop it!"

"Look at me, everybody!" shouted Grandma Josephine. "I'm flying! I'm a golden eagle!"

"I can fly faster than any of you!" cried Grandpa George, whizzing round and round, his nightgown billowing out behind him like the tail of a parrot.

"Grandpa George!" cried Charlie. "Please calm down. If we don't hurry, those astronauts will get there before us. Don't you want to see inside the Space Hotel, any of you?"

"Out of my way!" shouted Grandma Georgina, blowing herself back and forth. "I'm a jumbo jet!"

"You're a balmy old bat!" said Mr. Wonka.

In the end, the old people grew tired and out of breath, and everyone settled quietly into a floating position. "All set, Charlie and Grandpa Joe, sir?" said Mr. Wonka.

"All set, Mr. Wonka," Charlie answered, hovering near the ceiling.

"I'll give the orders," said Mr. Wonka. "I'm the pilot. Don't fire your rockets until I tell you. And don't forget who is who. Charlie, you're port. Grandpa Joe, you're starboard." Mr. Wonka pressed one of his own two buttons and immediately booster rockets began firing underneath the Great Glass Elevator. The Elevator leaped forward, but swerved violently to the right. "Hard a-port!" yelled Mr. Wonka. Charlie pressed his button. His rockets fired. The Elevator swung back into line. "Steady as you go!" cried Mr. Wonka. "Starboard ten degrees! . . . Steady! . . . Steady! . . . Keep her there! . . ."

Soon they were hovering directly underneath the tail of the enormous silvery Space Hotel. "You see that little square door with the bolts on it?" said Mr. Wonka. "That's the docking entrance. It won't be long now. Port a fraction . . . Steady! . . . Starboard a bit! . . . Good . . . Good . . . Easy does it . . . We're nearly there . . ."

To Charlie, it felt rather as though he were in a tiny rowboat underneath the stern of the biggest ship in the world. The Space Hotel towered over them. It was enormous. "I can't wait," thought Charlie, "to get inside and see what it's like."

4

The President

HALF A MILE BACK, Shuckworth, Shanks and Showler were keeping the television camera aimed all the time at the Glass Elevator. And across the world, millions and millions of people were clustered around their T.V. screens, watching tensely the drama being acted out two hundred and forty miles above the earth. In his study in the White House sat Lancelot R. Gilligrass, President of the United States of America, the most powerful man on earth. In this moment of crisis, all his most important advisers had been summoned urgently to his presence, and there they all were now, following closely on the giant television screen every move made by this dangerous-looking glass capsule and its eight desperate-looking astronauts. The entire Cabinet was present. The Chief of the Army was there, together with four other generals. There was the Chief of the Navy and the Chief of the Air Force and a sword swallower from Afghanistan, who was the President's best friend. There was the President's Chief Financial Advisor, who was standing in the middle of the room trying to balance the budget on top of his head, but it kept falling off. Standing nearest of all to the President was the Vice-President, a huge lady of eighty-nine with a whiskery chin. She had been the President's nurse when he was a baby and her name was Miss Tibbs. Miss Tibbs was the power behind the throne. She stood no nonsense from anyone. Some people said she was as strict with the President now as when he was a little boy. She was the terror of the White House and even the Head of the F.B.I. broke into a sweat when summoned to her presence. Only the President was allowed to call her Nanny. The President's famous cat, Mrs. Taubsypuss, was also in the room.

There was absolute silence now in the Presidential study. All eyes were riveted on the T.V. screen as the small glass object, with its booster rockets firing, slid smoothly up behind the giant Space Hotel.

"They're going to link up!" shouted the President. "They're going on board our Space Hotel!"

"They're going to blow it up!" cried the Chief of the Army. "Let's blow *them* up first, crash bang wallop bang-bang-bang-bang-bang." The Chief of the Army was wearing so many medal ribbons they covered the entire front of his tunic on both sides and spread down onto his pants as well. "Come on, Mr. P.," he said. "Let's have some really super-duper explosions!"

"Silence, you silly boy!" said Miss Tibbs, and the Chief of the Army slunk into a corner.

"Listen," said the President. "The point is this. *Who are they? And where do they come from?* Where's my Chief Spy?"

"Here, sir, Mr. President, sir," said the Chief Spy. He had

a false moustache, a false beard, false eyelashes, false teeth and a falsetto voice.

"Knock-knock," said the President.

"Who's there?" said the Chief Spy.

"Courteney."

"Courteney who?"

"Courteney one yet?" said the President.

There was a brief silence.

"The President asked you a question," said Miss Tibbs in an icy voice. "Have you Courteney one yet?"

"No, ma'am, not yet," said the Chief Spy, beginning to twitch.

"Well, here's your chance," snarled Miss Tibbs.

"Quite right," said the President. "Tell me immediately who those people are in that glass capsule!"

"Ah-ha," said the Chief Spy, twirling his false moustache. "That is a very difficult question."

"You mean you don't know?"

"I mean I do know, Mr. President. At least I think I know. Listen. We have just launched the finest hotel in the world. Right?"

"Right."

"And who is so madly jealous of this wonderful hotel of ours that he wants to blow it up?"

"Miss Tibbs," said the President.

"Wrong," said the Chief Spy. "Try again."

"Well," said the President, thinking deeply. "In that case, could it not perhaps be some other hotel owner who is envious of our lovely hotel?"

"Brilliant!" cried the Chief Spy. "Go on, sir! You're getting warm!"

"It's Mr. Waldorf," said the President. "Or Mr. Astoria?"

"Warmer and warmer, Mr. President!"

"Mr. Ritz!"

"You're hot, sir! You're boiling hot! Go on!"

"I've got it!" cried the President. "It's Mr. Hilton!"

"Well done, sir!" said the Chief Spy.

"Are you sure it's him?"

"Not sure, but it's certainly a warm possibility, Mr. President. After all, Mr. Hilton's got hotels in just about every country in the world but he hasn't got one in space. And we have. He must be madder than a maggot!"

"By gum, we'll soon fix this!" snapped the President, grabbing one of the eleven telephones on his desk. "Hello," he said into the phone. "Hello hello hello! Where's the operator?" He jiggled furiously on the little thing you jiggle when you want the operator. "Operator, where are you?"

"They won't answer you now," said Miss Tibbs. "They're all watching television."

"Well, *this* one'll answer!" said the President, snatching up a bright red telephone. This was the hot line direct to the Premier of Soviet Russia in Moscow. It was always open and only used in terrible emergencies. "It's just as likely to be the Russians as Mr. Hilton," the President went on. "Don't you agree, Nanny?"

"It's bound to be the Russians," said Miss Tibbs.

"Premier Yugetoff speaking," said the voice from Moscow. "What's on your mind, Mr. President?"

"Knock-knock," said the President.

"Who's there?" said the Soviet Premier.

"Warren."

"Warren who?"

"Warren Peace by Leo Tolstoy," said the President. "Now see here, Yugetoff. You get those astronauts of yours off that Space Hotel of ours this instant! Otherwise, I'm afraid we're going to have to show you just where you get off, Yugetoff!"

"Those astronauts are not Russians, Mr. President."

"He's lying," said Miss Tibbs.

"You're lying," said the President.

"Not lying, sir," said Premier Yugetoff. "Have you looked closely at those astronauts in the glass box? I myself cannot see them too clearly on my T.V. screen, but one of them, the little one with the pointed beard and the top hat, has a distinctly Chinese look about him. In fact, he reminds me very much of my friend the Prime Minister of China."

"Great garbage!" cried the President, slamming down the red phone and picking up a porcelain one. The porcelain phone went directly to the Head of the Chinese Republic in Peking.

"Hello hello hello!" said the President.

"Wing's Fish and Vegetable Store in Shanghai," said a small distant voice. "Mr. Wing speaking."

"Nanny!" cried the President, banging down the phone. "I thought this was a direct line to the Premier!"

"It is," said Miss Tibbs. "Try again."

The President picked up the receiver. "Hello!" he yelled.

"Mr. Wong speaking," said a voice at the other end.

"Mister who?" screamed the President.

"Mr. Wong, assistant stationmaster, Chunking, and if you asking about ten o'clock tlain, ten o'clock tlain no lunning today. Boiler burst."

The President threw the phone across the room at the Postmaster General. It hit him in the stomach. "What's the matter with this thing?" shouted the President.

"It is very difficult to phone people in China, Mr. President," said the Postmaster General. "The country's so full of Wings and Wongs, every time you wing you get the wong number."

"You're not kidding," said the President.

The Postmaster General replaced the telephone on the desk. "Try it just once more, Mr. President, please," he said. "I've tightened the screws underneath."

The President again picked up the receiver.

"Gleetings, honorable Mr. Plesident," said a soft faraway voice. "Here is Assistant-Plemier Chu-On-Dat speaking. How can I do for you?"

"Knock-knock," said the President.

"Who der?"

"Ginger."

"Ginger who?"

"Ginger yourself much when you fell off the Great Wall of China?" said the President. "Okay, Chu-On-Dat. Let me speak to Premier How-Yu-Bin."

"Much regret Premier How-Yu-Bin not here just this second, Mr. Plesident."

"Where is he?"

"He outside mending a flat tire on his bicycle."

"Oh no, he isn't," said the President. "You can't fool me, you crafty old mandarin! At this very minute he's boarding our magnificent Space Hotel with seven other rascals to blow it up!"

"Excuse pleese, Mr. Plesident. You make big mistake."

"No mistake!" barked the President. "And if you don't call them off right away I'm going to tell my Chief of the Army to blow them all sky high! So chew on that, Chu-On-Dat!"

"Hooray!" said the Chief of the Army. "Let's blow everyone up! Bang-bang! Bang-bang!"

"Silence!" barked Miss Tibbs.

"I've done it!" cried the Chief Financial Adviser. "Look at me, everybody! I've balanced the budget!" And indeed he had. He stood proudly in the middle of the room with the enormous two-hundred-billion-dollar budget balanced beautifully on the top of his bald head. Everyone clapped. Then suddenly the voice of astronaut Shuckworth cut in urgently on the radio loudspeaker in the President's study. "They've linked up and gone on board!" shouted Shuckworth. "And they've taken in the bed . . . I mean the bomb!"

The President sucked in his breath sharply. He also sucked in a big fly that happened to be passing at the time. He choked. Miss Tibbs thumped him on the back. He swallowed the fly and felt better. But he was very angry. He seized pencil and paper and began to draw a picture. As he drew, he kept muttering, "I won't have flies in my office! I won't put up with them!" His advisers waited eagerly for what was coming. They knew that the great man was about to give the world yet another of his brilliant inventions. The last had been the Gilligrass Left-Handed Corkscrew, which had been hailed by left-handers across the nation as one of the greatest blessings of the century.

"There you are!" said the President, holding up the paper. "This is the Gilligrass Patent Fly-Trap!" They all crowded round to look.

"The fly climbs up the ladder on the left," said the President. "He walks along the plank. He stops. He sniffs. He smells something good. He peers over the edge and sees the sugar lump. 'Ah-ha!' he cries. 'Sugar!' He is just about to climb down the string to reach it when he sees the basin of water below. 'Ho-ho!' he says. 'It's a trap! They want me to fall in!' So he walks on, thinking what a clever fly he is. But as you see, I have left out one of the rungs in the ladder he goes down by, so he falls and breaks his neck."

"Tremendous, Mr. President!" they all exclaimed. "Fantastic! A stroke of genius!"

"I wish to order one hundred thousand for the Army immediately," said the Chief of the Army.

"Thank you," said the President, making a careful note of the order.

"I repeat," said the frantic voice of Shuckworth over the loudspeaker, "they've gone on board and taken the bomb with them!"

"Stay well clear of them, Shuckworth," ordered the

President. "There's no point in getting your boys blown up as well."

And now, all over the world, the millions of watchers waited more tensely than ever in front of their television sets. The picture on their screens, in vivid color, showed the sinister little glass box securely linked up to the underbelly of the gigantic Space Hotel. It looked like some tiny baby animal clinging to its mother. And when the camera zoomed closer, it was clear for all to see that the glass box was completely empty. All eight of the desperadoes had climbed into the Space Hotel and they had taken their bomb with them.

5

Men from Mars

THERE WAS NO FLOATING inside the Space Hotel. The gravity-making machine saw to that. So once the docking had been triumphantly achieved, Mr. Wonka, Charlie, Grandpa Joe and Mr. and Mrs. Bucket were able to walk out of the Great Glass Elevator into the lobby of the Hotel. As for Grandpa George, Grandma Georgina and Grandma Josephine, none of them had had their feet on the ground for over twenty years and they certainly weren't going to change their habits now. So when the floating stopped, they all three plopped right back into bed again and insisted that the bed, with them in it, be pushed into the Space Hotel.

Charlie gazed around the huge lobby. On the floor there was a thick green carpet. Twenty tremendous chandeliers hung shimmering from the ceiling. The walls were covered with valuable pictures and there were big soft armchairs all over the place. At the far end of the room there were five elevator doors. The group stared in silence at all this luxury. Nobody dared to speak. Mr. Wonka had warned them that every word they uttered would be picked up by Space Control in Houston, so they had better be careful. A faint humming noise came from somewhere below the floor, but that only made the silence more spooky. Charlie took hold of Grandpa Joe's hand and held it tight. He wasn't sure he liked this very much. They had broken into the greatest machine ever built by man, the property of the United States Government, and if they were discovered and captured as they surely would be in the end, what would happen to them then? Jail for life? Yes, or something worse.

Mr. Wonka was writing on a little pad. He held up the pad. It said: ANYBODY HUNGRY?

The three old ones in the bed began waving their arms and nodding and opening and shutting their mouths. Mr. Wonka turned the paper over. On the other side it said: THE KITCHENS OF THIS HOTEL ARE LOADED WITH LUSCIOUS FOOD, LOBSTERS, STEAKS, ICE CREAM. WE SHALL HAVE A FEAST TO END ALL FEASTS.

Suddenly, a tremendous booming voice came out of a loudspeaker hidden somewhere in the room. "ATTENTION!" boomed the voice, and Charlie jumped. So did Grandpa Joe. Everybody jumped, even Mr. Wonka. "ATTENTION THE EIGHT FOREIGN ASTRONAUTS! THIS IS SPACE CONTROL

IN HOUSTON, TEXAS, U.S.A.! YOU ARE TRESPASSING ON AMERICAN PROPERTY! YOU ARE ORDERED TO IDENTIFY YOURSELVES IMMEDIATELY! SPEAK NOW!"

"Ssshhh!" whispered Mr. Wonka, finger to lips.

There followed a few seconds of awful silence. Nobody moved except Mr. Wonka who kept saying "Ssshhh! Ssshhh!"

"WHO ... ARE ... YOU?" boomed the voice from Houston, and the whole world heard it. "I REPEAT ... WHO ... ARE ... YOU?" shouted the urgent angry voice, and five hundred million people crouched in front of their television sets waiting for an answer to come from the mysterious strangers inside the Space Hotel. The television was not able to show a picture of these mysterious strangers. There was no camera in there to record the scene. Only the words came through. The T.V. watchers saw nothing but the outside of the giant hotel in orbit, photographed of course by Shuckworth, Shanks and Showler, who were following behind. For half a minute the world waited for a reply.

But no reply came.

"SPEAK!" boomed the voice, getting louder and louder and ending in a fearful frightening shout that rattled Charlie's eardrums. "SPEAK! SPEAK! SPEAK!" Grandma Georgina shot under the sheet. Grandma Josephine stuck her fingers in her ears. Grandpa George buried his head in the pillow. Mr. and Mrs. Bucket, both petrified, were once again in each other's arms. Charlie was clutching Grandpa Joe's hand, and the two of them were staring at Mr. Wonka and begging him with their eyes to do something. Mr.

Wonka stood very still, and although his face looked calm, you can be quite sure his clever inventive brain was spinning like a dynamo.

"THIS IS YOUR LAST CHANCE!" boomed the voice. "WE ARE ASKING YOU ONCE MORE ... WHO ... ARE ... YOU? REPLY IMMEDIATELY! IF YOU DO NOT REPLY WE SHALL BE FORCED TO REGARD YOU AS DANGEROUS ENEMIES. WE SHALL THEN PRESS THE EMERGENCY FREEZER SWITCH AND THE TEMPERATURE IN THE SPACE HOTEL WILL DROP TO MINUS ONE HUNDRED DEGREES CENTIGRADE. ALL OF YOU WILL BE INSTANTLY DEEP-FROZEN. YOU HAVE FIFTEEN SECONDS TO SPEAK. AFTER THAT YOU WILL TURN INTO ICICLES ... ONE ... TWO ... THREE ..."

"Grandpa," whispered Charlie as the counting continued, "we must do something. We *must!* Quick!"

"SIX!" said the voice. "SEVEN! ... EIGHT! ... NINE! ..."

"Mr. Wonka had not moved. He was still gazing straight ahead, still quite cool, perfectly expressionless. Charlie and Grandpa Joe were staring at him in horror. Then, all at once, they saw the tiny twinkling wrinkles of a smile appear around the corners of his eyes. He sprang to life. He spun round on his toes, skipped a few paces across the floor and then, in a frenzied unearthly sort of scream, he cried, "FIMBO FEEZI!"

The loudspeaker stopped counting. There was silence. All over the world there was silence.

Charlie's eyes were riveted on Mr. Wonka. He was going to speak again. He was taking a deep breath. "BUNGO BUNI!" he screamed. He put so much force into his voice that the effort lifted him right up onto the tips of his toes.

"BUNGO BUNI

DAFU DUNI

YUBEE LUNI!"

Again the silence.

The next time Mr. Wonka spoke, the words came out

so fast and sharp and loud they were like bullets from a machine gun. "ZOONK-ZOONK-ZOONK-ZOONK-ZOONK!" he barked. The noise echoed around and around the lobby of the Space Hotel. It echoed around the world.

Mr. Wonka now turned and faced the far end of the lobby where the loudspeaker voice had come from. He walked a few paces forward as a man would, perhaps, who wanted a more intimate conversation with his audience. And this time, the tone was much quieter, the words came more slowly, but there was a touch of steel in every syllable:

> "KIRASUKU MALIBUKU,
> WEEBEE WIZE UN YUBEE KUKU!
>
> ALIPENDA KAKAMENDA,
> PANTZ FORLDUN IFNO SUSPENDA!
>
> FUNIKIKA KANDERIKA,
> WEEBEE STRONGA YUBEE WEEKA!
>
> POPOKOTA BORUMOKA
> VERI RISKI YU PROVOKA!
>
> KATIKATI MOONS UN STARS
> FANFANISHA VENUS MARS!"

Mr. Wonka paused dramatically for a few seconds. Then he took an enormous deep breath and in a wild and fearsome voice, he yelled out:

"KITIMBIBI ZOONK!

FIMBOLEEZI ZOONK!

GUGUMIZA ZOONK!

FUMIKAKA ZOONK!

ANAPOLALA ZOONK ZOONK ZOONK!"

The effect of all this on the world below was electric. In the Control Room in Houston, in the White House in Washington, in palaces and city buildings and mountain shacks from America to China to Peru, the five hundred million people who heard that wild and fearsome voice yelling out these strange and mystic words all shivered with fear before their television sets. Everybody began turning to everybody else and saying, "Who are they? What language was that? Where do they come from?"

In the President's study in the White House, Vice-President Tibbs, the members of the Cabinet, the Chiefs of the Army and the Navy and the Air Force, the sword swallower from Afghanistan, the Chief Financial Advisor and Mrs. Taubsypuss the cat all stood tense and rigid. They were more than a little afraid. But the President himself kept a cool head and a clear brain. "Nanny!" he cried. "Oh, Nanny, what on earth do we do now?"

"I'll get you a nice warm glass of milk," said Miss Tibbs.

"I hate the stuff," said the President. "Please don't make me drink it!"

"Then summon the Chief Interpreter," said Miss Tibbs.

"Summon the Chief Interpreter!" said the President. "Where is he?"

"Right here, Mr. President," said the Chief Interpreter.

"What language was that creature spouting up there in the Space Hotel? Be quick! Was it Eskimo?"

"Not Eskimo, Mr. President."

"Ha! Then it was Tagalog! Either Tagalog or Ugro!"

"Not Tagalog, Mr. President. Not Ugro, either."

"Was it Tulu, then? Or Tungus or Tupi?"

"Definitely not Tulu, Mr. President. And I'm quite sure it wasn't Tungus or Tupi."

"Don't stand there telling him what it *wasn't,* you idiot!" said Miss Tibbs. "Tell him what it *was!*"

"Yes, ma'am, Miss Vice-President, ma'am," said the Chief Interpreter, beginning to shake. "Believe me, Mr. President," he went on, "it was not a language I have ever heard before."

"But I thought you knew every language in the world."

"I do, Mr. President."

"Don't lie to me, Chief Interpreter. How can you possibly know every language in the world when you don't know this one?"

"It is not a language of this world, Mr. President."

"Nonsense, man!" barked Miss Tibbs. "I understood some of it myself!"

"These people, Miss Vice-President, ma'am, have obviously tried to learn just a few of our easier words, but the rest of it is a language that has never been heard before on this earth!"

"Screaming scorpions!" cried the President. "You mean to tell me they could be coming from . . . from . . . from *somewhere else?*"

"Precisely, Mr. President."

"Like where?" said the President.

"Who knows?" said the Chief Interpreter. "But did you not notice, Mr. President, how they used the words Venus and Mars?"

"Of course I noticed it," said the President. "But what's that got to do with it? . . . Ah-ha! I see what you're driving at! Good gracious me! Men from Mars!"

"And Venus," said the Chief Interpreter.

"That," said the President, "could make for trouble."

"I'll say it could!" said the Chief Interpreter.

"He wasn't talking to you," said Miss Tibbs.

"What do we do now, General?" said the President.

"Blow 'em up!" cried the General.

"You're always wanting to blow things up," said the President crossly. "Can't you think of something *else?*"

"I like blowing things up," said the General. "It makes such a lovely noise. *Woomph-woomph!*"

"Don't be a fool!" said Miss Tibbs. "If you blow these people up, Mars will declare war on us! So will Venus!"

"Quite right, Nanny," said the President. "We'd be troculated like turkeys, every one of us! We'd be mashed like potatoes!"

"I'll take 'em on!" shouted the Chief of the Army.

"Shut up!" snapped Miss Tibbs. "You're fired!"

"Hooray!" said all the other generals. "Well done, Miss Vice-President, ma'am!"

Miss Tibbs said, "We've *got* to treat these fellows gently. The one who spoke just now sounded extremely cross. We've got to be polite to them, butter them up, make them happy. The last thing we want is to be invaded by men from Mars. You've got to talk to them, Mr. President. Tell Houston we want another direct radio link with the Space Hotel! And hurry!"

6
Invitation to the White House

"THE PRESIDENT OF THE UNITED STATES will now address you!" announced the loudspeaker voice in the lobby of the Space Hotel.

Grandma Georgina's head peeped cautiously out from under the sheets. Grandma Josephine took her fingers out of her ears and Grandpa George lifted his face from the pillow.

"You mean he's actually going to speak to us?" whispered Charlie.

"Ssshhh," said Mr. Wonka. "Listen."

"Dear friends," said the well-known Presidential voice over the loudspeaker. "Dear, *dear* friends! Welcome to Space Hotel 'U.S.A.' Greetings to the brave astronauts from Mars and Venus . . ."

"Mars and Venus!" whispered Charlie. "You mean he thinks we're from . . ."

"Ssshh-ssshh-ssshh!" said Mr. Wonka. He was doubled up with silent laughter, shaking all over and hopping from one foot to the other.

"You have come a long way," the President continued, "so why don't you come just a tiny bit farther and pay *us* a visit down here on our humble little earth? I invite all eight of you to stay with me here in Washington as my honored guests. You could land that wonderful glass space machine of yours on the lawn in back of the White House. We shall have the red carpet out and ready. I do hope you know enough of our language to understand me. I shall wait most anxiously for your reply."

There was a click and the President went off the air.

"What a fantastic thing!" whispered Grandpa Joe. The White House, Charlie! We're invited to the White House as honored guests!"

Charlie caught hold of Grandpa Joe's hands and the two of them started dancing round and round the lobby of the hotel. Mr. Wonka, still shaking with laughter, went and sat down on the bed and signaled everyone to gather round close so they could whisper without being heard by the hidden microphones.

"They're scared to death," he whispered. "They won't bother us any more now. So let's have that feast we were talking about and afterward we can explore the hotel."

"Aren't we going to the White House?" whispered Grandma Josephine. "I want to go to the White House and stay with the President."

"My dear old dotty dumpling," said Mr. Wonka. "You look as much like a man from Mars as a bedbug! They'd know at once they'd been fooled. We'd be arrested before we could say how d'you do."

Mr. Wonka was right. There could be no question of accepting the President's invitation and they all knew it.

"But we've got to say *something* to him," Charlie whispered. "He must be sitting down there in the White House this very minute waiting for an answer."

"Make an excuse," said Mr. Bucket.

"Tell him we're otherwise engaged," said Mrs. Bucket.

"Ask him for a rain check," said Grandpa Joe.

"You are right," whispered Mr. Wonka. "It is rude to ignore an invitation." He stood up and walked a few paces from the group. For a moment or two he remained quite still, gathering his thoughts. Then once again Charlie saw those tiny twinkling, smiling wrinkles around the corners of the eyes, and when he began to speak, his voice this time was like the voice of a giant, deep and devilish, very loud and very slow:

> *"In the quelchy quaggy sogmire,*
> *In the mashy mideous harshland,*
> *At the witchy hour of gloomness,*
> *All the grobes come oozing home.*
>
> *You can hear them softly slimeing,*
> *Glissing hissing o'er the slubber,*
> *All those oily boily bodies*
> *Oozing onward in the gloam.*
>
> *So start to run! Oh, skid and daddle,*
> *Through the slubber slush and sossel!*
> *Skip jump hop and try to skaddle!*
> *All the grobes are on the roam!"*

In his study two hundred and forty miles below, the President turned white as the White House. "Jumping jack-rabbits!" he cried. "I think they're after us!"

"Oh, *please* let me blow them up!" said the ex-Chief of the Army.

"Silence!" said Miss Tibbs. "Go stand in the corner!"

In the lobby of the Space Hotel, Mr. Wonka had merely paused in order to think up another verse, and he was just about to start off again when a frightful piercing scream stopped him cold. The screamer was Grandma Josephine. She was sitting up in bed and pointing with a shaking finger at the elevators at the far end of the lobby. She screamed a second time, still pointing, and all eyes turned toward the elevators. The door of the one on the left was sliding slowly open and the watchers could clearly see that there was something . . . something thick . . . something brown . . . something not exactly brown, but greenish-brown . . . something with slimy skin and large eyes . . . squatting inside the elevator!

7

Something Nasty in the Elevators

GRANDMA JOSEPHINE had stopped screaming now. She had gone rigid with shock. The rest of the group by the bed, including Charlie and Grandpa Joe, had become as still as stone. They dared not move. They dared hardly breathe.

And Mr. Wonka, who had swung quickly around to look when the first scream came, was as dumbfounded as the rest. He stood motionless, gaping at the thing in the elevator, his mouth slightly open, his eyes stretched wide as two wheels. What he saw, what they all saw, was this:

It looked more than anything like an enormous egg balanced on its pointed end. It was as tall as a big boy and wider than the fattest man. The greenish-brown skin had a shiny wettish appearance and there were wrinkles in it. About three-quarters up, in the widest part, there were two large round eyes as big as teacups. The eyes were white, but each had a brilliant red pupil in the center. The red pupils were resting on Mr. Wonka. But now they began traveling slowly across to Charlie and Grandpa Joe and the others by the bed, settling upon them and gazing at them with a cold malevolent stare. The eyes were everything. There were no other features, no nose or mouth or ears, but the entire egg-shaped body was itself moving very, very slightly, pulsing and bulging gently here and there as though the skin were filled with some thick fluid.

At this point, Charlie suddenly noticed that the next elevator was coming down. The indicator numbers above the door were flashing . . . 6 . . . 5 . . . 4 . . . 3 . . . 2 . . . 1 . . . L (for lobby). There was a slight pause. The door slid open, and there, inside the second elevator was another enormous slimy wrinkled greenish-brown egg with eyes.

Now the numbers were flashing above all three of the remaining elevators. Down they came—down, down, down . . . And soon, at precisely the same time, they reached the lobby floor and the doors slid open. Five open doors now . . . one creature in each . . . five in all . . . and five pairs of eyes with brilliant red centers all watching Mr. Wonka and watching Charlie and Grandpa Joe and the others.

There were slight differences in size and shape between the five, but all had the same greenish-brown wrinkled skin and the skin was rippling and pulsing.

For about thirty seconds nothing happened. Nobody stirred, nobody made a sound. The silence was terrible. So was the suspense. Charlie was so frightened he felt himself shrinking inside his skin. Then he saw the creature in the left-hand elevator suddenly starting to change shape! Its body was slowly becoming longer and longer, and thinner and thinner, going up and up toward the roof of the elevator, not straight up, but curving a little to the left, making a snakelike curve that was curiously graceful, up to the left and then curling over the top to the right and coming down again in a half circle; then the bottom end began to grow out as well, like a tail, creeping along the floor . . . creeping along the floor to the left . . . until at last the creature, which had originally looked like a huge egg, now looked like a long curvy serpent standing up on its tail.

Then the one in the next elevator began stretching itself in much the same way, and what a weird and oozy thing it was to watch! It was twisting itself into a shape that was a bit different from the first, balancing itself almost but not quite on the tip of its tail.

Then the three remaining creatures began stretching themselves all at the same time, each one elongating itself slowly upward, growing taller and taller, thinner and thinner, curving and twisting, stretching and stretching, curling and bending, balancing either on the tail or the head or both, and turned sideways now, so that only one eye was visible. When they had all stopped stretching and bending, this was how they finished up:

"Scram!" shouted Mr. Wonka. "Get out quick!"

People have never moved faster than Grandpa Joe and Charlie and Mr. and Mrs. Bucket at that moment. They all got behind the bed and started pushing like crazy. Mr. Wonka ran in front of them shouting "Scram! Scram! Scram!" And in ten seconds flat all of them were out of the lobby and back inside the Great Glass Elevator. Frantically, Mr. Wonka began undoing bolts and pressing buttons. The door of the Great Glass Elevator snapped shut and the whole thing leaped sideways. They were away! And of course all of them, including the three old ones in the bed, floated up again into the air.

8

The Vermicious Knids

"OH, MY GOODNESS ME!" gasped Mr. Wonka. "Oh, my sainted pants! Oh, my painted ants! Oh, my crawling cats! I hope never to see anything like *that* again!" He floated over to the white button and pressed it. The booster rockets fired. The Elevator shot forward at such a speed that soon the Space Hotel was out of sight far behind.

"But who *were* those awful creatures?" Charlie asked.

"You mean you didn't know?" cried Mr. Wonka. "Well, it's a good thing you didn't. If you'd had even the faintest idea of what horrors you were up against, the marrow would have run out of your bones! You'd have been fossilized with fear and glued to the ground! Then they'd have gotten you! You'd have been a cooked cucumber! You'd have been rasped into a thousand tiny bits, grated like cheese and flocculated alive! They'd have made necklaces from your knucklebones and bracelets from your teeth! Because those creature, my dear ignorant boy, are the most brutal, vindictive, venemous, murderous beasts in the entire universe!" Here Mr. Wonka paused and ran the tip of a pink tongue all the way around his lips. "VERMICIOUS KNIDS!" he cried. "That's what they were!" He sounded the K . . . K'NIDS, like that.

"I thought they were grobes," Charlie said. "Those oozy-woozy grobes you were telling the President about."

"Oh, no, I just made those up to scare the White House," Mr. Wonka answered. "But there is nothing made up about Vermicious Knids, believe you me. They live, as everybody knows, on the planet Vermes, which is eighteen thousand four hundred and twenty-seven million miles away, and they are very, very clever brutes indeed. The Vermicious Knid can turn itself into any shape it wants. It has no bones. Its body is really one huge muscle, enormously strong, but very stretchy and squishy, like a mixture of rubber and putty with steel wires inside. Normally it is egg-shaped, but it can just as easily give itself two legs like a human, or four legs like a horse. It can become as round as a ball or as long as a kite-string. From fifty yards away, a fully grown Vermicious Knid could stretch out its neck and bite your head off without even getting up!"

"Bite your head off with what?" said Grandma Georgina. "I didn't see any mouth."

"They have other things to bite with," said Mr. Wonka darkly.

"Such as what?" said Grandma Georgina.

"Ring off," said Mr. Wonka. "Your time's up. But listen, everybody. I've just had a funny thought. There I was kidding around with the President and pretending we were creatures from some other planet and by golly, there actually *were* creatures from some other planet on board!"

"Do you think there were many?" Charlie asked. "More than the five we saw?"

"Thousands!" said Mr. Wonka. "There are five hundred rooms in that Space Hotel and there's probably a family of them in every room!"

"Somebody's going to get a nasty shock when they go on board!" said Grandpa Joe.

"They'll be eaten like peanuts," said Mr. Wonka. "Every one of them."

"You don't really mean that, do you, Mr. Wonka?" Charlie said.

"Of course I mean it," said Mr. Wonka. "These Vermicious Knids are the terror of the Universe. They travel through space in great swarms, landing in other stars and planets and destroying everything they find. There used to be some rather nice creatures living on the moon a long time ago. They were called Poozas. But the Vermicious Knids ate the lot. They did the same on Venus and Mars and many other planets."

"Why haven't they come down to our earth and eaten us?" Charlie asked.

"They've tried to, Charlie, many times, but they've never made it. You see, all around our earth there is a vast

❖ 55 ❖

envelope of air and gas, and anything hitting *that* at high speed gets red-hot. Space capsules are made of special heatproof metal, and when they make a reentry, their speeds are reduced right down to about two thousand miles an hour, first by retro-rockets and then by something called 'friction.' But even so, they get badly scorched. Knids, which are not heatproof at all, and don't have any retro-rockets, get sizzled up completely before they're halfway through. Have you ever seen a shooting star?"

"Lots of them," Charlie said.

"Actually, they're not shooting stars at all," said Mr. Wonka. "They're Shooting Knids. They're Knids trying to enter the earth's atmosphere at high speed and going up in flames."

"What rubbish," said Grandma Georgina.

"You wait," said Mr. Wonka. "You may see it happening before the day is done."

"But if they're so fierce and dangerous," Charlie said, "why didn't they eat us up right away in the Space Hotel? Why did they waste time twisting their bodies into letters and writing SCRAM?"

"Because they're show-offs," Mr. Wonka replied. "They're tremendously proud of being able to write like that."

"But why say SCRAM when they wanted to catch us and eat us?"

"It's the only word they know," Mr. Wonka said.

"Look!" screamed Grandma Josephine, pointing through the glass. "Over there!"

Before he even looked, Charlie knew exactly what he was going to see. So did the others. They could tell by the high hysterical note in the old lady's voice.

And there it was, cruising effortlessly alongside them, a simply colossal Vermicious Knid, as thick as a whale, as long as a truck, with the most brutal vermicious look in its eye. It was no more than a dozen yards away, egg-shaped, slimy, greenish brown, with one malevolent red eye (the only one visible) fixed intently upon the people floating inside the Great Glass Elevator.

"The end has come!" screamed Grandma Georgina.

"He'll eat us all!" cried Mrs. Bucket.

"In one gulp," said Mr. Bucket.

"We're done for, Charlie," said Grandpa Joe. Charlie nodded. He couldn't speak or make a sound. His throat was seized up with fright.

But this time Mr. Wonka didn't panic. He remained perfectly calm. "We'll soon get rid of that," he said and he pressed six buttons all at once and six booster rockets went off simultaneously under the Elevator. The Elevator leaped forward like a stung horse, faster and faster, but the great green greasy Knid kept pace alongside it with no trouble at all.

"Make it go away!" yelled Grandma Georgina. "I can't stand it looking at me!"

"Dear lady," said Mr. Wonka, "it can't possibly get in here. I don't mind admitting I was a trifle alarmed back there in the Space Hotel. And with good reason. But here we have nothing to fear. The Great Glass Elevator is shockproof, waterproof, bombproof, bulletproof and Knidproof. So just relax and enjoy it."

"Oh, you Knid, you are vile and vermicious!"
cried Mr. Wonka.

"You are slimy and soggy and squishous!
But what do we care
'Cause you can't get in here,
So hop it and don't get ambitious!"

At this point, the massive Knid outside turned and started cruising away from the Elevator. "There you are!" cried Mr. Wonka, triumphant. "It heard me! It's going home!" But Mr. Wonka was wrong. When the creature was about a hundred yards away, it stopped, hovered for a moment, then went smoothly in reverse, coming back toward the Elevator with its rear-end (which was the pointed end of the egg) now in front. Even going backward, its acceleration was unbelievable. It was like some monstrous bullet coming at them and it came so fast nobody had time even to cry out.

CRASH! It struck the Glass Elevator with the most enormous bang and the whole thing shivered and shook, but the glass held and the Knid bounced off like a rubber ball.

"What did I tell you!" shouted Mr. Wonka, triumphant. "We're safe as sausages in here!"

"He'll have a nasty headache after that," said Grandpa Joe.

"It's not his head, it's his bottom!" said Charlie. "Look Grandpa, there's a big bump coming up on the pointed end where he hit! It's turning black and blue!"

And so it was. A purple bruisy bump the size of a small automobile was appearing on the pointed rear-end of the giant Knid. "Hello, you dirty great beast!" cried Mr. Wonka.

"Hello, you great Knid! Tell us, how do you do?
You're a rather strange color today.
Your bottom is purple and lavender blue.
Should it really be looking that way?

Are you not feeling well? Are you going to faint?
Is it something we cannot discuss?
It must be a very unpleasant complaint,
For your fanny's as big as a bus!

Let me get you a doctor. I know just the man
For a Knid with a nasty disease.
He's a butcher by trade which is not a bad plan,
And he charges quite reasonable fees.

Ah! Here he is now! Doc, you really are kind
To travel so far into space.
There's your patient, the Knid with the
        purple behind!
Do you think it's a desperate case?

'Great heavens above! It's no wonder he's pale!'
Said the doc with a horrible grin.
'There's a sort of balloon on the end of his tail!
I must prick it at once with a pin!'

So he got out a thing like an Indian spear,
With feathers all over the top,
And he lunged and he caught the Knid smack
        in the rear,
But alas, the balloon didn't pop!

Cried the Knid, 'What on earth am I going to do
With this painful preposterous lump?
I can't remain standing the whole summer
    through!
And I cannot sit down on my rump!'

'It's a bad case of rear-ache,' the medico said,
'And it's something I cannot repair.
If you want to sit down, you must sit on
    your head,
With your bottom high up in the air!'"

9
Gobbled Up

ON THE DAY when all this was happening, no factories
were open anywhere in the world. All offices and schools
were closed. Nobody moved away from the television
screens, not even for a couple of minutes to get a Coke or
to feed the baby. The tension was unbearable. Everybody
heard the American President's invitation to the men
from Mars to visit him in the White House. And they
heard the weird rhyming reply, which sounded rather
threatening. They also heard a piercing scream (Grandma
Josephine), and a little later on, they heard someone
shouting, "Scram! Scram! Scram!" (Mr. Wonka). Nobody
could make head or tail of the shouting. They took it to

be some kind of Martian language. But when the eight mysterious astronauts suddenly rushed back into their glass capsule and broke away from the Space Hotel, you could almost hear the great sigh of relief that rose up from the peoples of the earth. Telegrams and messages poured into the White House congratulating the President upon his brilliant handling of a frightening situation.

The President himself remained calm and thoughtful. He sat at his desk rolling a small piece of wet chewing gum between his finger and thumb. He was waiting for the moment when he could flick it at Miss Tibbs without her seeing him. He flicked it and missed Miss Tibbs but hit the Secretary of the Interior on the tip of his nose.

"Do you think the men from Mars have accepted my invitation to the White House?" the President asked.

"Of course they have," said the Foreign Secretary. "It was a brilliant speech, sir."

"They're probably on their way down here right now," said Miss Tibbs. "Go and wash that nasty sticky chewing gum off your fingers quickly. They could be here any minute."

"Let's have a song first," said the President. "Please sing another one about me, Nanny."

THE NURSE'S SONG

This mighty man of whom I sing,
The greatest of them all,
Was once a teeny little thing,
Just eighteen inches tall.

I knew him as a tiny tot,
I nursed him on my knee.
I used to sit him on the pot
And wait for him to wee.

I always washed between his toes,
And cut his little nails.
I brushed his hair and wiped his nose
And weighed him on the scales.

Through happy childhood days
    he strayed,
As all nice children should.
I smacked him when he disobeyed,
And stopped when he was good.

It soon began to dawn on me
He wasn't very bright,
Because when he was twenty-three
He couldn't read or write.

'What shall we do?' his parents sob.
'The boy has got the vapors!
He couldn't even get a job
Delivering the papers!'

'Ah-ha,' I said, 'this little clot
Could be a politician.'
'Nanny,' he cried, 'Oh Nanny, what
A super proposition!'

'Okay,' I said, 'let's learn and note
The art of politics.
Let's teach you how to miss the boat
And how to drop some bricks,
And how to win the people's vote
And lots of other tricks.

Let's learn to make a speech a day
Upon the T.V. screen,
In which you never never say
Exactly what you mean.
And most important, by the way,
Is not to let your teeth decay,
And keep your fingers clean.'

And now that I am eighty-nine,
It's too late to repent.
The fault was mine the little swine
Became the President.

"Bravo Nanny!" cried the President, clapping his hands. "Hooray!" shouted the others. "Well done, Miss Vice-President, ma'am! Brilliant! Tremendous!"

"My goodness!" said the President. "Those men from Mars will be here any moment! What on earth are we going to give them for lunch? Where's my Chief Cook?"

The Chief Cook was a Frenchman. He was also a French spy and at this moment he was listening at the keyhole of the President's study. *"Ici, Monsieur le Président!"* he said, bursting in.

"Chief Cook," said the President. "What do men from Mars eat for lunch?"

"Mars Bars," said the Chief Cook.

"Baked or boiled?" asked the President.

"Oh, *baked*, of course, Monsieur le Président. You will ruin a Mars Bar by boiling!"

The voice of astronaut Shuckworth cut in over the

loudspeaker in the President's study. "Request permission to link up and go aboard Space Hotel?" he said.

"Permission granted," said the President. "Go right ahead, Shuckworth. It's all clear now. . . . Thanks to me."

And so the large Commuter Capsule, piloted by Shuckworth, Shanks and Showler, with all the hotel managers and assistant managers and hall porters and pastry chefs and bellhops and waitresses and chambermaids on board, moved in smoothly and linked up with the giant Space Hotel.

"Hey, there! We've lost our television picture," called the President.

"I'm afraid the camera got smashed against the side of the Space Hotel, Mr. President," Shuckworth replied. The President said a very rude word into the microphone and ten million children across the nation began repeating it gleefully and got smacked by their parents.

"All astronauts and one hundred fifty hotel staff safely aboard Space Hotel!" Shuckworth reported over the radio. "We are now standing in the lobby!"

"And what do you think of it all?" asked the President. He knew the whole world was listening in, and he wanted Shuckworth to say how wonderful it was. Shuckworth didn't let him down.

"Gee, Mr. President, it's just *great!*" he said. "It's *unbelievable!* It's so *enormous!* And so . . . it's kind of hard to find words to describe it, it's so truly grand—especially the chandeliers and the carpets and all! I have the Chief Hotel Manager, Mr. Walter W. Wall, beside me now. He would like the honor of a word with you, sir."

"Put him on," said the President.

"Mr. President, sir, this is Walter Wall. What a sumptuous hotel this is! The decorations are superb!"

"Have you noticed that all the carpets are wall to wall, Mr. Walter Wall?" said the President.

"I have indeed, Mr. President."

"All the wallpaper is wall to wall, too, Mr. Walter Wall."

"Yes, sir, Mr. President! Isn't that something! It's going to be a real pleasure running a beautiful like this! *Hey! What's going on over there? Something's coming out of the elevators! Help!*" Suddenly the loudspeaker in the President's study gave out a series of the most ghastly screams and yells. *"Ayeeeee! Owwwww! Ayeeeee! Hel-l-l-lp! Hel-l-l-l-lp! Hel-l-l-l-l-l-l-p!"*

"What on earth's going on?" said the President. *"Shuckworth! Are you there, Shuckworth? . . . Shanks! Showler! Mr. Walter Wall! Where are you all? What's happening?"*

The screams continued. They were so loud the President had to put his fingers in his ears. Every house in the world that had a television or radio receiver heard those awful screams. There were other noises, too. Loud grunts and snortings and crunching sounds. Then there was silence.

Frantically, the President called the Space Hotel on the radio. Houston called the Space Hotel. The President called Houston. Houston called the President. Then both of them called the Space Hotel again. But answer came there none. Up there in space all was silent.

"Something nasty's happened," said the President.

"It's those men from Mars," said the ex-Chief of the Army. "I *told* you to let me blow them up."

"Silence!" snapped the President. "I've got to think."

The loudspeaker began to crackle. "Hello!" it said. "Hello hello hello! Are you receiving me, Space Control in Houston?"

The President grabbed the mike on his desk. "Leave this to me, Houston!" he shouted. "President Gilligrass here, receiving you loud and clear! Go ahead!"

"Astronaut Shuckworth here, Mr. President, back aboard the Commuter Capsule—*thank heavens!*"

"What happened, Shuckworth? Who's with you?"

"We're most of us here, Mr. President, I'm glad to say. Shanks and Showler are with me, and a whole bunch of other folks. I guess we lost maybe a couple of dozen people altogether, pastry chefs, hall porters, that sort of thing. It sure was a scramble getting out of that place alive!"

"What do you mean you *lost* two dozen people?" shouted the President. "How did you lose them?"

"Gobbled up!" replied Shuckworth. "One gulp and that was it! I saw a big six-foot-tall assistant manager being swallowed up just like you'd swallow a lump of ice cream, Mr. President! No chewing—nothing. Just down the hatch!"

"But *who?*" yelled the President. "Who are you talking about? Who did the swallowing?"

"Hold it!" cried Shuckworth. "Oh, my lord, here they all come now! They're coming after us! They're swarming out of the Space Hotel! They're coming out in swarms! You'll have to excuse me a moment, Mr. President. No time to talk right now!"

10

Commuter Capsule in Trouble— Knid Attack Number One

WHILE SHUCKWORTH, Shanks and Showler were being chased out of the Space Hotel by the Knids, Mr. Wonka's Great Glass Elevator was orbiting the earth at tremendous speed. Mr. Wonka had all his booster rockets firing and the Elevator was reaching speeds of thirty-four thousand miles an hour instead of the normal seventeen thousand. They were trying, you see, to get away from that huge angry Vermicious Knid with the purple behind. Mr. Wonka wasn't afraid of it, but Grandma Josephine was petrified. Every time she looked at it, she let out a piercing scream and clapped her hands over her eyes. But of course thirty-four thousand miles an hour is dawdling to a Knid. Healthy young Knids think nothing of traveling a million miles between lunch and supper, and then another million before breakfast the next day. How else could they commute between the plant Vermes and

other stars? Mr. Wonka should have known this and saved
his rocket power, but he kept right on going and giant
Knid kept right on cruising effortlessly alongside, glaring
into the Elevator with its wicked red eye. "You people
have bruised my backside," the Knid seemed to be saying,
"and in the end I'm going to get you for that."

They had been streaking around the earth like this
for forty-five minutes when Charlie, who was floating
comfortably beside Grandpa Joe near the ceiling, said
suddenly, "There's something ahead! Can you see it,
Grandpa? Straight in front of us!"

"I can, Charlie, I can. . . . Good heavens! It's the Space
Hotel!"

"It can't be, Grandpa. We left it miles behind us long
ago."

"Ah-ha," said Mr. Wonka. "We've been going so fast
we've gone all the way around the earth and caught up
with it again. A splendid effort!"

"And there's the Commuter Capsule! Can you see it, Grandpa? It's just behind the Space Hotel!"

"There's something else there, too, Charlie, if I'm not mistaken!"

"I know what those are!" screamed Grandma Josephine. "They're Vermicious Knids! Turn back at once!"

"Reverse!" yelled Grandma Georgina. "Go the other way!"

"Dear lady," said Mr. Wonka. "This isn't an automobile on the highway. When you are in orbit, you cannot stop and you cannot go backward."

"I don't care about that!" shouted Grandma Josephine. "Put on the brakes! Stop! Back-pedal! The Knids'll get us!"

"Now let's for heaven's sake *stop* this nonsense once and for all," Mr. Wonka said sternly. "You know very well my Elevator is completely Knidproof. You have nothing to fear."

They were closer now and they could see the Knids pouring out from the tail of the Space Hotel and swarming like wasps around the Commuter Capsule.

"They're attacking it!" cried Charlie. "They're after the Commuter Capsule!"

It was a fearsome sight. The huge green egg-shape Knids were grouping themselves into squadrons with about twenty Knids to a squadron. Then each squadron formed itself into a line abreast, with one yard between Knids. Then, one after another, the squadrons began attacking the Commuter Capsule. They attacked in reverse with their pointed rear-ends in front and they came in at a fantastic speed.

WHAM! One squadron attacked, bounced off and wheeled away.

CRASH! Another squadron smashed against the side of the Commuter Capsule.

"Get us out of here, you madman!" screamed Grandma Josephine. "What are you waiting for?"

"They'll be coming after *us* next!" yelled Grandma Georgina. "For heaven's sake, man, turn back!"

"I doubt very much if that capsule of theirs is Knid-proof," said Mr. Wonka.

"Then we must help them!" cried Charlie. "We've got to do something! There are a hundred and fifty people inside that thing!"

Down on the earth, in the White House study, the President and his advisers were listening in horror to the voices of the astronauts over the radio.

"They're coming at us in droves!" Shuckworth was shouting. "They're bashing us to bits!"

"But *who?*" yelled the president. "You haven't even told us who's attacking you!"

"These dirty great greenish-brown brutes with red eyes!" shouted Shanks, butting in. "They're shaped like enormous eggs and they're coming at us backwards."

"Backwards?" cried the President. "Why backwards?"

"Because their bottoms are even more pointy than

their tops!" shouted Shuckworth. "Look out! Here comes another lot! BANG! We won't be able to stand this much longer, Mr. President! The waitresses are screaming and the chambermaids are all hysterical and the bellhops are being sick and the hall porters are saying their prayers. What shall we do, Mr. President, sir, what on earth shall we do?"

"Fire your rockets, you idiot, and make a reentry!" shouted the President. "Come back to earth immediately!"

"That's impossible!" cried Showler. "They've busted our rockets! They've smashed them to smithereens!"

"We're cooked, Mr. President!" shouted Shanks. "We're done for! Because even if they don't succeed in destroying the capsule, we'll have to stay up here in orbit for the rest of our lives! We can't make a reentry without rockets!"

The President was sweating and the sweat ran all the way down the back of his neck and inside his collar.

"Any moment now, Mr. President," Shanks went on, "we're going to lose contact with you altogether! There's another lot coming at us from the left and they're aiming straight for our radio antenna. Here they come! I don't think we'll be able to . . ." The voice cut. The radio went dead.

"Shanks!" cried the President. "Where are you, Shanks? . . . Shuckworth! Shanks! Showler! . . . Showlworth! Shucks! Shankler! . . . Shankworth! Showl! Shuckler! Why don't you answer me?!"

Up in the Great Glass Elevator where they had no radio and could hear nothing of these conversations, Charlie was saying, "Surely their only hope is to make a reentry and dive back to earth quickly."

"Yes," said Mr. Wonka. "But in order to reenter the earth's atmosphere they've got to kick themselves out of orbit. They've got to change course and head downward and to do that they need rockets! But their rocket tubes are all dented and bent! You can see that from here! They're crippled!"

"Why can't we tow them down?" Charlie asked.

Mr. Wonka jumped. Even though he was floating, he somehow jumped. He was so excited he shot upward and hit his head on the ceiling. Then he spun round three times in the air and cried, "Charlie! You've got it! That's it! We'll tow them out of orbit! To the buttons, quick!"

"What do we tow them with?" asked Grandpa Joe. "Our neckties?"

"Don't you worry about a little thing like that!" cried Mr. Wonka. "My Great Glass Elevator is ready for anything! In we go! Into the breach, dear friends, into the breach!"

"Stop him!" screamed Grandma Josephine.

"You be quiet, Josie," said Grandpa Joe. "There's someone over there needs a helping hand and it's our job to give it. If you're frightened, you'd better just close your eyes tight and stick your fingers in your ears."

11
The Battle of the Knids

"GRANDPA JOE, SIR!" shouted Mr. Wonka. "Kindly jet yourself over to the far corner of the Elevator there and turn that handle! It lowers the rope!"

"A rope's no good, Mr. Wonka! The Knids will bite through a rope in one second!"

"It's a steel rope," said Mr. Wonka. "It's made of reinscorched steel. If they try to bite through *that,* their teeth will splinter like spillikins! To your buttons, Charlie! You've got to help me maneuver. We're going right over the top of the Commuter Capsule and then we'll try to hook onto it somewhere and get a firm hold!"

Like a battleship going into action, the Great Glass Elevator with booster rockets firing moved smoothly in over the top of the enormous Commuter Capsule. The Knids immediately stopped attacking the Capsule and went for the Elevator. Squadron after squadron of giant Vermicious Knids flung themselves furiously against Mr. Wonka's marvelous machine. WHAM! CRASH! BANG! The noise was thunderous and terrible. The Elevator was tossed about the sky like a leaf, and inside it, Grandma Josephine, Grandma Georgina and Grandpa George, floating in their nightshirts, were all yowling and screeching and flapping their arms and calling for help. Mrs. Bucket had wrapped her arms around Mr. Bucket and was clasping him so tightly that one of his shirt buttons punctured his skin. Charlie and Mr. Wonka, as cool as two cantaloupes, were up near the ceiling working the booster-rocket controls, and Grandpa Joe, shouting war cries and throwing curses at the Knids, was down below turning the handle that unwound the steel rope. At the same time, he was watching the rope through the glass floor of the Elevator.

"Starboard a bit, Charlie," shouted Grandpa Joe. "We're right on top of her now! . . . Forward a couple of yards, Mr. Wonka! . . . I'm trying to get the hook hooked around that stumpy thing sticking out in front there! . . . Hold it! . . . I've got it. . . . That's it. . . . Forward a little now and see if it holds! . . . More! . . . More! . . ." The big steel rope tightened. It held! And now, wonder of wonders, with her booster rockets blazing, the Elevator began to tow the huge Commuter Capsule forward and away!

"Full speed ahead!" shouted Grandpa Joe. "She's going to hold! She's holding! She's holding fine!"

"All boosters firing!" cried Mr. Wonka, and the Elevator leaped ahead. Still the rope held. Mr. Wonka jetted himself down to Grandpa Joe and shook him warmly by the hand. "Well done, sir," he said. "You did a brilliant job under heavy fire!"

Charlie looked back at the Commuter Capsule some thirty yards behind them on the end of the tow line. It had little windows up front, and in the windows he could clearly see the flabbergasted faces of Shuckworth, Shanks and Showler. Charlie waved to them and gave them the thumbs-up signal. They didn't wave back. They simply gaped. They couldn't believe what was happening.

Grandpa Joe blew himself upward and hovered beside Charlie, bubbling with excitement. "Charlie, my boy," he said. "We've been through a few funny things together lately, but never anything like this!"

"Grandpa, where are the Knids? They've suddenly vanished."

Everyone looked round. The only Knid in sight was their old friend with the purple behind, still cruising alongside in its usual place, still glaring into the Elevator.

"*Just* a minute!" cried Grandma Josephine. "What's *that* I see over there?" Again they looked, and this time, sure enough, away in the distance, in the deep blue sky of outer space, they saw a massive cloud of Vermicious Knids wheeling and circling like a fleet of bombers.

"If you think we're out of the woods yet, you're crazy!" shouted Grandma Georgina.

"I fear no Knids!" said Mr. Wonka. "We've got them beaten now!"

"Poppyrot and pigwash!" said Grandma Josephine. "Any moment now they'll be at us again! Look at them! They're coming in! They're coming closer!"

This was true. The huge fleet of Knids had moved in at incredible speed and was now flying level with the Great Glass Elevator, a couple of hundred yards away on the right-hand side. The one with the bump on its rear-end was much closer, only twenty yards away on the same side.

"It's changing shape!" cried Charlie. "That nearest one! —what's it going to do? It's getting longer and longer!" And indeed it was. The mammoth egg-shaped body was slowly stretching itself out like chewing gum, becoming longer and longer and thinner and thinner, until in the end it looked exactly like a long slimy-green serpent as thick as a thick tree and as long as a football field. At the front end were the eyes, big and white with red centers, at the back a kind of tapering tail and at the very end of the tail was the enormous round swollen bump it had gotten when it crashed against the glass.

The people floating inside the Elevator watched and waited. Then they saw the long ropelike Knid turning and coming straight but quite slowly toward the Great Glass Elevator. Now it began actually wrapping its ropy body around the Elevator itself. Once around it went . . . then twice around, and very horrifying it was to be inside and to see the soft green body squishing against the outside of the glass no more than a few inches away.

"It's tying us up like a parcel!" yelled Grandma Josephine.

"Bunkum!" said Mr. Wonka.

"It's going to crush us in its coils!" wailed Grandma Georgina.

"Never!" said Mr. Wonka.

Charlie glanced quickly back at the Commuter Capsule. The sheet-white faces of Shuckworth, Shanks and Showler were pressed against the glass of the little windows, terror-struck, stupefied, stunned, their mouths open, their expressions frozen like fishfingers. Once again, Charlie gave them the thumbs-up signal. Showler

acknowledged it with a sickly grin, but that was all.

"Oh, oh, oh!" screamed Grandma Josephine. "Get that beastly squishy thing away from here!"

Having curled its body twice around the Elevator, the Knid now proceeded to tie a knot with its two ends, a good strong knot, left over right, then right over left. When it had pulled the knot tight, there remained about five yards of one end hanging loose. This was the end with the eyes on it. But it didn't hang loose for long. It quickly curled itself into the shape of a huge hook and the hook stuck straight out sideways from the Elevator as though waiting for something else to hook itself onto it.

While all this was going on, nobody had noticed what the other Knids were up to. "Mr. Wonka!" Charlie cried. "Look at the others! What *are* they doing?"

What indeed?

These, too, had all changed shape and had become longer, but not nearly so long or so thin as the first one. Each of them had turned itself into a kind of thick rod and the rod was curled around at both ends—at the tail end and at the head end—so that it made a double-ended hook. And now all the hooks were linking up into one long chain—one thousand Knids, all joining together and curving around in the sky to make a chain of Knids half a mile long or more! And the Knid at the very front of the chain (who's front hook was not, of course, hooked up to anything) was leading them in a wide circle and sweeping in toward the Great Glass Elevator.

"Hey!" shouted Grandpa Joe. "They're going to hook up with this brute who's tied himself around us!"

"And tow us away!" cried Charlie.

"To the planet Vermes," gasped Grandma Josephine. "Eighteen thousand four hundred and twenty-seven million miles from here!"

"They can't do that!" cried Mr. Wonka. "*We're* doing the towing around here!"

"They're going to link up, Mr. Wonka!" Charlie said. "They really are! Can't we stop them? They're going to tow us away and they're going to tow the people we're towing away as well!"

"Do something, you old fool!" shrieked Grandma Georgina. "Don't just float about looking at them!"

"I must admit," said Mr. Wonka, "that for the first time in my life I find myself at a bit of a loss."

They all stared in horror through the glass at the long chain of Vermicious Knids. The leader of the chain was coming closer and closer. The hook, with two big angry eyes on it, was out and ready. In thirty seconds it would link up with the hook of the Knid wrapped around the Elevator.

"I want to go home!" wailed Grandma Josephine. "Why can't we all go home?"

"Great thundering tomcats!" cried Mr. Wonka. "*Home* is right! What on earth am I thinking of! Come on, Charlie! Quick! REENTRY! You take the yellow button! Press it for all you're worth! I'll handle this lot!" Charlie and Mr. Wonka literally flew to the buttons. "Hold your hats!" shouted Mr. Wonka. "Grab your gizzards! We're going down!"

Rockets started firing out of the Elevator from all sides. It tilted and gave a sickening lurch and then plunged downward into the earth's atmosphere at a simply colossal speed. *"Retro-rockets!"* bellowed Mr. Wonka.

"I mustn't forget to fire the retro-rockets!" He flew over to another series of buttons and started playing on them like a piano.

The Elevator was now streaking downward head first, upside down, and all the passengers found themselves floating upside down as well.

"Help!" screamed Grandma Georgina. "All the blood's going to my head!"

"Then turn yourself the other way up," said Mr. Wonka. "That's easy enough, isn't it?"

Everyone blew and puffed and turned somersaults in the air until at last they were all the right way up. "How's the tow rope holding, Grandpa?" Mr. Wonka called out.

"They're still with us, Mr. Wonka, sir! The rope's holding fine."

It was an amazing sight—The Great Elevator streaking down toward the earth with the huge Commuter Capsule in tow behind it. But the long chain of Knids was coming after them, following them down, keeping pace with them easily, and now the hook of the leading Knid in the chain was actually reaching out and grasping for the hook made by the Knid on the Elevator.

"We're too late!" screamed Grandma Georgina. "They're going to link up and haul us back!"

"I think not," said Mr. Wonka. "Don't you remember what happens when a Knid enters the earth's atmosphere at high speed? He gets red-hot. He burns away in a long fiery trail. He becomes a Shooting Knid. Soon these dirty beasts will start popping like popcorn!"

As they streaked on downward, sparks began to fly off the sides of the Elevator. The glass glowed pink, then red, then scarlet. Sparks also began to fly off the long chain of Knids, and the leading Knid in the chain started to shine like a red-hot poker. So did all the others. So did the great slimy brute coiled around the Elevator itself. This one, in fact, was trying frantically to uncoil itself and get away, but it was having trouble untying the knot, and in another ten seconds it began to sizzle. Inside the Elevator they could actually hear the sizzling. It made a noise like bacon frying. And exactly the same sort of thing was happening to the other one thousand Knids in the chain. The tremendous heat was simply sizzling them up. They were red-hot, every one of them. Then suddenly, they became white-hot and they gave out a dazzling white light.

"They're shooting Knids!" cried Charlie.

"What a splendid sight," said Mr. Wonka. "It's better than fireworks."

In a few seconds more, the Knids had blown away in a cloud of ashes and it was all over. "We've done it!" cried Mr. Wonka. "They've been roasted to a crisp! They've been frizzled to a fritter! We're saved!"

"What do you mean saved?" said Grandma Josephine. "We'll all be frizzled ourselves if this goes on any longer! We'll be barbecued like beefsteaks! Look at that glass! It's hotter than a fizzgig!"

"Have no fears, dear lady," answered Mr. Wonka. "My Elevator is air-conditioned, ventilated, aerated and automated in every possible way. We're going to be all right now."

"I haven't the faintest idea what's been going on," said Mrs. Bucket, making one of her rare speeches. "But whatever it is, I don't like it."

"Aren't you enjoying it, Mother?" Charlie asked her.

"No," she said. "I'm not. Nor is your father."

"What a great sight it is!" said Mr. Wonka. "Just look at the earth down there, Charlie, getting bigger and bigger!"

"And us going to meet it at two thousand miles an hour!" groaned Grandma Georgina. "How are you going to slow down for heaven's sake? You didn't think of that, did you?"

"He's got parachutes," Charlie told her. "I'll bet he's got great big parachutes that open just before we hit."

"*Parachutes!*" said Mr. Wonka with contempt. "Parachutes are only for astronauts and sissies! And anyway, we don't want to *slow down*. We want to *speed up*. I've told you already we've got to be going at an absolutely tremendous speed when we hit. Otherwise, we'll never punch our way in through the roof of the Chocolate Factory."

"How about the Commuter Capsule?" Charlie asked anxiously.

"We'll be letting them go in a few seconds now," Mr. Wonka answered. "They *do* have parachutes, three of them, to slow them down on the last bit."

"How do you know we won't land in the Pacific Ocean?" said Grandma Josephine.

"I don't," said Mr. Wonka. "But we all know how to swim, do we not?"

"This man," shouted Grandma Josephine, "is crazy as a crumpet!"

"He's cracked as a crawfish!" cried Grandma Georgina.

Down and down plunged the Great Glass Elevator. Nearer and nearer came the earth below. Oceans and continents rushed up to meet them, getting bigger every second. . . .

"Grandpa Joe, sir! Throw out the rope! Let it go," ordered Mr. Wonka. "They'll be all right now so long as their parachutes are working."

"Rope gone!" called out Grandpa Joe, and the huge Commuter Capsule, on its own now, began to swing away to one side. Charlie waved to the three astronauts in the front window. None of them waved back. They were still sitting there in a kind of shocked daze, gaping at the old ladies and the old men and the small boy floating about in the Glass Elevator.

"It won't be long now," said Mr. Wonka, reaching for a row of tiny pale blue buttons in one corner. "We shall soon know whether we are alive or dead. Keep very quiet please for this final part. I have to concentrate awfully hard, otherwise we'll come down in the wrong place."

They plunged into a thick bank of clouds and for ten seconds they could see nothing. When they came out of the clouds, the Commuter Capsule had disappeared, and the earth was very close, and there was only a great spread of land beneath them with mountains and forests . . . then fields and trees . . . then a small town.

"There it is!" shouted Mr. Wonka. "My Chocolate Factory! My beloved Chocolate Factory!"

"You mean *Charlie's* Chocolate Factory," said Grandpa Joe.

"That's *right!*" said Mr. Wonka, addressing Charlie. "I'd clean forgotten! I do apologize to you my dear boy! Of course it's yours! And here we go!"

Through the glass floor of the Elevator, Charlie caught a quick glimpse of the huge red roof and the tall chimneys of the giant factory. They were plunging straight down onto it.

"Hold your breath!" shouted Mr. Wonka. "Hold your nose! Fasten your seat belts and say your prayers! We're going through the roof!"

12
Back to the Chocolate Factory

AND THEN THE NOISE of splintering wood and broken glass and absolute darkness and the most awful crunching sounds as the Elevator rushed on and on, smashing everything before it.

All at once, the crashing noises stopped and the ride became smoother and the Elevator seemed to be traveling on guides or rails, twisting and turning like a roller coaster.

And when the lights came on, Charlie suddenly realized that for the last few seconds he hadn't been floating at all. He had been standing normally on the floor. Mr. Wonka was on the floor, too, and so was Grandpa Joe and Mr. and Mrs. Bucket, and also the big bed. As for Grandma Josephine, Grandma Georgina and Grandpa George, they must have fallen right back onto the bed because they were now all three on top of it and scrabbling to get under the blanket.

"We're through!" yelled Mr. Wonka. "We've done it! We're in!" Grandpa Joe grabbed him by the hand and said, "Well done, sir! How splendid! What a magnificent job!"

"Where in the world are we now?" said Mrs. Bucket.

"We're back, Mother!" Charlie cried. "We're in the Chocolate Factory!"

"I'm very glad to hear it," said Mrs. Bucket. "But didn't we come rather a long way round?"

"We had to," said Mr. Wonka, "to avoid the traffic."

"I have never met a man," said Grandma Georgina, "who talks so much absolute nonsense!"

"A little nonsense now and then, is relished by the wisest men," Mr. Wonka said.

"Why don't you pay some attention to where this crazy elevator's going!" shouted Grandma Josephine. "And stop footling about!"

"A little footling round about, will stop you going up the spout," said Mr. Wonka.

"What did I tell you!" cried Grandma Georgina. "He's round the twist! He's bogged as a beetle! He's dotty as a dingbat! He's got rats in the roof! I want to go home!"

"Too late," said Mr. Wonka. "We're there!" The Elevator stopped. The doors opened and Charlie found himself looking out once again at the great Chocolate Room with the chocolate river and the chocolate waterfall, where everything was eatable—the trees, the leaves, the grass, the pebbles and even the rocks. And there to meet them were hundreds and hundreds of tiny Oompa-Loompas, all waving and cheering. It was a sight that took one's breath away. Even Grandma Georgina was stunned into silence for a few seconds. But not for long.

"Who in the world are all those peculiar little men?" she said.

"They're Oompa-Loompas," Charlie told her. "They're wonderful. You'll love them."

"Ssshh," said Grandpa Joe. "Listen, Charlie. The drums are starting up. They're going to sing."

"Alleluia!" sang the Oompa-Loompas.
"Oh alleluia and hooray!

Our Willy Wonka's back today!
We thought you'd never make it home!
We thought you'd left us all alone!
We knew that you would have to face
Some frightful creatures up in space.
We even thought we heard the crunch
Of someone eating you for lunch ..."

"All right!" shouted Mr. Wonka, laughing and raising both hands. "Thank you for your welcome. Will some of you please help to get this bed out of here?"

Fifty Oompa-Loompas ran forward and pushed the bed with the three old ones in it out of the elevator. Mr. and Mrs. Bucket, both looking completely overwhelmed by it all, followed the bed out. Then came Grandpa Joe, Charlie and Mr. Wonka.

"Now," said Mr. Wonka, addressing Grandpa George, Grandma Georgina and Grandma Josephine. "Up you hop out of that bed and let's get cracking. I'm sure you'll all want to lend a hand running the factory."

"Who, us?" said Grandma Josephine.

"Yes, you," said Mr. Wonka.

"You must be joking," said Grandma Georgina.

"I never joke," said Mr. Wonka.

"Now just you listen to me, sir," said old Grandpa George, sitting up straight in bed. "You've gotten us into quite enough tubbles and trumbles for one day!"

"I've gotten you out of them, too," said Mr. Wonka proudly. "And I'm going to get you out of that bed as well, you see if I don't!"

13
How Wonka-Vite Was Invented

"I HAVEN'T BEEN out of this bed in twenty years and I'm not getting out now for anybody," said Grandma Josephine firmly.

"Nor me," said Grandma Georgina.

"You were out of it just now, every one of you," said Mr. Wonka.

"That was floating," said Grandpa George. "We couldn't help it."

"We never put our feet on the floor," said Grandma Josephine.

"Try it," said Mr. Wonka. "You might surprise yourself."

"Go on, Josie," said Grandpa Joe. "Give it a try. I did. It was easy."

"We're perfectly comfortable where we are, thank you very much," said Grandma Josephine.

Mr. Wonka sighed and shook his head very slowly and very sadly. "Oh well," he said, "so that's that." He laid his head on one side and gazed thoughtfully at the three old people in the bed, and Charlie, watching him closely, saw those bright little eyes of his beginning to spark and twinkle once again.

Ha-Ha, thought Charlie. What's coming now?

"I suppose," said Mr. Wonka, placing the tip of one finger on the point of his nose and pressing gently, "I suppose, because this is a very special case . . . I suppose

I *could* spare you just a tiny little bit of . . ." He stopped and shook his head.

"A tiny little bit of what?" said Grandma Josephine sharply.

"No," said Mr. Wonka. "It's pointless. You seem to have decided to stay in that bed no matter what happens. And anyway, the stuff is much too precious to waste. I'm sorry I mentioned it." He started to walk away.

"Hey!" shouted Grandma Georgina. "You can't start something and not go on with it! *What* is too precious to waste?"

Mr. Wonka stopped. Slowly he turned around. He looked long and hard at the three old people in the bed. They looked back at him, waiting. He kept silent a little longer, allowing their curiosity to grow. The Oompa-Loompas stood absolutely still behind him, watching.

"What is this thing you're talking about?" said Grandma Georgina.

"Get on with it, for heaven's sake!" said Grandma Josephine.

"Very well," Mr. Wonka said at last. "I'll tell you. And listen carefully because this could change your whole lives. It could even change *you.*"

"I don't want to be *changed!*" shouted Grandma Georgina.

"May I go on, madam? Thank you. Not long ago, I was fooling about in my Inventing Room, stirring stuff around and mixing things up the way I do every afternoon at four o'clock, when suddenly I found I had made something that seemed very unusual. This thing I had made kept changing color as I looked at it, and now and again it gave a little jump, it actually jumped up in the air, as though it were alive. 'What have we here?' I cried, and I rushed it quickly to the Testing Room and gave some to the Oompa-Loompa who was on duty there at the time. The result was immediate! It was flabbergasting! It was unbelievable! It was also rather unfortunate."

"What happened?" said Grandma Georgina, sitting up.

"What indeed," said Mr. Wonka.

"Answer her question," said Grandma Josephine. "What happened to the Oompa-Loompa?"

"Ah," said Mr. Wonka. "Yes . . . well . . . there's no point in crying over spilled milk, is there? I realized, you see, that I had stumbled upon a new and tremendously powerful vitamin, and I also knew that if only I could make it safe, if only I could stop it doing to others what it did to that Oompa-Loompa . . ."

"What *did* it do to that Oompa-Loompa?" said Grandma Georgina sternly.

"The older I get, the deafer I become," said Mr. Wonka. "Do please raise your voice a trifle next time. Thank you so much. Now then. I simply *had* to find a way of making this stuff safe, so that people could take it without, er . . ."

"Without *what?*" snapped Grandma Georgina.

"Without a leg to stand on," said Mr. Wonka. "So I rolled up my sleeves and set to work once more in the Inventing Room. I mixed and I mixed. I must have tried just about every mixture under the moon. By the way, there is a little hole in one wall of the Inventing Room which connects directly with the Testing Room next door, so I was always able to keep passing stuff through for testing to whichever brave volunteer happened to be on duty. Well, the first few weeks were pretty depressing and we won't talk about them. Instead, let me tell you what happened on the one hundred and thirty-second day of my labors. That morning, I had changed the mixture drastically, and this time the little pill I produced at the end of it all was not nearly so active or alive as the others had been. It kept changing color, yes, but only from lemon yellow to blue, then back to yellow again. And when I placed it on the palm of my hand, it didn't jump about like a grasshopper. It only quivered, and then ever so slightly.

"I ran to the hole in the wall that led to the Testing Room. A very old Oompa-Loompa was on duty there that morning. He was a bald, wrinkled, toothless old fellow. He was in a wheelchair. He had been in the wheelchair for at least fifteen years.

"'This is test number one hundred and thirty-two!' I said, chalking it up on the board.

"I handed him the pill. He looked at it nervously. I couldn't blame him for being a bit jittery after what had happened to the other one hundred and thirty-one volunteers."

"What *had* happened to them?" shouted Grandma Georgina. "Why don't you answer the question instead of skidding around it on two wheels?"

"Who knows the way out of a rose?" said Mr. Wonka. "So this brave old Oompa-Loompa took the pill and with the help of a little water, he gulped it down. Suddenly, the most amazing thing happened. Before my very eyes, queer little changes began taking place in the way he looked. A moment earlier, he had been practically bald, with just a fringe of snowy white hair around the sides and the back of his head. But now the fringe of white hair was turning gold and all over the top of his head new gold hair was beginning to sprout, like grass. In less than half a minute, he had grown a splendid new crop of long golden hair. At the same time, many of the wrinkles started disappearing from his face, not all of them, but about half, enough to make him look a good deal younger, and all of this must have given him a nice tickly feeling because he started grinning at me, then laughing, and as soon as he opened his mouth, I saw the strangest sight of all. Teeth were growing up out from those old toothless gums, good white teeth, and they were coming up so fast I could actually see them getting bigger and bigger.

"I was too flabbergasted to speak. I just stood there with my head poking through the hole in the wall, staring at the little Oompa-Loompa. I saw him slowly lifting himself out of his wheelchair. He tested his legs on the ground. He stood up. He walked a few paces. Then he looked up at me and his face was bright. His eyes were huge and bright as two stars.

"'Look at me,' he said softly. 'I'm walking! It's a miracle!'

"'It's Wonka-Vite!' I said. 'The great rejuvenator! It makes you young again. How old do you feel now?'

"He thought very carefully about this question, then he said, 'I feel almost exactly how I felt when I was fifty years old.'

"'How old were you just now, before you took the Wonka-Vite?' I asked him.

"'Seventy last birthday,' he answered.

"'That means,' I said, 'it has made you twenty years younger.'

"'It has, it has!' he cried, delighted. 'I feel as frisky as a froghopper!'

"'Not frisky enough,' I told him. 'Fifty is still pretty old. Let us see if I can't help you a bit more. Stay right where you are. I'll be back in a twink.'

"I ran to my workbench and quickly made one more pill of Wonka-Vite, using exactly the same mixture as before.

"'Swallow this,' I said, passing the second pill through the hatch. There was no hesitating this time. Eagerly, he popped it into his mouth and chased it down with a drink of water. And behold, within half a minute, another twenty years had fallen away from his face and body and he was now a slim and sprightly young Oompa-Loompa of thirty. He gave a whoop of joy and started dancing around the room, leaping high in the air and coming down on his toes. 'Are you happy?' I asked him.

"'I'm ecstatic!' he cried, jumping up and down. 'I'm happy as a horse in a hayfield!' He ran out of the Testing Room to show himself off to his family and friends.

"Thus was Wonka-Vite invented," said Mr. Wonka. "And thus was it made safe for all to use."

"Why don't you use it yourself, then?" said Grandma Georgina. "You told Charlie you were getting too old to run the factory, so why don't you just take a couple of pills and get forty years younger? Tell me that?"

"Anyone can ask questions," said Mr. Wonka. "It's the answers that count. Now then, if the three of you in the bed would care to try a dose . . ."

"Just one minute!" said Grandma Josephine, sitting up straight. "First I'd like to take a look at this seventy-year-old Oompa-Loompa who is now back to thirty."

Mr. Wonka flicked his fingers. A tiny Oompa-Loompa, looking young and perky, ran forward out of the crowd and did a marvelous little dance in front of the three old people in the big bed. "Two weeks ago, he was seventy years old and in a wheelchair," Mr. Wonka said proudly. "And look at him now!"

"The drums, Charlie!" said Grandpa Joe. "Listen! They're starting up again!"

Far away down on the bank of the chocolate river, Charlie could see the Oompa-Loompa band striking up once more. There were twenty Oompa-Loompas in the band, each with an enormous drum twice as tall as himself, and they were beating a slow mysterious rhythm that soon had all the other hundreds of Oompa-Loompas swinging and swaying from side to side in a kind of trance. They began to chant:

> *"If you are old and have the shakes,*
> *If all your bones are full of aches,*
> *If you can hardly walk at all,*
> *If living drives you up the wall*
> *If you're a grump and full of spite,*
> *If you're a human parasite,*
> *Then what you need is Wonka-Vite!*
> *Your eyes will shine, your hair will grow,*
> *Your face and skin will start to glow.*
> *Your rotten teeth will all drop out*

And in their place new teeth will sprout.
Those rolls of fat around your hips
Will vanish, and your wrinkled lips
Will get so soft and rosy pink
That all the boys will smile and wink
And whisper secretly that this
Is just the girl they want to kiss!
But wait! For that is not the most
Important thing of which to boast.
Good looks you'll have, we've told you so,
But looks aren't everything, you know.
Each pill, as well, to you will give
An extra twenty years to live!
So come, old friends, and do what's right!
Let's make your lives as bright as bright!
Let's take a dose of this delight!
This heavenly magic dynamite!
You can't go wrong, you must go right!
It's Willy Wonka's Wonka-Vite!"

14

Recipe for Wonka-Vite

"HERE IT IS!" cried Mr. Wonka, standing at the end of the bed and holding high in one hand a little bottle. "The most valuable bottle of pills in the world! And that, by the way," he said, giving Grandma Georgina a saucy glance, "is why I haven't taken any myself. They are far too valuable to waste on me."

He held the bottle out over the bed. The three old ones sat up and stretched their scrawny necks, trying to catch a glimpse of the pills inside. Charlie and Grandpa Joe also came forward to look. So did Mr. and Mrs. Bucket. The label said:

WONKA-VITE
Each pill will make you YOUNGER by exactly 20 years
CAUTION!
Do not take more than the amount recommended by
Mr. Wonka

They could all see the pills through the glass. They were a brilliant yellow, shimmering and quivering inside the bottle. Vibrating is perhaps a better word. They were vibrating so rapidly that each pill became a blur and you couldn't see its shape. You could see only its color. You got the impression that there was something very small but incredibly powerful, something not quite of this world, locked up inside them and fighting to get out.

"They're wriggling," said Grandma Georgina. "I don't like things that wriggle. How do we know they won't go on wriggling inside us after we've swallowed them? Like those Mexican jumping beans of Charlie's I swallowed a couple of years back. You remember that, Charlie?"

"I told you not to eat them, Grandma."

"They went on jumping about inside me for a month," said Grandma Georgina. "I couldn't sit still."

"If I'm going to eat one of those pills, I sure as heck want to know what's in it first," said Grandma Josephine.

"I don't blame you," said Mr. Wonka. "But the recipe is extremely complicated. Wait a minute. I've got it written down somewhere . . ." He started digging around in the pockets of his coattails. "I know it's here somewhere," he said. "I couldn't have lost it. I keep all my most valuable and important things in these pockets. The trouble is, there's such a lot of them . . ." He started emptying the pockets and placing the contents on the bed—a home-made catapult, a Yo-Yo, a trick fried egg made of rubber, a slice of salami, a tooth with a filling in it, a stinkbomb, a packet of itching powder . . . "It must be here, it must be, it *must*," he kept muttering. "I put it away so carefully. . . . Ah! *Here* it is!" He unfolded a crumpled piece of paper, smoothed it out, held it up, and began to read as follows:

RECIPE FOR MAKING WONKA-VITE

Take a block of finest chocolate weighing one ton (or twenty sackfuls of broken chocolate, whichever is the easier). Place chocolate in very large cauldron and melt over red-hot furnace. When melted, lower heat slightly so as not to burn the chocolate, but keep it boiling. Now add the following, in precisely the order given, stirring well all the time and allowing each item to dissolve before adding the next:

THE HOOF OF A MANTICORE

THE TRUNK (AND THE SUITCASE) OF AN ELEPHANT

THE YOLKS OF THREE EGGS FROM A WHIFFLEBIRD

A WART FROM A WART HOG

THE HORN OF A COW (IT MUST BE A LOUD HORN)

THE FRONT TAIL OF A COCKATRICE

SIX OUNCES OF SPRUNGE FROM A YOUNG SLIMESCRAPER

TWO HAIRS (AND ONE RABBIT) FROM THE HEAD OF A

    HIPPOCAMPUS

THE BEAK OF A RED-BREASTED WILBATROSS

A CORN FROM THE TOE OF A UNIHORN

THE FOUR TENTACLES OF A QUADROPUS

THE HIP (AND THE PO AND THE POT) OF A HIPPOPOTAMUS

THE SNOUT OF A PROGHOPPER

A MOLE FROM A MOLE

THE HIDE (AND THE SEEK) OF A SPOTTED WHANGDOODLE

THE WHITES OF TWELVE EGGS FROM A TREESQUEAK

❖ 103 ❖

THE THREE FEET OF A SNOZZWANGER (IF YOU CAN'T
GET THREE FEET, ONE YARD WILL DO)
THE SQUARE ROOT OF A SOUTH AMERICAN ABACUS
THE FANGS OF A VIPER (IT MUST BE A VINDSHIELD
VIPER)
THE CHEST (AND THE DRAWERS) OF A WILD GROUT

*When all the above are thoroughly dissolved, boil for a
further twenty-seven days but do not stir. At the end of
this time, all liquid will have evaporated and there will
be left in the bottom of the cauldron only a hard brown
lump about the size of a football. Break this open with
a hammer and in the very center of it you will find a
small round pill. This pill is* WONKA-VITE.

15

Good-Bye, Georgina

WHEN MR. WONKA had finished reading the recipe, he
carefully folded the paper and put it back into his pocket.
"A very, *very* complicated mixture," he said. "So can you
wonder it took me so long to get it just right?" He held the
bottle up high and gave it a little shake and the pills rattled loudly inside it, like glass beads. "Now, sir," he said,
offering the bottle first to Grandpa George. "Will you take
one pill or two?"

"Will you solemnly swear," said Grandpa George, "that

it will do what you say it will and nothing else?"

Mr. Wonka placed his free hand on his heart. "I swear it," he said.

Charlie edged forward. Grandpa Joe came with him. The two of them always stayed close together. "Please excuse me for asking," Charlie said, "but are you really absolutely sure you've got it *quite right?*"

"Whatever makes you ask a funny question like that?" said Mr. Wonka.

"I was thinking of the gum you gave to Violet Beauregarde," Charlie said.

"So *that's* what's bothering you!" cried Mr. Wonka. "But don't you understand, my dear boy, that I never *did* give that gum to Violet? She snatched it without permission. And I shouted, 'Stop! Don't! Spit it out!' But the silly girl took no notice of me. Now Wonka-Vite is altogether different. I am *offering* these pills to your grandparents. I am *recommending* them. And when taken according to my instructions, they are as safe as sugar candy!"

"Of course they are!" cried Mr. Bucket. "What are you waiting for, all of you?"

An extraordinary change had come over Mr. Bucket since he had entered the Chocolate Room. Normally, he was a pretty timid sort of person. A lifetime devoted to screwing caps onto the tops of toothpaste tubes in a toothpaste factory had turned him into a rather shy and quiet man. But the sight of the marvelous Chocolate Factory had made his spirit soar. What is more, this business of the pills seemed to have given him a terrific kick. "Listen!" he cried, going up to the edge of the bed. "Mr. Wonka's offering you a new life! Grab it while you can!"

"It's a delicious sensation," Mr. Wonka said. "And it's very quick. You will lose a year a second. Exactly one year falls away from you every second that goes by." He stepped forward and placed the bottle of pills gently in the middle of the bed. "So here you are, my dears," he said. "Help yourselves!"

"Come on!" cried all the Oompa-Loompas together.
"Come on, old friends, and do what's right!
Come make your lives as bright as bright!
Just take a dose of this delight!
This heavenly magic dynamite!
You can't go wrong, you must go right!
IT'S WILLY WONKA'S WONKA-VITE!"

This was too much for the old people in the bed. All three of them made a dive for the bottle. Six scrawny hands shot out and started scrabbling to get hold of it. Grandma Georgina got it. She gave a grunt of triumph and unscrewed the cap and tipped all the little brilliant yellow pills onto the blanket on her lap. She cupped her hands around them so the others couldn't reach out and snatch them. "All right!" she shouted excitedly, counting them quickly. "There's twelve pills here. That's six for me and three for each of you!"

"Hey! That's not fair!" shrilled Grandma Josephine. "It's four for each of us!"

"Four each is right!" cried Grandpa George. "Come on, Georgina! Hand over my share!"

Mr. Wonka shrugged his shoulders and turned his back on them. He hated squabbles. He hated it when people got grabby and selfish. Let them fight it out among themselves, he thought, and he walked away. He walked slowly down toward the chocolate waterfall. It was an unhappy truth, he told himself, that nearly all people in the world behave badly when there is something really big at stake. Money is the thing they fight over most. But these pills were bigger than money. They could do things for you no amount of money could ever do. They were worth at least a million dollars a pill. He knew plenty of very rich men who would gladly pay that much in order to become twenty years younger. He reached the riverbank below the waterfall and he stood there gazing at the great gush and splash of melted chocolate pouring down. He had hoped the noise of the waterfall would drown the arguing voices of the old grandparents in the bed, but it didn't. Even with his back to them, he still couldn't help hearing most of what they were saying.

"I had them first!" Grandma Georgina was shouting. "So they're mine to hand out!"

"Oh no they're not!" shrilled Grandma Josephine. "He didn't give them to you! He gave them to all three of us!"

"I want my share and no one's going to stop me getting it!" yelled Grandpa George. "Come on, woman! Hand them over!"

Then came the voice of Grandpa Joe, cutting in sternly through the rabble. "Stop this at once!" he ordered. "All three of you! You're behaving like savages!"

"You keep out of this, Joe, and mind your own business!" said Grandma Josephine.

"Now you be careful, Josie," Grandpa Joe went on. "Four is too many for one person anyway."

"That's right," Charlie said. "*Please,* Grandma, why don't you just take one or two each, like Mr. Wonka said, and that'll leave some for Grandpa Joe and mother and father."

"Yes!" cried Mr. Bucket. "I'd love one."

"Oh, wouldn't it be wonderful," said Mrs. Bucket, "to be twenty years younger and not have aching feet anymore! Couldn't you spare just one for each of us, Mother?"

"I'm afraid not," said Grandma Georgina. "These pills are especially reserved for us three in the bed. Mr. Wonka said so."

"I want my share!" shouted Grandpa George. "Come on, Georgina! Dish them out!"

"Hey, let me go, you brute!" cried Grandma Georgina. "You're hurting me! Ow! . . . All right! *All right!* I'll share them if you'll stop twisting my arm. . . . That's better. . . . Here's four for Josephine . . . four for George . . . and four for me."

"Good," said Grandpa George. "Now who's got some water?"

Without looking around, Mr. Wonka knew that three Oompa-Loompas would be running to the bed with three glasses of water. Oompa-Loompas were always ready to help. There was a brief pause, and then:

"Well, here goes!" cried Grandpa George.

"Young and beautiful, that's what I'll be!" shouted Grandma Josephine.

"Farewell, old age!" cried Grandma Georgina. "All together now! Down the hatch!"

Then there was silence. Mr. Wonka was itching to turn

around and look, but he forced himself to wait. Out of the corner of one eye he could see a group of Oompa-Loompas, all motionless, their eyes fixed intently in the direction of the big bed over by the elevator. Then Charlie's voice broke the silence. *"Wow!"* he was shouting. "Just look at *that!* That's fantastic! It's . . . it's incredible!"

"I can't believe it!" Grandpa Joe was yelling. "They're getting younger and younger! They really are! Just *look* at Grandpa George's hair!"

"And his teeth!" cried Charlie. "Hey, Grandpa! You're getting lovely white teeth all over again!"

"Mother!" shouted Mrs. Bucket to Grandma Georgina. "Oh, Mother! You're beautiful! You're so young! And just *look* at Dad!" she went on, pointing at Grandpa George. "Isn't he the handsomest thing?"

"What's it feel like, Josie?" asked Grandpa Joe excitedly. "Tell us what it feels like to be back to thirty again! . . . Wait a minute! You look younger than thirty! You can't be a day more than twenty now! . . . But that's enough, isn't it? . . . I would stop there if I were you. Twenty's quite young enough!"

Mr. Wonka shook his head sadly and passed a hand over his eyes. Had you been standing very close to him you would have heard him murmuring softly under his breath, "Oh, deary deary me, here we go again . . ."

"Mother!" cried Mrs. Bucket, and now there was a shrill note of alarm in her voice. "Why don't you stop, Mother? You're going too far! You're way under twenty! You can't be more than fifteen! You're . . . you're . . . you're ten! *You're getting smaller, Mother!"*

"Josie!" shouted Grandpa Joe. "Hey, Josie! Don't do it, Josie! You're shrinking! You're a little girl! Stop her, somebody! Quick!"

"They're *all* going too far!" cried Charlie.

"They took too much," said Mr. Bucket.

"Mother's shrinking faster than any of them," wailed Mrs. Bucket. *"Mother! Can't you hear me, Mother? Can't you stop?"*

"My heavens, isn't it quick!" said Mr. Bucket, who seemed to be the only one enjoying it. "It really is a year a second!"

"But they've hardly got any more years left!" wailed Grandpa Joe.

"Mother's no more than four now," Mrs. Bucket cried out. "She's three . . . two . . . one . . . *Gracious me!* What's happening to her? Where's she gone? Mother! Georgina! Where are you? Mr. Wonka, come quickly! Come here, Mr. Wonka! Something frightful's happened! Something's gone wrong. My old mother's disappeared!"

Mr. Wonka sighed and turned around and walked slowly and quite calmly back toward the bed.

"Where's my mother?" bawled Mrs. Bucket.

"Look at Josephine!" cried Grandpa Joe. "Just look at her! I ask you!"

Mr. Wonka looked first at Grandma Josephine. She was sitting in the middle of the huge bed, bawling her head off. "Wa! Wa! Wa!" she said. "Wa! Wa! Wa! Wa! Wa!"

"She's a screaming baby!" cried Grandpa Joe. "I've got a screaming baby for a wife!"

"The other one's Grandpa George!" Mr. Bucket said,

smiling happily. "The slightly bigger one there crawling around. He's my wife's father."

"That's right! He's my father!" wailed Mrs. Bucket. "And where's Georgina, my old mother? She's vanished! She's nowhere, Mr. Wonka! She's absolutely nowhere! I saw her getting smaller and smaller and in the end she got so small she just disappeared into thin air. What I want to know is where has she *gone?* And how in the world are we going to get her back?"

"Ladies and gentlemen," said Mr. Wonka, coming up close and raising both hands for silence. "*Please,* I beg you, do not ruffle yourselves! There's nothing to worry about."

"You call it nothing!" cried poor Mrs. Bucket. "When my old mother's gone up the spout and my father's a howling baby . . ."

"A lovely baby," said Mr. Wonka.

"I quite agree," said Mr. Bucket.

"What about my Josie?" cried Grandpa Joe.

"What *about* her?" said Mr. Wonka.

"Well . . ."

"A great improvement, sir," said Mr. Wonka, "don't you agree?"

"Oh, yes!" said Grandpa Joe. "I mean *NO!* What am I saying? She's a howling baby!"

"But in perfect health," said Mr. Wonka. "May I ask you, sir, how many pills she took?"

"Four," said Grandpa Joe glumly. "They all took four."

Mr. Wonka made a wheezing noise in his throat and a look of great anguish came over his face. "Why oh why can't people be more sensible?" he said sadly. "Why don't they *listen* to me when I tell them something? I explained very carefully beforehand that each pill makes the taker exactly twenty years younger. So if Grandma Josephine took four of them, she automatically became younger by four times twenty, which is . . . wait a minute now . . . four twos are eight . . . add a nought . . . that's eighty . . . so she automatically became younger by eighty years. How old, sir, was your wife, if I may ask, before this happened?"

"She was eighty last birthday," Grandpa Joe answered. "She was eighty and three months."

"There you are, then!" cried Mr. Wonka, flashing a happy smile. "The Wonka-Vite worked perfectly. She is now precisely three months old! And a plumper, rosier infant I've never set eyes on!"

"Nor me," said Mr. Bucket. "She'd win a prize in any baby competition."

"*First* prize," said Mr. Wonka.

"Cheer up, Grandpa," said Charlie, taking the old man's hand in his. "Don't be sad. She's a beautiful baby."

"Madam," said Mr. Wonka, turning to Mrs. Bucket. "How old, may I ask, was Grandpa George, your father?"

"Eighty-one," wailed Mrs. Bucket. "He was eighty-one exactly."

"Which makes him a great big bouncing one-year-old boy now," said Mr. Wonka happily.

"How splendid!" said Mr. Bucket to his wife. "You'll be the first person in the world to change her father's diapers!"

"He can change his own rotten diapers!" said Mrs. Bucket. "What I want to know is *where's my mother? Where's* Grandma *Georgina?*"

"Ah-ha," said Mr. Wonka, "Oh-ho. . . . Yes, indeed, where oh where has Georgina gone? How old please, was the lady in question?"

"Seventy-eight," Mrs. Bucket told him.

"Well, of *course!*" laughed Mr. Wonka. "That explains it!"

"What explains what?" snapped Mrs. Bucket.

"My dear madam," said Mr. Wonka. "If she was only seventy-eight and she took enough Wonka-Vite to make her eighty years younger, then naturally she's vanished. She's bitten off more than she could chew! She's taken off more years than she had!"

"Explain yourself," said Mrs. Bucket.

"Simple arithmetic," said Mr. Wonka. "Subtract eighty from seventy-eight and what do you get?"

"Minus two!" said Charlie.

"Hooray!" said Mr. Bucket. "My mother-in-law's minus two years old!"

"Impossible!" said Mrs. Bucket.

"It's true," said Mr. Wonka.

"And where is she now, may I ask?" said Mrs. Bucket.

"That's a good question," said Mr. Wonka. "A very good question. Yes, indeed. Where is she now?"

"You don't have the foggiest idea, do you?"

"Of course I do," said Mr. Wonka. "I know exactly where she is."

"Then tell me!"

"You must try to understand," said Mr. Wonka, "that if she is now minus two, she's got to add two more years before she can start again from nought. She's got to wait it out."

"Where does she wait?" said Mrs. Bucket.

"In the Waiting Room, of course," said Mr. Wonka.

BOOM-BOOM! said the drums of the Oompa-Loompa band. BOOM-BOOM! BOOM-BOOM! And all the Oompa-Loompas, all the hundreds of them standing there in the Chocolate Room began to sway and hop and dance to the rhythm of the music. "Attention please!" they sang.

Attention please! Attention, please!
Don't dare to talk! Don't dare to sneeze!
Don't doze or daydream! Stay awake!
Your health, your very life's at stake!
Ho-ho, you say, they can't mean me.
Ha-ha, we answer, wait and see.
Did any of you ever meet
A child called Goldie Pinklesweet?
Who on her seventh birthday went
To stay with Granny down in Kent.
At lunchtime on the second day
Of dearest little Goldie's stay,
Granny announced, 'I'm going down
To do some shopping in the town.'
(D'you know why Granny didn't tell
The child to come along as well?
She's going to the nearest inn
To buy herself a double gin.)
So out she creeps. She shuts the door.
And Goldie, after making sure
That she is really by herself,
Goes quickly to the medicine shelf,
And there, her little greedy eyes
See pills of every shape and size,

Such fascinating colors, too—
Some green, some pink, some brown, some blue.
'All right,' she says, 'let's try the brown.'
She takes one pill and gulps it down.
'Yum-yum!' she cries. 'Hooray! What fun!
They're chocolate-coated, every one!'
She gobbles five, she gobbles ten,
She stops her gobbling only when
The last pill's gone. There are no more.
Slowly she rises from the floor.
She stops. She hiccups. Dear, oh dear,
She starts to feel a trifle queer.
You see, how could young Goldie know,
For nobody had told her so,
That Grandmama, her old relation
Suffered from frightful constipation.
This meant that every night she'd give
Herself a powerful laxative,
And all the medicines that she'd bought,
Were naturally of this sort.
The pink and red and blue and green
Were all extremely strong and mean,
But far more fierce and meaner still,
Was Granny's little chocolate pill.
Its blast effect was quite uncanny.
It used to shake up even Granny.
In point of fact she did not dare
To use them more than twice a year.
So can you wonder little Goldie
Began to feel a wee bit moldy?
Inside her tummy, something stirred.

A funny gurgling sound was heard,
And then, oh dear, from deep within,
The ghastly rumbling sounds begin!
They rumbilate and roar and boom!
They bounce and echo round the room!
The floorboards shake and from the wall
Some bits of paint and plaster fall.
Explosions, whistles, awful bangs
Were followed by the loudest clangs.
(A man next door was heard to say,
'A thunderstorm is on the way.')
But on and on the rumbling goes.
A window cracks, a lamp bulb blows.
Young Goldie clutched herself and cried,
'There's something wrong with my inside!'
This was, we very greatly fear,
The understatement of the year.
For wouldn't any child feel crummy,
With loud explosions in her tummy?
Granny, at half past two, came in,
Weaving a little from the gin,
But even so she quickly saw
The empty bottle on the floor.
'My precious laxatives!' she cried.
'I don't feel well,' the girl replied.
Angrily Grandma shook her head.
'I'm really not surprised,' she said.
'Why can't you leave my pills alone?'
With that, she grabbed the telephone
And shouted, 'Listen, send us quick

An ambulance! A child is sick!
It's number fifty, Fontwell Road!
Come fast! I think she might explode!'
We're sure you do not wish to hear
About the hospital and where
They did a lot of horrid things
With stomach pumps and rubber rings.
Let's answer what you want to know:
Did Goldie live or did she go?
The doctors gathered round her bed,
'There's really not much hope,' they said
'She's going, going, gone!' they cried.
She's had her chips! She's dead! She's died!'
'I'm not so sure,' the child replied,
And all at once she opened wide
Her great big bluish eyes and sighed,
And gave the anxious docs a wink,
And said, 'I'll be okay, I think.'
So Goldie lived and back she went
At first to Granny's place in Kent.
Her father came the second day
And fetched her in a Chevrolet,
And drove her to their home in Dover.
But Goldie's troubles were not over.
You see, if someone takes enough
Of any highly dangerous stuff,
One will invariably find
Some traces of it left behind.
It pains us greatly to relate
That Goldie suffered from this fate.

She'd taken such a massive fill
Of this unpleasant kind of pill,
It got into her blood and bones,
It messed up all her chromosomes,
It made her constantly upset,
And she could never really get
The beastly stuff to go away.
And so the girl was forced to stay
For seven hours every day
Within the everlasting gloom
Of what we call The Ladies Room.
And there she sits and dreams of glory,
Alone inside the lavatory.
So now, before it is too late.
Take heed of Goldie's dreadful fate.
And seriously, all jokes apart,
Do promise us across your heart
That you will never help yourself
To medicine from the medicine shelf.

16
Vita-Wonk and Minusland

"IT's UP TO YOU, Charlie, my boy," said Mr. Wonka. "It's your factory. Shall we let your Grandma Georgina wait it out for the next two years, or shall we try to bring her back right now?"

"You don't really mean you might be able to bring her back?" cried Charlie.

"There's no harm in trying, is there . . . if that's the way you want it?"

"Oh yes, of course I do! For Mother's sake especially. Can't you see how sad she is?"

Mrs. Bucket was sitting on the edge of the big bed, dabbing her eyes with a hanky. "My poor old mother," she kept saying. "She's minus two and I won't see her again for months and months and months, if ever at all." Behind her, Grandpa Joe, with the help of an Oompa-Loompa, was feeding his three-month-old wife, Grandma Josephine, from a bottle. Alongside them, Mr. Bucket was spooning something called "Wonka's Squdgemallow Baby Food" into one-year-old Grandpa George's mouth but mostly all over his chin and chest. "Big deal," he was muttering angrily. "What a lousy rotten bust-up this is! They tell me I'm going to the chocolate factory to have a good time and I finish up being a mother to my father-in-law."

"Everything's under control, Charlie," said Mr. Wonka, surveying the scene. "They're doing fine. They don't need us here. Come along! We're off to hunt for Grandma!" He caught Charlie by the arm and went dancing toward the open door of the Great Glass Elevator. "Hurry up, my dear boy, hurry up!" he cried. "We've got to hustle if we're going to get there before!"

"Before *what*, Mr. Wonka?"

"Before she gets subtracted, of course! All Minuses are subtracted! Don't you know any arithmetic at all?"

They were in the Elevator now and Mr. Wonka was

searching among the hundreds of buttons for the one he wanted. "*Here* we are!" he said, placing his finger delicately upon a tiny ivory button on which it said "MINUSLAND."

The doors slid shut. And then, with a fearful whistling whirring sound the great machine leaped away to the right. Charlie grabbed Mr. Wonka's legs and held on tight. Mr. Wonka pulled a jump seat out of the wall and said, "Sit down, Charlie, quick, and strap yourself in tight! This journey's going to be rough and choppy!" There were straps on either side of the seat and Charlie buckled himself firmly in. Mr. Wonka pulled out a second seat for himself and did the same.

"We are going a long way down," he said. "Oh, such a long way down we are going."

The Elevator was gathering speed. It twisted and swerved. It swung sharply to the left, then it went right, then left again, and it was heading downward all the time—down and down and down. "I only hope," said Mr. Wonka, "The Oompa-Loompas aren't using the other Elevator today."

"What other elevator?" asked Charlie.

"The one that goes the opposite way on the same track as this."

"Holy snakes, Mr. Wonka! You mean we might have a collision?"

"I've always been lucky so far, my boy. Hey! Take a look out there! Quick!"

Through the window, Charlie caught a glimpse of what seemed like an enormous quarry with a steep craggy-brown rock-face, and all over the rock-face there were hundreds of Oompa-Loompas working with picks and pneumatic drills.

"Rock candy," said Mr. Wonka. "That's the richest deposit of rock candy in the world."

The Elevator sped on. "We're going deeper, Charlie. Deeper and deeper. We're about two hundred thousand feet down already." Strange sights were flashing by outside but the Elevator was traveling at such terrific speed that only occasionally was Charlie able to recognize anything at all. Once, he thought he saw in the distance a cluster of tiny houses shaped like upside-down cups, and there were streets in between the houses and Oompa-Loompas walking in the streets. Another time, as they were passing some sort of a vast red plain dotted with things that looked like oil derricks, he saw a great spout of brown liquid spurting out of the ground high into the air. "A gusher!" cried Mr. Wonka, clapping his hands. "A whacking great gusher! How splendid! Just when we needed it!"

"A what?" said Charlie.

"We've struck chocolate again, my boy. That'll be a rich new field. Oh, what a beautiful gusher! Just look at it go!"

On they roared, heading downward more steeply than ever now, and hundreds, literally hundreds of astonishing sights kept flashing by outside. There were giant cogwheels turning and mixers mixing and bubbles bubbling and vast orchards of toffee-apple trees and lakes the size of football fields filled with blue and gold and green liquid, and everywhere there were Oompa-Loompas!

"You realize," said Mr. Wonka, "that what you saw earlier on when you went around the factory with all those naughty little children was only a tiny corner of the establishment. It goes down for miles and miles. And as soon as possible I shall show you all the way around slowly and properly. But that will take three weeks. Right now we have other things to think about and I have important things to tell you. Listen carefully to me, Charlie. I must talk fast, for we'll be there in a couple of minutes.

"I suppose you guessed," Mr. Wonka went on, "what happened to all those Oompa-Loompas in the Testing Room when I was experimenting with Wonka-Vite. Of course you did. They disappeared and became Minuses just like your Grandma Georgina. The recipe was miles too strong. One of them actually became minus eighty-seven! Imagine that!"

"You mean he's got to wait eighty-seven years before he can come back?" Charlie asked.

"That's what kept bugging me, my boy. After all, one can't allow one's best friends to wait around as miserable Minuses for eighty-seven years."

"And get subtracted as well," said Charlie. "That would be frightful."

"Of course it would, Charlie. So what did I do? 'Willy Wonka,' I said to myself, 'if you can invent Wonka-Vite to make people younger, then surely to goodness you can also invent something else to make people older!'"

"Ah-ha!" cried Charlie. "I see what you're getting at. Then you could turn the Minuses quickly back into Pluses and bring them home again."

"Precisely, my dear boy, precisely—always supposing, of course, that I could *find out* where the Minuses had gone to!"

The Elevator plunged on, diving steeply toward the center of the earth. All was blackness outside now. There was nothing to be seen.

"So once again," Mr. Wonka went on, "I rolled up my sleeves and set to work. Once again I squeezed my brain, searching for the new recipe. I had to create *age* . . . to make people *old, older, oldest.* . . . 'Ha-ha!' I cried, for now the ideas were beginning to come. 'What is the oldest living thing in the world? What lives longer than anything else?'"

"A tree," Charlie said.

"Right you are, Charlie! But what kind of a tree? Not the Douglas Fir. Not the Giant Redwood. Not the Sequoia. No, no, my boy. It is a tree called the Bristlecone Pine that grows upon the slopes of Wheeler Peak in Nevada, U.S.A. You can find Bristlecone Pines on Wheeler Peak today that are over four thousand years old! This is a fact, Charlie. Ask any dendrochronologist you like (and look that word up in the dictionary when you get home, will you please?). So that started me off. I jumped into the Great Glass Elevator and rushed all over the world collecting special items from the oldest living things . . .

A PINT OF SAP FROM A 4000-YEAR-OLD BRISTLECONE
   PINE.
THE TOENAIL CLIPPINGS FROM A 168-YEAR-OLD RUSSIAN
   FARMER CALLED PETROVITCH GREGOROVITCH.
AN EGG LAID BY A 200-YEAR-OLD TORTOISE BELONGING
   TO THE KING OF TONGA.
THE TAIL OF A 51-YEAR-OLD HORSE IN ARABIA.
THE WHISKERS OF A 36-YEAR-OLD CAT CALLED
   CRUMPETS.
AN OLD FLEA WHICH HAD LIVED ON CRUMPETS FOR
   36 YEARS.
THE TAIL OF A 207-YEAR-OLD GIANT RAT FROM TIBET.
THE BACK TEETH OF A 97-YEAR-OLD GRIMALKIN LIVING
   IN A CAVE ON MOUNT POPACATAPETAL.
THE KNUCKLEBONES OF A 700-YEAR-OLD CATTALOO
   FROM PERU . . .

All over the world, Charlie, I tracked down very old and ancient animals and took an important little bit of something from each one of them—a hair or an eyebrow, or sometimes it was no more than an ounce or two of toe-jam scraped from between its toes while it was sleeping. I tracked down THE WHISTLE-PIG, THE BOBOLINK, THE SKROCK, THE POLLYFROG, THE GIANT CURLICUE, THE STINGING SLUG AND

THE VENEMOUS SQUERKLE WHO CAN SPIT POISON RIGHT INTO YOUR EYE FROM 50 YARDS AWAY. But there's no time to tell you about them all now, Charlie. Let me just say quickly that in the end, after lots of boiling and bubbling and mixing and testing in my Inventing Room, I produced one tiny cupful of oily black liquid and gave four drops of it to a brave twenty-year-old Oompa-Loompa volunteer to see what happened."

"What did happen?" Charlie asked.

"It was fantastic!" cried Mr. Wonka. "The moment he swallowed it, he began wrinkling and shriveling up all over and his hair started dropping off and his teeth started falling out and before I knew it, he had suddenly become an old fellow of seventy-five! And thus, my dear Charlie, was Vita-Wonk invented!"

"Did you rescue all the Oompa-Loompa Minuses, Mr. Wonka?"

"Every single one of them, my boy! One hundred and thirty-one all told! Mind you, it wasn't quite as easy as all that. There were lots of snags and complications along the way. Good heavens! We're nearly there. I *must* stop talking now and watch where we're going."

Charlie realized that the Elevator was no longer rushing and roaring. It was hardly moving at all now. It seemed to be drifting. "Undo your straps," Mr. Wonka said. "We must get ready for action." Charlie undid his straps and stood up and peered out. It was an eerie sight. They were drifting in a heavy gray mist and the mist was swirling and swishing around them as though driven by winds from many sides. In the distance, the mist was darker and almost black and it seemed to be swirling more fiercely than ever over there. Mr. Wonka slid open the doors. "Stand back!" he said. "Don't fall out, Charlie, whatever you do!"

The mist came into the Elevator. It had the fusty reeky smell of an old underground dungeon. The silence was overpowering. There was no sound at all, no whisper of wind, no voice of creature or insect, and it gave Charlie a queer frightening feeling to be standing there in the middle of this gray inhuman nothingness—as though he were in another world altogether, in some place where man should never be.

"Minusland," whispered Mr. Wonka. "This is it, Charlie. The problem now is to find her. We may be lucky. And then again, we may not."

17

Rescue in Minusland

"I DON'T LIKE IT here at all," Charlie whispered. "It gives me the willies."

"Me too," Mr. Wonka whispered back. "But we've got a job to do, Charlie, and we must go through with it."

The mist was condensing now on the glass walls of the Elevator, making it difficult to see out except through the open doors.

"Do any other creatures live here, Mr. Wonka?"

"Plenty of Gnoolies."

"Are they dangerous?"

"If they bite you, they are. You're a gonner, my boy, if you're bitten by a Gnooly."

The Elevator drifted on, rocking gently from side to side. The gray-black oily fog swirled around them.

"What does a Gnooly look like, Mr. Wonka?"

"They don't *look* like anything, Charlie. They can't."

"You mean you've never seen one?"

"You can't *see* Gnoolies, my boy. You can't even feel them . . . until they puncture your skin. Then it's too late. They've got you."

"You mean there might be swarms of them all around us this very moment?" Charlie asked.

"There might," said Mr. Wonka.

Charlie felt his skin beginning to creep. "Do you die at once?" he asked.

"First you become subtracted. . . . A little later you are divided . . . but very slowly. It takes a long time . . . it's long division and it's very painful. After that, you become one of them."

"Couldn't we shut the door?" Charlie asked.

"I'm afraid not, my boy. We'd never see her through the glass. There's too much mist and moisture. She's not going to be easy to pick out anyway."

Charlie stood at the open door of the Elevator and stared into the swirling vapors. This, he thought, is what hell must be like. Hell without heat. There was something unholy about it all, something unbelievably diabolical. It was all so deathly quiet, so desolate and empty. At the same time, the constant movement, the twisting and swirling of the misty vapors, gave one the feeling that some very powerful force, evil and malignant, was at work all around. Charlie felt a jab on his arm! He jumped! He almost jumped out of the Elevator! "Sorry," said Mr. Wonka. "It's only me."

"Oh-h-h!" Charlie gasped. "For a second, I thought . . ."

"I know what you thought, Charlie. . . . And by the way, I'm awfully glad you're with me. How would you like to come here alone as I did . . . as I had to many times?"

"I wouldn't," said Charlie.

"There she is," said Mr. Wonka, pointing. "No, she isn't! Oh, dear! I could have sworn I saw her for a moment right over there on the edge of that dark patch. Keep watching Charlie."

"There!" said Charlie. *"Over there! Look!"*

"Where?" said Mr. Wonka. "Point to her, Charlie!"

"She's . . . she's gone again. She sort of faded away," Charlie said.

They stood at the open door of the Elevator, peering into the swirly gray vapors.

"There! Quick! Right there!" Charlie cried. *"Can't you see her?"*

"Yes, Charlie! I see her! I'm moving up close now." Mr. Wonka reached behind him and began touching a number of buttons.

"Grandma!" Charlie cried out. "We've come to get you, Grandma!"

They could see her faintly through the mist, but oh so

faintly. And they could see the mist through *her* as well. She was transparent. She was hardly there at all. She was no more than a shadow. They could see her face and just the faintest outline of her body swathed in a nightgown. But she wasn't upright. She was floating lengthwise in the swirling vapor.

"Why is she lying down?" Charlie whispered.

"Because she's a Minus, Charlie. Surely you know what a minus sign looks like. . . . Like that." Mr. Wonka drew a horizontal line in the air with his finger.

The Elevator glided close. The ghostly shadow of Grandma Georgina's face was no more than a yard away now. Charlie reached out through the door to touch her but there was nothing there to touch. His hand went right through her skin. "Grandma!" he gasped. She began to drift away.

"Stand back!" ordered Mr. Wonka, and suddenly, from some secret place inside his coat-tails he whisked out a spraygun. It was one of those old-fashioned things people used to use for spraying fly spray around the room before Aerosol cans came along. He aimed the spraygun straight at the shadow of Grandma Georgina and he pumped the handle hard *once . . . twice . . . three times!* Each time, a fine black spray spurted out from the nozzle of the gun. Instantly, Grandma Georgina disappeared.

"A bulls-eye!" cried Mr. Wonka, jumping up and down with excitement. "I got her with both barrels. I plussed her good and proper. That's Vita-Wonk for you."

"Where's she gone?" Charlie asked.

"Back where she came from, of course. To the factory. She's a Minus no longer, my boy! She's a one hundred per-

cent red-blooded Plus! Come along now! Let's get out of here quickly before the Gnoolies find us!" Mr. Wonka jabbed a button. The doors closed and the Great Glass Elevator shot upward for home.

"Sit down and strap yourself in again, Charlie," said Mr. Wonka. "We're going flat out this time."

The Elevator roared and rocketed up toward the surface of the earth. Mr. Wonka and Charlie sat side by side on their little jump seats, strapped in tight. Mr. Wonka started tucking the spraygun back into that enormous pocket somewhere in his coat-tails. "It's such a pity one has to use a clumsy old thing like this," he said. "But there's simply no other way of doing it. Ideally, of course, one would measure out exactly the right number of drops into a teaspoon and feed it carefully into the mouth. But it's impossible to feed anything into a Minus. It's like trying to feed one's own shadow. That's why I've got to use a spraygun. Spray 'em all over, my boy! That's the only way!"

"It worked fine, though, didn't it?" Charlie said.

"Oh, it worked all right, Charlie! It worked beautifully! All I'm saying is there's bound to be a slight overdose . . ."

"I don't quite know what you mean, Mr. Wonka."

"My dear boy, if it only takes four drops of Vita-Wonk to turn a young Oompa-Loompa into and old man . . ." Mr. Wonka lifted his hands and let them fall limply onto his lap.

"You mean Grandma may have gotten too much?" asked Charlie, turning slightly pale.

"I'm afraid that's putting it rather mildly," said Mr. Wonka.

"But why did you give her such a lot of it then?" said Charlie, getting more and more worried. "Why did you spray her three times? She must have gotten pints and pints of it!"

"*Gallons!*" cried Mr. Wonka, slapping his thighs. "Gallons and gallons! But don't let a little thing like that bother you, my dear Charlie! The important part of it is we've got her back! She's a Minus no longer. She's a lovely Plus!

> *"She's as plussy as plussy can be!*
> *She's more plussy than you or than me!*
> *The question is how,*
> *Just how old is she now?*
> *Is she more than a hundred and three?"*

18
The Oldest Person in the World

"WE RETURN IN TRIUMPH, Charlie!" cried Mr. Wonka as the Great Glass Elevator began to slow down. "Once more your dear family will all be together again!"

The Elevator stopped. The doors slid open. And there was the Chocolate Room and the chocolate river and the Oompa-Loompas and in the middle of it all the great bed belonging to the old grandparents. "Charlie!" said Grand-pa Joe, rushing forward. "Thank heaven you're back!" Charlie hugged him. Then he hugged his mother and father. "Is she here?" he said. "Grandma Georgina?"

Nobody answered. Nobody did anything except Grand-pa Joe, who pointed to the bed. He pointed but he didn't look where he was pointing. None of them looked at the bed—except Charlie. He walked past them all to get a bet-ter view, and he saw at one end the two babies, Grandma Josephine and Grandpa George, both tucked in and sleep-ing peacefully. At the other end . . .

"Don't be alarmed," said Mr. Wonka running up and placing a hand on Charlie's arm. "She's bound to be just a teeny bit over-plussed. I warned you about that."

"What have you done to her?" cried Mrs. Bucket. "My poor old mother!"

Propped up against the pillows at the other end of the bed was the most extraordinary thing Charlie had ever seen. Was it some ancient fossil? It couldn't be that because it was moving slightly. And now it was making sounds. Croaking sounds—the kind of sounds a very old frog might make if it knew a few words. "Well well well," it croaked. "If it isn't dear Charlie."

"Grandma!" cried Charlie. *"Grandma Georgina! Oh . . . Oh . . . Oh!"*

Her tiny face was like a pickled walnut. There were such masses of creases and wrinkles that the mouth and eyes and even the nose were sunken almost out of sight. Her hair was pure white and her hands, which were resting on top of the blanket, were just little lumps of wrinkly skin.

The presence of this ancient creature seemed to have terrified not only Mr. and Mrs. Bucket, but Grandpa Joe as well. They stood well back, away from the bed. Mr. Wonka, on the other hand, was as happy as ever. "My dear lady!" he cried advancing to the edge of the bed and clasping one of those tiny wrinkled hands in both of his. "Welcome home! And how are you feeling on this bright and glorious day?"

"Not too bad," croaked Grandma Georgina. "Not too bad at all, considering my age."

"Good for you!" said Mr. Wonka. "Atta girl! All we've got to do now is find out exactly how old you are! Then we shall be able to take further action!"

"You're taking no further action around here," said Mrs. Bucket, tight-lipped. "You've done enough damage already!"

"But my dear old muddleheaded mugwump," said Mr. Wonka, turning to Mrs. Bucket. "What does it matter that the old girl has become a trifle too old? We can put that right in a jiffy! Have you forgotten about Wonka-Vite and how every tablet makes you twenty years younger? We shall bring her back! We shall transform her into a blossoming blushing maiden in the twink of an eye!"

"What good is that when her husband's not even out of diapers yet?" wailed Mrs. Bucket, pointing a finger at the one-year-old Grandpa George, so peacefully sleeping.

"Madam," said Mr. Wonka, "let us do one thing at a time."

"I forbid you to give her that beastly Wonka-Vite!" said Mrs. Bucket. "You'll turn her into a Minus again just as sure as I'm standing here!"

"I don't want to be a Minus," croaked Grandma Georgina. "If I ever have to go back to that beastly Minusland again, the Gnoolies will griddle me."

"Fear not," said Mr. Wonka. "This time *I myself* will supervise the giving of the medicine. I shall personally see to it that you get the correct dosage. But listen very carefully now! I cannot work out how many pills to give you until I know exactly how old you are! That's obvious, isn't it?"

"It is not obvious at all," said Mrs. Bucket. "Why can't you give her one pill at a time and play it safe?"

"Impossible, madam. In very serious cases such as this, Wonka-Vite doesn't work at all when given in small doses. You've got to throw everything at her in one go. You've got to hit her with it hard. A single pill wouldn't even begin to shift her. She's too far gone for that. It's all or nothing."

"No," said Mrs. Bucket firmly.

"Yes," said Mr. Wonka. "Dear lady, please listen to me. If you have a very severe headache and you need *three* aspirins to cure it, it's no good taking only one at a time and waiting four hours between each. You'll never cure yourself that way. You've got to gulp them all down in one go. It's the same with Wonka-Vite. May I proceed?"

"Oh, all *right*, I suppose you'll have to," said Mrs. Bucket.

"Good," said Mr. Wonka, giving a little jump and twirling his feet in air. "Now then, how old are you, my dear Grandma Georgina?"

"I don't know," she croaked. "I lost count of that years and years ago."

"Don't you have *any* idea?" said Mr. Wonka.

"Of course I don't," gibbered the old woman. "Nor would you if you were as old as I am."

"Think!" said Mr. Wonka. "You've *got* to think!"

The tiny old wrinkled brown walnut face wrinkled itself up more than ever. The others stood waiting. The Oompa-Loompas, enthralled by the sight of this ancient object, were all edging closer and closer to the bed. The two babies slept on.

"Are you, for example, a hundred?" said Mr. Wonka. "Or a hundred and ten? Or a hundred and twenty?"

"It's no good," she croaked. "I never did have a head for numbers."

"This is a *catastrophe!*" cried Mr. Wonka. "If you can't tell me how old you are, I can't help you! I dare not risk an overdose!"

Gloom settled upon the entire company, including for once Mr. Wonka himself. "You've messed it up good and proper this time, haven't you?" said Mrs. Bucket.

"Grandma," Charlie said, moving forward to the bed. "Listen, Grandma. Don't worry about exactly how old you might be. Try to think of a *happening* instead. Think of something that *happened* to you. Anything you like . . . as far back as you can. It may help us."

"Lots of things happened to me, Charlie. So many many things happened to me . . ."

"But can you *remember* any of them, Grandma?"

"Oh, I don't know, my darling. I suppose I could remember one or two if I thought hard enough."

"Good, Grandma, good!" said Charlie eagerly. "Now what is the very earliest thing you can remember in your whole life?"

"Oh, my dear boy, that really would be going back a few years, wouldn't it?"

"When you were little, Grandma, like me. Can't you remember anything you did when you were little?"

The tiny sunken black eyes glimmered faintly and a sort of smile touched the corners of the almost invisible little slit of a mouth. "There was a ship," she said. "I can remember a ship. I couldn't ever forget that ship . . ."

"Go on, Grandma! A ship? What sort of a ship? Did you sail in her?"

"Of course I sailed in her, my darling. We all sailed in her."

"Where from? Where to?" Charlie went on eagerly.

"Oh no, I couldn't tell you that. I was just a tiny little girl." She lay back on the pillow and closed her eyes. Charlie watched her, waiting for something more. Everybody waited. No one moved.

"It had a lovely name, that ship. There was something beautiful, so beautiful about that name. But of course I couldn't possibly remember it . . ."

Charlie, who had been sitting on the edge of the bed, suddenly jumped up. His face was shining with excitement. "If I said the name, Grandma, would you remember it then?"

"I might Charlie . . . yes, I think I might . . ."

"The Mayflower!" cried Charlie.

The old woman's head jerked up off the pillow. *"That's it!"* she croaked. "You've *got* it, Charlie! The *Mayflower.* . . . Such a lovely name . . ."

"Grandpa!" Charlie called out, dancing with excitement. "What year did the *Mayflower* sail?"

"The *Mayflower* sailed out of Plymouth Harbor on September 6, 1620," said Grandpa Joe.

"Plymouth," croaked the old woman. "That rings a bell, too. Yes, it might easily have been Plymouth."

"Sixteen hundred and twenty!" cried Charlie. "Oh, my heavens above! That means you're . . . you do it, Grandpa!"

"Well now," said Grandpa Joe. "Take sixteen hundred and twenty away from nineteen hundred and seventy-two . . . that leaves . . . don't rush me now, Charlie. That leaves three hundred and fifty-two."

"Jumping jackrabbits!" yelled Mr. Bucket. "She's three hundred and fifty-two years old!"

"She's more," said Charlie. "How old did you say you were, Grandma, when you sailed on the *Mayflower?* Were you about eight?"

"I think I was even younger than that, my darling. I was only a little bitty girl, probably no more than six."

"Then she's *three hundred and fifty-eight!*" gasped Charlie.

"That's Vita-Wonk for you," said Mr. Wonka proudly. "I told you it was powerful stuff."

"Three hundred and fifty-eight," said Mr. Bucket. "It's unbelievable!"

"Just imagine the things she must have seen in her lifetime," said Grandpa Joe.

"My poor old mother!" wailed Mrs. Bucket. "What on earth . . ."

"Patience, dear lady," said Mr. Wonka. "Now comes the interesting part. Bring on the Wonka-Vite!"

An Oompa-Loompa ran forward with a large bottle and gave it to Mr. Wonka. He put it on the bed. "How young does she want to be?" he asked.

"Seventy-eight," said Mrs. Bucket firmly. "Exactly where she was before all this nonsense started."

"Surely she'd like to be a bit younger than that?" said Mr. Wonka.

"Certainly not!" said Mrs. Bucket. "It's too risky!"

"Too risky, too risky!" croaked Grandma Georgina. "You'll only minus me again if you try to be clever!"

"Have it your own way," said Mr. Wonka. "Now then, I've got to do a few sums." Another Oompa-Loompa trotted forward, holding up a blackboard. Mr. Wonka took a piece of chalk from his pocket and wrote:

Present age of person.... 358
Age she wants to be
   (subtract this) ___ 78
Number of years younger
   she must become = 280
If each pill of Wonka-Vite makes
you 20 years younger, we must divide
280 by 20 to find out   14
how many pills to give: 20)280

"Fourteen pills of Wonk-Vite exactly," said Mr. Wonka. The Oompa-Loompa took the blackboard away. Mr. Wonka picked up the bottle from the bed and opened it and counted out fourteen of the little brilliant yellow pills. "Water!" he said. Another Oompa-Loompa ran forward with a glass of water. Mr. Wonka tipped all fourteen pills into the glass. The water bubbled and frothed. "Drink it while it's fizzing," he said, holding the glass up to Grandma Georgina's lips. "All in one gulp!"

She drank it.

Mr. Wonka sprang back and took a large brass clock from his pocket. "Don't forget," he cried, "it's a year a second! She's got two hundred and eighty years to lose!

That'll take her four minutes and forty seconds! Watch the centuries fall away!"

The room was so silent they could hear the ticking of Mr. Wonka's clock. At first nothing much happened to the ancient person lying on the bed. She closed her eyes and lay back. Now and again, the puckered skin of her face gave a twitch and her little hands jerked up and down, but that was all.

"One minute gone!" called Mr. Wonka. "She's sixty years younger."

"She looks just the same to me," said Mr. Bucket.

"Of course she does," said Mr. Wonka. "What's a mere sixty years when you're over three hundred to start with!"

"Are you all right, Mother?" said Mrs. Bucket anxiously. "Talk to me, Mother!"

"Two minutes gone!" called Mr. Wonka. "She's one hundred and twenty years younger!"

And now definite changes were beginning to show in the old woman's face. The skin was quivering all over and some of the deepest wrinkles were becoming less and less deep, the mouth less sunken, the nose more prominent.

"Mother!" cried Mrs. Bucket. "Are you all right? Speak to me, Mother, please!"

Suddenly, with a suddenness that made everyone jump, the old woman sat bolt upright in bed and shouted, *"We've beaten them! Yorktown's surrendered! We've kicked them out, those dirty British!"*

"She's going crazy!" said Mr. Bucket.

"Not at all," said Mr. Wonka. "She's going through the eighteenth century."

"Three minutes gone," said Mr. Wonka.

Every second now she was growing slightly less and less shriveled, becoming more and more lively. It was a marvelous thing to watch.

"Gettysburg!" she cried. *"General Lee is on the run!"*

And a few seconds later she let out a great wail of anguish and said, "He's dead, he's dead, he's dead!"

"Who's dead?" said Mr. Bucket, craning forward.

"Lincoln!" she wailed. *"There goes the train ..."*

"She must have seen it!" said Charlie. "She must have been there!"

"She *is* there," said Mr. Wonka. "At least she was a few seconds ago."

"Will someone please explain to me," said Mrs. Bucket, "what on earth ..."

"Four minutes gone!" said Mr. Wonka. "Only forty seconds left! Only forty more years to lose!"

"Grandma!" cried Charlie, running forward. "You're looking almost exactly like you used to! Oh, I'm so glad!"

"Just as long as it all stops when it's meant to," said Mrs. Bucket.

"I'll bet it doesn't," said Mr. Bucket. "Something always goes wrong."

"Not when *I'm* in charge of it, sir," said Mr. Wonka. "Time's up. She is now seventy-eight years old! How do you feel, dear lady? Is everything all right?"

"I feel tolerable," she said. "Just tolerable. But that's no thanks to you, you meddling old mackerel!"

There was again, the same cantankerous grumbling old Grandma Georgina that Charlie had known so well before it all started. Mrs. Bucket flung her arms around her and began weeping with joy. The old woman pushed her aside and said, "What, may I ask, are those two silly babies doing at the other end of the bed?"

"One of them's your husband," said Mr. Bucket.

"Rubbish!" she said. "Where *is* George?"

"I'm afraid it's true, Mother," said Mrs. Bucket. "That's him on the left. The other one's Josephine."

"You . . . you chiseling old cheeseburger!" she shouted, pointing a fierce finger at Mr. Wonka. "What in the name of . . ."

"Now now now now now!" said Mr. Wonka. "Let us not for mercy's sake have another row so late in the day. If everyone will keep their hair on and leave this to Charlie and me, we shall have them exactly where they used to be in the flick of a fly's wing!"

19

The Babies Grow Up

"BRING ON THE VITA-WONK!" said Mr. Wonka. "We'll soon fix these two babies."

An Oompa-Loompa ran forward with a small bottle and a couple of silver teaspoons.

"Wait just one minute!" snapped Grandma Georgina. "What sort of devilish dumpery are you up to now?"

"It's all right, Grandma," said Charlie. "I promise you it's all right. Vita-Wonk does the opposite to Wonka-Vite. It makes you older. It's what we gave *you* when you were a Minus. It saved you!"

"You gave me too much!" snapped the old woman.

"We had to, Grandma."

"And now you want to do the same to Grandpa George!"

"Of course we don't," said Charlie.

"I wound up three hundred and fifty-eight years old," she went on. "What's to stop you making another little mistake and giving him *fifty times more than you gave me?* Then I'd suddenly have a twenty-thousand-year-old caveman in bed beside me! *Imagine that,* and him with a big knobby club in one hand and dragging me around by my hair with the other. No, thank you!"

"Grandma," Charlie said patiently. "With you we had to use a spray because you were a Minus. You were a ghost. But here Mr. Wonka can . . ."

"Don't talk to me about that man!" she cried. "He's batty as a bullfrog!"

"No, Grandma, he is *not!* And here he can measure it out exactly right, drop by drop, and feed it into their mouths. That's true isn't it, Mr. Wonka?"

"Charlie," said Mr. Wonka. "I can see that the factory is going to be in good hands when I retire. You learn very fast. I am so pleased I chose you, my dear boy, so very pleased. Now then, what's the verdict? Do we leave them as babies or do we grow them up with Vita-Wonk?"

"You go ahead, Mr. Wonka," said Grandpa Joe. "I'd like

you to grow my Josie up so she was just the same as before—eighty years old."

"Thank you, sir," said Mr. Wonka. "I appreciate the confidence you place in me. But what about the other one, Grandpa George?"

"Oh, all *right,* then," said Grandma Georgina. "But if he ends up a caveman I don't want him in *this* bed anymore!"

"That's settled then," said Mr. Wonka. "Come along, Charlie! We'll do them both together. You hold one spoon and I'll hold the other. I shall measure out four drops and four drops only into each spoon and we'll wake them up and pop it into their mouths."

"Which one shall I do, Mr. Wonka?"

"You do Grandma Josephine, the tiny one. I'll do Grandpa George, the one-year-old. Here's your spoon."

Charlie took the spoon and held it out. Mr. Wonka opened the bottle and dripped four drops of oily black liquid into Charlie's spoon. Then he did the same to his own. He handed the bottle back to the Oompa-Loompa.

"Shouldn't someone hold the babies while you give it?" said Grandpa Joe. "I'll hold Grandma Josephine."

"Are you mad?" said Mr. Wonka. "Don't you realize that Vita-Wonk acts instantly? It's not one year a second like Wonka-Vite. Vita-Wonk is as quick as lightning! The moment the medicine is swallowed–ping!–and it all happens! The getting bigger and the growing older and everything else all happens in one second. So don't you see, my dear sir," he said to Grandpa Joe, "that one moment you'd be holding a tiny baby in your arms and just one second later you'd find yourself staggering about with an eighty-year-old woman and you'd drop her like a ton of bricks on the floor!"

"I see what you mean," said Grandpa Joe.

"All set, Charlie?"

"All set, Mr. Wonka." Charlie moved around the bed to where the tiny sleeping baby lay. He placed one hand behind her head and lifted it. The baby awoke and started yelling. Mr. Wonka was on the other side of the bed doing the same to one-year-old George. "Both together now, Charlie!" said Mr. Wonka. "Ready, steady, *go!* Pop it in." Charlie pushed his spoon into the open mouth of the baby and tipped the drops down her throat.

"Make sure she swallows it!" cried Mr. Wonka. "It won't work until it gets into their tummies!"

It is difficult to explain what happened next, and whatever it was, it only lasted for one second. A second is about as long as it takes you to say aloud and quickly, "one-two-three-four-five." And that is how long it took, with Charlie watching closely, for the tiny baby to grow and swell and wrinkle into the eighty-year-old Grandma Josephine. It was a frightening thing to see. It was like an explosion. A small baby suddenly exploded into an old woman, and Charlie all at once found himself staring straight into the well-known and much-loved wrinkly old face of his Grandma Josephine. *"Hello,* my darling," she said. "Where have *you* come from?"

"Josie!" cried Grandpa Joe, rushing forward. "How marvelous! You're back!"

"I didn't know I'd been away," she said.

Grandpa George had also made a successful comeback. "You were better-looking as a baby," Grandma Georgina said to him. "But I'm glad you've grown up again, George . . . for one reason."

"What's that?" asked Grandpa George.

"You won't wet the bed anymore."

20
How to Get Someone Out of Bed

"I AM SURE," said Mr. Wonka, addressing Grandpa George, Grandma Georgina and Grandma Josephine, "I am quite sure the three of you, after all that, will now want to jump out of bed and lend a hand in running the Chocolate Factory."

"Who, us?" said Grandma Josephine.

"Yes, you," said Mr. Wonka.

"Are you crazy?" said Grandma Georgina. "I'm staying right here where I am in this nice comfortable bed, thank you very much!"

"Me, too!" said Grandpa George.

At that moment, there was a sudden commotion among the Oompa-Loompas at the far end of the Chocolate Room. There was a buzz of excited chatter and a lot of running about and waiving of arms, and out of all this a single Oompa-Loompa emerged and came rushing toward Mr. Wonka, carrying a huge envelope in his hands. He came up close to Mr. Wonka. He started whispering. Mr. Wonka bent down low to listen.

"Outside the factory gates?" cried Mr. Wonka. *"Men! . . . What sort of men? . . . Yes, but do they look dangerous? . . . Are they acting dangerously? And a what? . . . A helicopter! . . . And these men came out of it? . . . They gave you this?"*

Mr. Wonka grabbed the huge envelope and quickly slit it open and pulled out the folded letter inside. There was absolute silence as he skimmed swiftly over what was written on the paper. Nobody moved. Charlie began to feel cold. He knew something dreadful was going to happen. There was a very definite smell of danger in the air. The men outside the gates, the helicopter, the nervousness of the Oompa-Loompas . . . He was watching Mr. Wonka's face, searching for a clue, for some change in expression that would tell him how bad the news was.

"Great whistling whangdoodles!" cried Mr. Wonka, leaping so high in the air that when he landed his legs gave way and he crashed onto his backside.

"Snorting snozzwangers!" he yelled, picking himself up and waving the letter about as though he were swatting mosquitoes. "Listen to this, all of you. Just you listen to this!" He began to read aloud:

THE WHITE HOUSE

WASHINGTON D.C.

TO MR. WILLY WONKA.

SIR

TODAY THE ENTIRE NATION, INDEED THE WHOLE WORLD IS REJOICING AT THE SAFE RETURN OF OUR COMMUTER CAPSULE FROM SPACE WITH 136 SOULS ON BOARD. HAD IT NOT BEEN FOR THE HELP THEY RECEIVED FROM AN UNKNOWN SPACESHIP, THESE 136 PEOPLE WOULD NEVER HAVE COME BACK. IT HAS BEEN REPORTED TO ME THAT THE COURAGE SHOWN BY THE EIGHT ASTRONAUTS ABOARD THIS UNKNOWN SPACESHIP WAS EXTRAORDINARY. OUR RADAR STATIONS, BY TRACKING THIS SPACESHIP ON ITS RETURN TO EARTH, HAVE DISCOVERED THAT IT SPLASHED DOWN IN A PLACE KNOWN AS WONKA'S CHOCOLATE FACTORY. THAT, SIR, IS WHY THIS LETTER IS BEING DELIVERED TO YOU.

I WISH NOW TO SHOW THE GRATITUDE OF THE NATION BY INVITING ALL EIGHT OF THOSE INCREDIBLY BRAVE ASTRONAUTS TO COME AND STAY IN THE WHITE HOUSE FOR A FEW DAYS AS MY HONORED GUESTS.

I AM ARRANGING A SPECIAL CELEBRATION PARTY IN THE BLUE ROOM THIS EVENING AT WHICH I MYSELF WILL PIN MEDALS FOR BRAVERY UPON ALL EIGHT OF THESE GALLANT FLIERS. THE MOST IMPORTANT PERSONS IN THE LAND WILL BE PRESENT AT THIS GATHERING TO SALUTE THE HEROES WHOSE DAZZLING DEEDS WILL BE WRITTEN FOREVER IN THE HISTORY OF OUR NATION. AMONG THOSE ATTENDING WILL BE THE VICE-PRESIDENT, MISS ELVIRA TIBBS, ALL THE MEMBERS OF MY CABINET, THE CHIEFS OF THE ARMY, THE NAVY AND THE AIR FORCE, ALL MEMBERS OF THE CONGRESS, A FAMOUS SWORD SWAL-LOWER FROM AFGHANISTAN WHO IS NOW TEACHING ME TO EAT MY WORDS (WHAT YOU DO IS YOU TAKE THE S OFF THE BEGINNING OF THE SWORD AND PUT IT ON THE END BEFORE YOU SWALLOW IT). AND WHO ELSE IS COM-ING? OH YES, MY CHIEF INTERPRETER, AND THE GOVER-NORS OF EVERY STATE IN THE UNION, AND OF COURSE MY CAT, MRS. TAUBSYPUSS.

A HELICOPTER AWAITS ALL EIGHT OF YOU OUTSIDE THE FACTORY GATES. I MYSELF AWAIT YOUR ARRIVAL AT THE WHITE HOUSE WITH THE VERY GREATEST PLEASURE AND IMPATIENCE.

I BEG TO REMAIN, SIR.

MOST SINCERELY YOURS

Lancelot R. Gilligrass.

LANCELOT R. GILLIGRASS
President of the United States

P.S. COULD YOU PLEASE BRING ME A FEW WONKA FUDGE-
MALLOW DELIGHTS. I LOVE THEM SO MUCH BUT EVERY-
BODY AROUND HERE KEEPS STEALING MINE OUT OF THE
DRAWER IN MY DESK. AND DON'T TELL NANNY.

Mr. Wonka stopped reading. And in the stillness that
followed Charlie could hear people breathing. He could
hear them breathing in and out much faster than usual.
And there were other things, too. There were so many
feelings and passions and there was so much sudden
happiness swirling around in the air it made his head
spin. Grandpa Joe was the first to say something. . . .
"*Yippeeeeeeeeee!*" he yelled out, and he flew across the
room and caught Charlie by the hands and the two of
them started dancing away along the bank of the choco-

late river. "We're going, Charlie!" sang Grandpa Joe. "We're going to the White House after all!" Mr. and Mrs. Bucket were also dancing and laughing and singing, and Mr. Wonka ran all over the room proudly showing the President's letter to the Oompa-Loompas. After a minute or so, Mr. Wonka clapped his hands for attention. "Come along, come along!" he called out. "We mustn't dilly! We mustn't dally! Come on, Charlie! And you, sir, Grandpa Joe! And Mr. and Mrs. Bucket! The helicopter is outside the gates! We can't keep it waiting!" He began hustling the four of them toward the door.

"*Hey!*" screamed Grandma Georgina from the bed. "What about us? We were invited too, don't you forget that!"

"It said *all eight of us* were invited!" cried Grandma Josephine.

"And that includes *me!*" said Grandpa George.

Mr. Wonka turned and looked at them. "Of course it includes you," he said. "But we can't possibly get that bed into a helicopter. It won't go through the door."

"You mean . . . you mean if we don't get out of bed we can't come?" said Grandma Georgina.

"That's exactly what I mean," said Mr. Wonka. "Keep going Charlie," he whispered, giving Charlie a little nudge. "Keep walking toward the door."

Suddenly, behind them, there was a great *swoosh* of blankets and sheets and a pinging of bedsprings as the three old people all exploded out of the bed together. They came sprinting after Mr. Wonka, shouting, "Wait for us! Wait for us!"

It was amazing how fast they were running across the floor of the great Chocolate Room. Mr. Wonka and Charlie and the others stood staring at them in wonder. They leaped across paths and over bushes like gazelles in springtime, with their bare legs flashing and their nightshirts flying out behind them.

Suddenly Grandma Josephine put the brakes on so

hard she skidded five yards before coming to a stop. "Wait!" she screamed. "We must be mad! We can't go to a famous party in the White House in our nightshirts! We can't stand there practically naked in front of all those people while the President pins medals all over us!"

"Oh-h-h-h!" wailed Grandma Georgina. "Oh, what *are* we going to do?"

"Don't you have any clothes with you at all?" asked Mr. Wonka.

"Of course we don't!" said Grandma Josephine. "We haven't been out of that bed for twenty years!"

"We can't go!" wailed Grandma Georgina. "We'll have to stay behind!"

"Couldn't we buy something from a store?" said Grandpa George.

"What with?" said Grandma Josephine. "We don't have any money!"

"Money!" cried Mr. Wonka. "Good gracious me, don't you go worrying about money! I've got plenty of *that!"*

"Listen," said Charlie. "Why couldn't we ask the helicopter to land on the roof of a big department store on the way over. Then you can all pop downstairs and buy exactly what you want!"

"Charlie!" cried Mr. Wonka, grasping him by the hand. "What *would* we do without you? You're brilliant! Come along everybody! We're off to stay in the White House!"

They all linked arms and went dancing out of the Chocolate Room and along the corridors and out through the front door into the open where the big helicopter was waiting near the factory gates. A group of extremely important-looking gentlemen came toward them and bowed.

"Well, Charlie," said Grandpa Joe. "It's certainly been a busy day."

"It's not over yet," Charlie said, laughing. "It hasn't even begun."

There's more to Roald Dahl than great stories...

Did you know that 10% of author royalties* from this book go to help the work of the Roald Dahl charities?

The Roald Dahl Foundation supports specialist pediatric Roald Dahl nurses throughout the UK caring for children with epilepsy, blood disorders, and acquired brain injury. It also provides practical help for children and young people with brain, blood, and literacy problems—all causes close to Roald Dahl during his lifetime—through grants to UK hospitals and charities as well as to individual children and their families.

The Roald Dahl Museum and Story Centre, based in Great Missenden just outside London, is in the Buckinghamshire village where Roald Dahl lived and wrote. At the heart of the Museum, created to inspire a love of reading and writing, is his unique archive of letters and manuscripts. As well as two fun-packed biographical galleries, the Museum boasts an interactive Story Centre. It is a place for family, teachers and their pupils to explore the exciting world of creativity and literacy.

www.roalddahlfoundation.org
www.roalddahlmuseum.org

The Roald Dahl Foundation (RDF) is a registered charity no. 1004230.

The Roald Dahl Museum and Story Centre (RDMSC) is a registered charity no. 1085853.

The Roald Dahl Charitable Trust, a newly established charity, supports the work of RDF and RDMSC.

* Donated royalties are net of commission